STICKING OUT

BOSTON BUCKS

CATHRYN FOX

ISBN Ebook: 978-1-998943-65-4

ISBN Print: 978-1-998943-66-1

CONNER

Two Years Ago:

Body tired, and head hurting from a hangover, I roll over in bed and glare at my buzzing phone. Whoever is calling can fuck right off. I'm not only hurting from drinking too much last night, but we just lost the Eastern Conference playoffs against Pittsburgh in the seventh game, and anyone who knows me knows better than to be calling today.

"Fuck off." I grumble and roll over, closing my eyes when my damn phone finally stops buzzing. Just when I'm about to doze off, my phone starts screaming at me all over again. "Shit." I reach out and grab my phone. When I see that it's my brother, I slide my finger across the screen, and grunt out, "This better be important."

"Hey, sorry about the playoffs." There's sincerity in his voice, but there's something else there as well, something that has me forgetting all about my hangover and sitting up in bed.

"Yeah, is that why you called?"

"No, uh..." A giggle sounds in the background, and when I hear my brother's muffled words, I realize he's covering the phone. Whatever is going on, he doesn't want me to hear, and I'm not sure I want to either, because I know he's on a work trip, away from home—away from his wife. The hairs on the back of my neck lift and I sit up straighter, checking the time as my heart jumps into my throat. "What's going on?" I ask, even though I'm not certain I want an answer.

"Listen..." His voice is clear again. "I need you to do me a favor."

Unease grips my stomach. "What kind of favor?"

"I was supposed to be home today, but I got tied up in New York."

Tied up?

More giggles sound, and my brain starts racing. My brother, who I adore and respect more than any other human on this planet, is a hockey scout for Harvard, and travels to numerous high schools across the country. If he's tied up in New York, it had better not be with some girl.

"Alec?"

"Yeah, listen." He clears his throat. Probably to cover up the rustling noises in the background, and I don't even want to think about what or who is making them. "Dani has an ultrasound appointment today. I was supposed to take her, but I can't make it. I called and she's not feeling so great. Would you mind taking her for me?"

"Who are you with?" I growl, pinching the bridge of my nose as I try to clear the fog from my brain.

He snorts out a laugh, but I know him well enough to realize it's his way of stalling. "It's nothing."

I resist the urge to blurt out—how the fuck can it be nothing? My brother is married to the most amazing woman on the planet, and she's pregnant with his child. I must be wrong. I must be hearing things. Yeah, the alcohol and partying must be messing with my brain. "Alec. What the fuck, man? What's happening?"

"Come on, bro. It's nothing. Just cleaning the pipes." More giggling bubbles through the phone. "You know Dani hasn't been feeling well lately, right?"

Really, that's his fucking justification for cheating? Anger, rage, and every other hostile emotion—that I've never felt toward my brother in my life—wells up inside me.

"No way, Alec. You're telling me your wife hasn't been putting out because she's pregnant and not well, and this is how you treat her?" How could he do this? This is the man who always stood up for me when I was a kid. He was protective and caring and beat the crap out of the other kids when they made fun of me because I couldn't read.

Conner Birch, thick as wood, dumb as a stump. Oh yeah, that's how they taunted me as they knocked on their heads like their heads were made of hardwood. If Alec is a protector by nature, as I've always known him to be, why isn't he protecting Dani when she needs it most? Fuck, if she were my wife, I'd run barefoot over glass if she needed me to.

"Just do me this one favor, bro." His voice is a little more labored, breathless, and my stomach turns, not wanting to think about why. "I'll be home tomorrow."

My head pounds harder as my blood runs cold. "You should stop what you're doing and come home now." I glance around my room as my vision clears—in more ways than one. Sure, I've had my head down and my blades on the ice, focused solely on my career for a while now, but how did I not see this coming? Maybe I could have done something, said something to him to stop this from happening.

"Will you do this for me or not?"

There's a hardness tinging his voice now, and while it's a simple question, I realize it's also a loaded one. Panic grips my stomach. Jesus. I'm now responsible for keeping his secret. I swallow the bile pushing into my throat.

"Jesus, bro. How old is she?"

"Old enough. I'm not an idiot."

While that is debatable, I shake my head and kick off my blankets. "What time is the appointment?" I'm supposed to meet up with Summer, the girl I've been seeing for the last six months, later this afternoon. She's a sophomore at Boston College and we met after a game one night. She's not a bunny, although she is a bit younger than me, and has a thing for llamas. Like a real weird thing for llamas. She has blankets, stuffed toys, and mugs with llamas on them. Hell, she even has llamas on her panties. Maybe I'll get to see that up close and personal later.

No wait, she messaged last night and said she couldn't make it —which, with nothing on the agenda today, is probably why I stayed out too late and drank too much last night. I hope her grandmother is doing okay. Summer said she hasn't been well and she's been staying with her. She even missed the game last night, but said she caught it on TV.

"Two. Can you take her?"

Jesus, that's in half an hour. Way to leave it to the last minute. "Yeah, I'll be there, for *her*."

Clearly picking up on my anger, he shoots back, "Bro, come on. Put yourself in my shoes."

"Oh, I am." Honestly my brother had shoes I knew I could never fill, and this...this fucking hurts. My idolization of him, for all he's done for me, is now battling with his infidelity...or infidelities. The less I know, the better.

"You can't tell me you wouldn't do the same," he shoots back.

"Pretty sure I can, bro." With that, I end the call and toss the phone to the foot of my bed like it's about to give me the plague. I exhale loudly, and wince as I turn toward my window, the bright afternoon sun hurting my eyes.

My phone pings, and thinking it might be Dani, I grab it only to read the text from my brother.

Alec: Thanks. I owe you.

It's not me he owes. No, it's Dani he owes and what he owes her is a big fucking apology, followed by months of groveling for forgiveness. Instead of answering, I focus on what needs to be done, and shoot off a message to Dani—all the while hating myself for even knowing my brother's secret.

. . .

Me: Hey, heard from Alec. He asked me to take you to your appointment. How are you feeling?

Dani: Probably better than you.

I chuckle. She knows me well. I know her well too. She was my friend in high school before my brother ever showed her any attention. She moved into our Boston neighborhood when she was a sophomore, like me. Alec was a senior, who had girls falling all over him. Why wouldn't he? He was the smartest guy I knew, going places, and doing things. Okay, maybe there was a tiny part of me that was envious at how easy schoolwork came to him, when I struggled so horribly. Even though I eventually got help with my dyslexia, I still have troubles, and I keep that part of my life hidden.

Me: I'm okay. I can take you.

Dani: I'm a big girl. I can go by myself. Don't worry about it. You probably want to commiserate with Summer today.

Me: She's with her grandmother and I need the distraction. Trust me.

Dani: Fine then, dinner is on me.

Me: You're not cooking dinner when you're not feeling well.

. . .

Dani: I have homemade lasagna in the freezer.

Me: If you insist.

Dani:

Me: See you shortly.

Dani: Merci.

I laugh at her use of French. She'd taken some courses at the local college. I'm not sure what her fascination with French is. Maybe it's because she moved around a lot as a kid, her folks even did a stint in Montreal, Canada. Or maybe she wants to go to Paris someday.

I stumble to my shower, wash quickly and before I dress, I swallow down a few pain meds. Fuck, I am never drinking again—said every guy the morning after he drank too much. I tug on a pair of clean jeans, and grab a T-shirt from my drawer. I pull it on as I hurry down my stairs and go straight for the coffee machine. I fill my travel mug and head outside.

Ten minutes later, I'm at my brother's house, and Dani is on her steps. She's smiling but it doesn't reach her eyes. Fuck, she looks like she's in pain. Does she know? She starts toward me, her steps slow, like it might hurt to walk.

Guilt clogs my throat as I jump from the car, circle the front and open her door. I take her heavy bag from her, and she slides into the car. I weigh the bag in my hand. "What do you have in here anyway?"

"A pregnant girl needs her things, Conner." Holding her stomach, she smiles again, but it's easy to tell she's hurting. I don't close her door. Instead, I kneel. "What is it?" Her chin quivers and I lose all ability to breathe as she looks away. "Dani?"

"I had spotting this morning, and bad cramping."

I lean in and put my arms around her and she grips my forearm, like it's her lifeline. Anger that my brother isn't here for her rages inside me. "It's okay. Everything is going to be okay." I know how much she wants this child so it has to be okay. Nothing can be wrong. She's a good person who does good things. She picks up dogs on her bus and runs a doggy day care, even staying late when the owners get stuck in traffic. The world can't let a woman like that down, right?

Maybe not, but my brother sure as fuck has.

She sniffs and laughs. "I'm sorry. I'm just so hormonal lately. Yesterday I ran out of Clarence's diet cookies on the bus and when he looked at me with those big, sad brown eyes, I broke out crying."

I smooth her hair back. "Clarence is smart and knows how to play you. You know that, right? I bet you gave him two when you got him to your daycare." I try to make light of it, wanting nothing but her happiness and when she laughs again and nods in agreement, I exhale.

"Yeah, I did."

I blink rapidly, pout and point to my face. "This, right here, is going to get me two slices of lasagna tonight, isn't it?"

She laughs again. "I'm such a pushover."

"Nah, you're just sweet, Dani."

She gives me a warm, grateful smile as she puts one hand on my face. "Thanks, Conner."

I lean into her hand, absorbing her warmth and as it wraps around my heart, I jerk back and stand, severing the intimate connection.

She's not yours, dude.

"Okay, let's get you to your appointment, and get you checked out."

I close her door, and sense her eyes on me as I circle the front of the car and slide back into the driver's seat. As I back out of her driveway, she asks, "Did you talk to Alec, or did he text?"

"Both, actually."

I avoid looking at her, and concentrate on the road. "He got tied up," she states.

"Yeah."

I glance at her hands as she links them, squeezing tight. Fuck. I drive to the downtown core, hurrying to reach the hospital, and squeeze my vehicle between two big trucks. I steal a glance at Dani, who is trying to appear calm, but her nervous energy is palpable.

I kill the ignition and reach for the door handle. Her hand lands on mine. "You don't have to come in. You can go grab a coffee or something." She glances around. "There's plenty of coffee shops around here."

The worry in her eyes speaks volumes. "Didn't you know?" I nod toward the hospital. "The coffee machines in these places have the best brew in the world."

She grins and nudges me. "Always motivated by the finer things in life, Conner."

As I take in her grin, I can't help but think she's one of the finer things in life. I've always known it. I thought my brother did too.

Her eyes narrow. "Are you okay?"

I put on a fast smile. "Yup, let's go." I hop from the car and when she closes her door, I hit the fob to lock it. I walk over to her and casually throw my arm over her shoulder. She weaves her fingers through mine, and we head inside the hospital. She registers and we take the elevator up to the fifth floor. She takes a seat and points to a spot down the hall. "Machine is down there."

I'm a bit reluctant to leave her, and I'm not exactly sure what my role is here. "You...uh...want me to come in with you?"

"No, that's okay."

I nod and saunter down the hall just as her name is called. I glance back over my shoulder to watch her walk away with a nurse. I grab a crappy coffee and take a seat in the waiting room, tugging my hat low, because one, I look and feel like shit, and two, I don't want anyone to recognize me. I normally love the fans. Right now, however, I'm too wound up to carry on any kind of conversation.

I finish my coffee, and toss it into a nearby trash can when the same nurse who'd taken Dani to her room appears, the lines on her forehead deep as she seeks me out.

"You're Conner?" she asks.

The coffee turns in my stomach. "Is Dani okay?"

"She wants to see you." Before I can even ask what's going on, the nurse is on the move and I hurry my steps to keep pace. I struggle to keep the panic down, because my gut is telling me something very bad is happening.

As my blood drains to my feet, I force my heavy legs to work quickly, and the second I enter the room, and see Dani on the bed, her face as white as the sheet she's laying on, a tortured sound crawls out of my throat. She reaches for me, and I hurry to her, taking her cold hand in mine. Tears fall down her cheeks.

"Alec...can you call him?" she manages to get out between sobs. "I need him."

I nod, and stumble into the hallway, pulling my phone from my pocket. Through blurry eyes, I punch in his number, and when he answers, sounding happy, relaxed...sated...rage grips my throat and pushes cruel words from my lungs. "You get your fucking ass home right now, or you're dead to me."

Little did I know that those words, spoken in the heat of the moment, were going to come true. If I had known, I never would have spoken them.

P^{resent Day:}

Here we are in game seven, three wins for the Bucks, three wins for the Panthers. But we're on home ice and the guys are feeding off the crowd tonight. The current score is two to one for the Bucks and the Panthers are on a power play with ten seconds left. I grab Brighton's hand as the Panthers pull their goalie, their center skating down the ice, ready to score on Brady. Conner, along with a couple other Bucks, are tight on his heels, but the guy they are chasing—Lazar—is fast and widening the lead.

"Ohmigod," Brighton cries out, as we hold our breath. Melanie might not be here tonight as that guy challenges her husband, Brady, but I know she's watching this all play out on TV and I'm sure she's on the edge of her seat, much like we are, even if she's home with their son Kayce.

"I can't look." I put one hand over my face, but peek through my fingers as Lazar takes the shot, only for Brady to stop it seconds before the buzzer goes off.

The packed arena goes wild, everyone jumping to their feet and screaming. The guys on the ice all start hugging each other, and I don't miss the way Conner glances up at me. Nervousness invades my stomach as our eyes meet. Tonight… well, tonight I am going to ask him for a favor. A big one. I've been building up to this for months and I told myself that if they won the cup tonight, they'd all be in a good mood, and it would be the perfect time to ask.

All the WAGs hug. Not that I'm a wife or girlfriend of any player, but I am best friends with Conner. We've been best friends since I moved into his neighborhood my freshman year. I almost blew that once in high school, though. I had a wicked crush on him and found the nerve to put it in writing —on a pretty sheet of pink paper. I left the letter on his bed one day. I waited for days for him to say something to me. God, those days were excruciating. When he never brought it up, I figured he wanted to stay in the friend zone, so that's where we stayed.

Thank God, it didn't ruin our friendship and while it would have been nice to have a conversation, that could have made things awkward. I guess in the end, he handled it correctly and it was shortly after that when his brother, the hottest senior in high school, started paying attention to me. Me— Miss Nobody. A girl who only sticks out in this crowd of women because I'm not hot like they are. Nope, I'm just plain Jane—a little too curvy—Danielle Birch. I never did go back to my maiden name after we lost Alec in that terrible car accident, the same day I lost my unborn baby.

But I can't think about that right now. After counselling, I've forced myself to move on, and moving on is exactly what I'm doing, and hopefully, my best friend Conner is going to help me with that.

Brighton grabs my hand. "Come on, let's go."

We all head to the ice as the cup is presented. Honestly, I'm not a WAG, and I don't feel like I should be on the ice, but I'm pretty sure Brighton wasn't having any of that. The families all gather around as the Conn Smythe award goes to Brady Fisher, and we all cheer. It's a whirlwind of activity as the guys take turns lifting the cup and skating it around the ice. It's so exciting, and I can't take my eyes off Conner when it's his turn.

Once the team takes the cup into the locker room, all the wives and girlfriends make their way outside, and win or lose, we've already rented out Kilting Around, a famous Scottish pub in town. Before I go, I wave to my in-laws, who are making their way off the ice. We'd hugged earlier before the game, but I can't leave without seeing them now.

"I'll meet you there. I have to go talk to Bill and Darcy." I hurry to them, and they pull me into their arms. Darcy has tears in her eyes and Bill does too, even though he's trying to hide them.

"Conner was amazing," I say as they squeeze me.

Darcy nods in agreement. "We are so proud of him." As she smiles a part of me tightens, because they were proud of Alec too, and were really looking forward to having a grandchild. I think they only had hope for the two of us, not really expecting Conner to settle down for a while, as he had a career to focus on. But I know Conner, and deep inside, he's always wanted a family. Now that he's settled in his career, I guess there's nothing holding him back, although he no longer talks about it. Nevertheless, I hope to someday give Darcy and Bill what they want.

"Are you guys coming to the pub to celebrate?"

Bill gives a dismissive wave. "My pub days are over, but you guys go and have fun."

"Okay, the girls are waiting. I'd better go."

"Barbecue soon," Darcy says and gives me another hug. I honestly love how close we still are. "Give Conner a hug and kiss for us."

Why would they want me to hug and kiss Conner? "You're going to see him soon, aren't you?"

She gives an almost sheepish smile. "Yes, of course." Okay, that was weird. "You'd better get going." I give a little wave and struggle through the crowd. Outside, the cool air falls over me and I zip up my coat, all the while trying not to get trampled by the rambunctious crowd, excited to party the night away.

Knowing the guys will be a while, a bunch of us made plans to meet them at the pub. Brighton finds me, and weaves her arm through mine as we head toward her big SUV. Yes, she's an SUV person now, with her two kids, and a big dog, and while others make fun of it, I am so damn envious.

All I ever wanted was to be a mother. My younger sister was the same. Dad was an attaché to the U.S. consulate, and we moved a lot. Our mom stayed home with us, and I loved that. Alec wanted a family too, which is why we got pregnant shortly after we married. My phone pings and ends my trip down memory lane. I pull it from my pocket to see that it's my sister.

I answer and she screams into the phone. I start laughing as I pull it away from my ear. I hear her husband Jared in the background. He's a good guy, a radiologist at Boston General, and honestly, my sister, with her three young kids, is living the life I've always wanted. I'm so happy for her and want the same, which is why I've been trying in-vitro. The only one who knows that secret is Conner. I haven't shared the details with anyone else. When I told him about my plans last year at Melanie's after exam celebration, he was shocked, and I'm not sure he ever warmed to the idea of me being a single mom, even though he knows how much I want kids.

"You're deafening me, Rylee."

"Sorry. I'm just so excited. Are you guys going out to celebrate?"

"We're heading to Kilting Around." I put my hand over my other ear to block the noise of the crowd. "You're welcome to join us."

"The kids are down and it's too late to get a sitter now. Besides, it's not like I can go too far when I'm breastfeeding and I can't even enjoy a drink." She sounds devastated, but I know she's not and I nod in agreement, once again a tinge of envy pinching my heart. "Why don't you guys come by tomorrow for a celebration dinner?" she suggests.

"I'll ask Conner and get back to you."

"Okay, go celebrate and give Conner a big hug and kiss from me."

Why does everyone want me to hug and kiss Conner?

"Hey," I hear Jared in the background. "You will not be extending hugs or kisses to Conner." He's trying to sound stern, but there's laughter in his voice. He and my sister are in love and he doesn't ever have to worry about her with another man. My stomach tightens at that thought. There was a time with Alec...

"Okay, give him a big hug and kiss from you," my sister laughs out.

"Cut it out. We're just friends." Conner will never see me as anything more than a friend, and I gave up on my crush on him years ago.

Did you, though, Dani?

"Have you never heard of friends with benefits?" I can just see the twist of Rylee's lips and the bob of her head as she says that to me.

"He's my brother-in-law," I counter, wanting to put an end to this conversation. But the truth is, if he agrees to what I'm going to ask him tonight, we'll be crossing a fine line, and I just hope it doesn't ruin what we have.

Brighton lets my arm go and waves to Josie. "Josie, over here." Josie comes rushing over, a big smile on her gorgeous face. She's a nurse, and sometimes when I look at these career women, I wonder how they look at me. Not that they've ever been anything but nice. It's just that they all have degrees and important jobs, whereas I run a doggy day care, and Josie's mastiff Apollo is one of the animals I pick up and drop off every day. A brain surgeon I am not.

"I have to go," I tell my sister.

"Just promise me you'll give him a hug and kiss."

"Goodbye, sis."

I laugh and end the call, and Josie arches a brow. "Everything okay?"

"Sisters," I groan with a laugh, and she watches me waiting for me to continue my explanation. "She was joking about me giving Conner a hug and a kiss." I expect her to laugh, but she doesn't. Instead, she nods, like that might actually be a good idea. "What?" I ask.

"It's not a bad idea." She pulls open the door to the back seat when we reach Brighton's big van with its three-row seating.

"What?" She can't be serious.

"That man needs to get out more. Have you noticed how grumpy he's been lately?"

"Pressure for the cup," I explain.

"Sure. Sure." She climbs into the vehicle and I follow her in. "Or maybe pressure is building up elsewhere."

I laugh. "Oh, Josie. I am so not his type."

"Yeah, maybe he doesn't like gorgeous, intelligent, supportive women."

Josie thinks I'm gorgeous, intelligent and supportive? I agree with the last one but not the first two.

She crinkles her nose. "I don't think he likes the bunnies anymore. I haven't seen him with any. I only ever see him with you."

My heart lurches. Oh, God, am I monopolizing all his time? Does he feel responsible for me after…Alec? I swallow hard, and the favor I was going to ask him begins to crumble before my eyes. I can almost feel it turn to dust in my hands. Conner needs to be getting out more, with a woman who isn't his best friend and sister-in-law. Have I been holding him back?

I buckle up as excitement fills the air and dread spreads in my stomach. Does Conner want to be hanging with the bunnies? If that's the case, I need a plan B for myself going forward.

Soon enough we all pile out of the SUV at Kilting Around, and there's a sign indicating it's closed for a private party, which is us. Inside, we fill the tables as more friends and family join the celebration. The place is loud and I'm grateful that it's helping drown out my darker thoughts. Drinks are poured and since I'm not pregnant, I grab a margarita and take a much-needed sip. Snacks fill the tables and I dig in, wanting to fill the hollow in my stomach.

A couple of hours later, cheers erupt in the pub as the guys begin to pour in, and I lift my gaze to find Conner seeking me out. Guilt takes a big bite out of my tongue as I swallow the words that have been dancing on the tip of it for a long time. I can't ask Conner for any kind of favor, especially if he's put his life on hold because he feels an obligation to me.

His blue eyes, eyes the same color as his brother's, light up when they find me and everything in the way he's currently looking at me makes me think I have it all wrong. I'm not a burden or obligation. I'm someone he wants to be around. Although I have no idea why he'd choose to spend time with me, when there's a horde of bunnies here all vying for his attention.

He steps up to me and throws his arms out. I jump from my chair and he wraps his arms around me and spins me in a circle.

"I'm so proud of you," I tell him and he sets me down. His head dips and for the briefest of seconds, when his gaze lands on my lips, I think he's going to kiss me. I wet my lips and he cocks his head, like he's trying to get a read on my actions.

My heart races, and when his lips connect with my forehead, I pull myself together. What the hell was I thinking? I don't know, but I hope he wasn't thinking that I wanted a kiss.

He reaches across the table and grabs a mozzarella stick. "I'm starved."

"Give me that." Brady snatches it from his hand and takes a big bite.

Conner playfully shoves him. "Hey."

"Okay, children, there are enough mozzarella sticks for everyone." Noah snatches one off the plate and holds it out to Conner. Conner reaches for it, and before he can get it, Noah takes a bite.

Conner shoves Noah and grumbles, "Fucker."

I laugh, take a mozzarella stick and put it in front of Conner's mouth. He stares at his friends and gloats as he takes a bite and mumbles, "At least someone loves me."

Jesse slaps Conner's back. "Aw, we love you too, dude."

Conner puts his hand on the small of my back, and guides me to my chair. It's a small gesture, one he's done often. It just feels different tonight. I don't know why. Maybe it's because my mind has been on sex lately—with the purpose of having a child, of course—but his touch does something ridiculously crazy to the neglected spot between my legs. I flinch, because everything about that feels wrong. Okay, well no, it feels right, which is why it's wrong. Does that even make sense?

He eyes me, and I avert my gaze and sit. The truth is, I haven't been with another man since Alec. Uh, yeah, and also he was my first. Like I said, I'm your average plain Jane, and not a woman who garners attention when walking down the street, or in a pub full of beautiful women.

The guys pull up chairs and sit next to us, and soon enough, the conversation returns to the win and the volume in the place rises to new heights. I'm okay with that. It makes my unease and quietness tonight less noticeable. I take a sip of my drink and note the way Conner is watching me. I plaster on a smile, which only makes his eyes narrow more.

Jesse says something funny and calls out to Conner. With his attention diverted, I turn to Josie and talk about the book we're reading for next week's book club. A few women come up to the table and put their hands all over the guys, even the married ones. The women at the table are confident in themselves and their men, so no scene is caused. The men are quick to shut down the unwanted advances, Conner included. It does, however, remind me he's a young single guy who should be out having fun.

"If you'll excuse me." I stand a little too quickly. Conner grabs my chair before it tumbles backward. I laugh awkwardly. "I don't know my own strength."

"You're strong from all those dogs you wrestle," Jesse points out. "When I take Apollo for a walk, he walks me, yet you have no troubles at all."

That's me. Plain. Curvy. Strong. All the traits a guy goes for. I glance at Conner. "I'll be right back."

He nods, and I get the sense he can tell I'm off tonight. I make a trip down the hall to the washroom, and stand before the mirror, fixing my hair and then washing my hands. I lean in and pinch my cheeks to add a bit of color, and when a few girls come in, showcasing gorgeous bodies in very little clothes, they smile at me and I smile back as I leave. I head back down the hall, and when I reach the bar, I wave to the bartender, asking for a big glass of water.

As I stand there, waiting for his attention, a big body presses against me, pinning me between the oak countertop and a wall of muscles. I don't need to turn to know it's Conner. His warm soapy scent, the same scent he's been using since we were kids, wraps around me.

He puts his mouth to my ear. "Hey, are you okay?"

I spin to face him and he inches back slightly. I gaze into his eyes, and everything about him messes with my body—which is wrong, dammit. Sure, I was going to ask him for a big favor but I was planning on keeping it all clinical.

My inner voice breaks out in hysterical laughter, and I shut it down. Yeah, I must be crazy to think I could have sex with this man and stay detached.

I smile and gesture with a nod. "Someone is trying to get your attention."

He glances over his shoulder, and eyes the pretty blonde. "Yeah." He turns back to me. "What's going on with you tonight, Dani?"

Just then the bartender slides a glass of water my way. His eyes go wide. "Wait..."

"No," I answer quickly, and glance at the blonde again. I'm about to tell him nothing is going on, and that he should go off and have some fun, but as I try to formulate the words, to arrange them into a coherent sentence, I find myself blurting out, "I want to have a baby." His head rears back and his eyes narrow.

"I know."

"In-vitro hasn't worked," I rush out quickly, even though there's a part of my brain trying to stop me from making a huge mistake. "And, I was...uh, wondering if maybe you could help a girl out."

CONNER

I reach around Dani and grip the counter to keep myself upright. "You want...me..." My fingers bite into the wood as my words stall in my throat.

"Technically." She gives a nervous little laugh as she pushes a strand of hair behind her ear and leans in to whisper, "It's your sperm I want."

My heart pounds in my ears, making it difficult to hear, because, obviously, what I'm hearing doesn't make sense. She's not asking me to be a sperm donor, right? I nearly laugh at that ridiculous thought.

She blinks rapidly, as I try not to stare at her like she just grew a second head. "In-vitro isn't working." Her words are rushed as she continues with, "And the doctor suggested I try it the good old-fashioned way."

I take two deep breaths, and as my racing brain slows, it begins to fill in the blanks and make sense out of what is happening here. "Oh, so you want me to fill a cup or tube or something, so you can...insert it?" Jesus, did I really just say that out loud? I should just shut the hell up because I have no idea how this all works.

"No, it would have to be, you know." She awkwardly bumps her fists together. "Me and you. Old fashioned. Like grandpa and grandma used to do it." She rolls her eyes, and a tortured sound climbs out of her throat. "I don't know why I just said it like that."

She said it like that because she's not in her right mind. She can't be. I inch back, letting go of the counter. "Dani…I don't think—"

"You're right," she blurts out and gives a flirty laugh, but it can't hide the pain in her eyes. "I was only kidding. Too many margaritas. Alcohol turns me into a joker." I'm about to tell her it doesn't, that I've never seen that happen, when she lifts up her glass. "Which is why I'm on to water."

By my count, she's had two drinks tonight, unless she was pounding them back before I got here and I don't think that was the case at all, I also don't think she was joking.

She wants a baby.

Holy shit, Dani just asked me to be her baby daddy.

"Dani," I begin and rub my chin.

"I was kidding." She gives me a little shove. "Go celebrate your win. This is huge, Conner."

"Dani…"

She pushes past me and walks back to the table, and I make a move to follow her when I'm surrounded by bunnies. Dani glances at me over her shoulder and her fake smile falters as Naomi puts her arm around me and goes up on her toes to give me a congratulatory kiss. By the time I manage to peel her off me, Dani's attention is on Josie and Brighton. She puts her arms in the air, and stretches, and I know that's her classic move for making her exit. A second later, she stands, pulls on her coat and slides her finger across the screen of her phone.

I hurry to her, and take it from her hands. "Going somewhere?"

"It's been a long week. I need sleep. You guys have fun." She points to the door as it opens and in walk a few more players. "I'm going to grab an Uber."

"I'll drive you." I slip her phone into her coat pocket, and she opens her mouth like she's going to protest when I glare at her. She can't ask me to be her baby daddy and then take an Uber home like nothing really happened here tonight. We need to talk. I'm not sure if everyone at the table can sense the storm going on inside of me, but they've mostly fallen quiet.

Dani puts her hand on my chest, like she's done a million times before, only tonight it feels...different. I can only chalk that up to what she just asked me, and right there, that's just one of the reasons I can't do this. I can't let anything come between us.

"Conner—"

"Catch up with you guys later," I tell the guys, as I tug on my coat. I turn my focus to Dani. "Ready?" I don't give her a chance to answer or protest. I put my hand on her back and guide her to the door. The night air whips around us, as I hurry my steps and begin the brisk walk to my car. Once there, I open the door for her and she slides in.

We're both quiet, lost in our own thoughts as I drive to Beacon Hill. I bought the big house here when I first signed with the Bucks a few years ago. It's too big for me, but it's an investment. I maneuver the downtown streets, which are filled with partygoers, and while I'm excited for our win, I'm no longer in the mood to party.

As we approach our neighborhood, Dani's soft voice pulls my attention.

"Conner."

"Yeah."

"I'm sorry."

I grip the steering wheel tighter. "You don't need to be sorry." Christ, I'd once swore that if Dani was my wife, I'd walk through burning fire for her. But she's not my wife. She married my brother. She'd chosen him.

But this is fucking important to her, dude.

The only thing she's ever wanted was a child, a family. "I just don't see how any of this could work." How could we raise a baby together? Technically, she's my sister-in-law, which makes this so twisted. Not to mention that I'm on the road during the NHL season. What kind of help could I actually be? Then again, the other guys manage.

But no... I mean, there was a time I wanted my own family, and there was a big part of me that was envious that Alec was doing all the things I wanted...but this...this is wrong. Besides, I sort of gave up on a family, not wanting to pass along my genes. What if my child ended up with my learning disorder and ended up suffering the way I had...still do?

"No, I mean..." She glances down and starts twisting the hem of her coat between her fingers. "It's...after Alec." My heart lurches at my brother's name, and once again equal measures of guilt, shame, sorrow and loss hit at the same time. "I don't want you to feel responsible for me. I don't think I realized how I kept you from other things, other women, until tonight—"

A burst of fierce heat moves through me. "Did someone say something to you?"

"Not in so many words, no. I just realized how much time you spend with me when you could be...out."

Out?

I steal a fast glance at her, but she's looking out the passenger side window. "What are you talking about?"

"You should be out having fun with the bunnies. I think the last girl I saw you with was Summer."

"We broke up." After my brother's death, and me trying to be strong for everyone, I had no time for Summer, and she just sort of faded into the background.

"I know." She shrugs and her shoulders hover around her ears. "But you're always hanging out with me. Like you owe it to your brother, or to me, or something. I don't know."

"I hang out with you because I want to, not because of some sense of obligation. We're friends, Dani. We've always been friends." All the more reason we can't have a baby together. I can't risk losing her.

"It's just...you should be having sex." She winces a bit when she says sex.

"You should be having sex too," I counter without thinking as my mind goes in a direction I'd fought hard in the past to never let it go. Maybe I'm going there tonight because she asked me to be her baby daddy—the old-fashioned way, like grandpa and grandma used to do. Okay, it's going to take a while to wash that image from my damn brain.

I reach across the seat and take her hand in mine. "I want to ask you something and I want you to tell me the truth." I narrow my gaze, and search her face.

She nods. Here goes nothing. "You weren't joking earlier, were you?" She looks down, but not before I catch the embarrassment in her eyes. "We've always been honest with each other. No secrets." *Yeah, like you've been honest with her, dude.* Fuck me. I've kept a horrible secret from her for two years. The only way I sleep at night is by telling myself there's no need for her to know. It won't change the past and will only hurt her. Besides, it's not like she's ever going to find out now. Alec is gone.

"I wasn't. I've given it a lot of thought, but clearly not enough thought. I think desperation is messing with my reasoning abilities."

"Why me?" I push out past a tight throat.

She goes quiet and every muscle tightens. Honestly, I don't expect her to say that it's me she wants—that it was me she always wanted, and somehow ended up with Alec. No, I don't expect that at all. I don't even want that.

Yeah, okay, dude. Chill the fuck out.

"It's just that we're friends and I trust you." Her brow is furrowed, tight as she swallows. "I know you. I know what you're made of."

What I'm made of?

All the reasons this is more complicated. Honestly, I can't make sense of it. Wouldn't that put our friendship on the line. That's not something I've ever wanted to mess with. I know things come in threes, and after losing my brother, Dani's baby...I've been waiting for the third ball to drop, and dammit, it's not going to be my relationship with her. I can't risk that.

But a baby is so damn important to her, dude.

Under her breath she murmurs, "DNA." I lean into her, and strain to figure out what it is she's saying. "DNA," she whispers again, and those three little letters hit me in the gut harder than that fucker Blake Danske in tonight's game.

Yeah, okay I get it. I'm made of the right DNA. DNA close to my brother's. Fuck, would she even want his DNA if she knew what he'd been doing behind her back when she was pregnant—when she was spotting and in trouble and needed him more than ever before. Probably not, but I can't tell her that.

I also can't tell her I don't have the right DNA. What if my offspring takes after me, and ends up getting bullied and beaten up, because he's 'thick in the head' as I've been called. I barely made it through high school. Dani knows I struggled. She just doesn't know why. I don't like to talk about it. Would she want my DNA if she knew I had a learning disorder? I guess the fact that she knew I struggled, and still asked, says there's a good chance she would want it. Jesus, she's that desperate for a piece of Alec.

I go quiet for a long time, and when I reach her house I pull into the driveway. I yawn, my body suddenly so very tired. "Thanks for the lift." She reaches for the handle, like she's about to scurry away. Fine. I reach for mine too and she stares at me when I exit and circle the front.

"What are you doing?"

Tension arcs between us and I hate it with every fiber of my being. "We should probably talk a little more about this."

"Honestly, Conner. It was a mistake." The sadness about her absolutely guts me, and I pull her into my arms. At first she's stiff, but then she relaxes into me, and puts her arms around me. Fuck, she's been through so much. Too much. Her body begins to shake, despite my warmth.

"Come on. Let's get you inside."

She nods and sniffs, so I keep my arm around her and walk her to the door. Since I have my own key, I unlock it and we step inside. The warmth of her place wraps around me like it always does and makes me feel right at home. I've always loved being at her place. This one and the one she grew up in. Her mother still makes the best cherry pie.

I take my coat off and hang it in the front closet and she slips out of hers and I take it from her. "Are you hungry?" she asks. "You didn't eat much at the pub."

"Too hyped up."

"I can heat us up some lasagna. I didn't eat much either."

No wonder. She was probably trying to figure out the best way to ask me to be her baby daddy. She stifles a yawn, and I put my hands on her shoulders and walk her to the kitchen, indicating for her to sit. "I'll heat it for us."

I open up her freezer and pull out the individually sized containers with the lasagna and toss them into the microwave. As they heat, I pour us both a glass of water and sit next to her. She watches me with careful eyes, like I'm about to berate or lecture her or something. She knows better than that, though.

I sit and my knees touch hers. "If the doc suggested the good old-fashioned way, have you thought about dating again?" Is it too soon to be asking that? Alec has been gone for two years, and she hasn't even cleaned his closet out yet. I guess we all grieve in our own ways, and the fact that she wants my DNA, because it's close to Alec's, well...she's still in love with him.

"Actually, I have thought about it."

My stomach tightens. Goddammit, why do I hate the idea of her in another man's arms? It was bad enough seeing her with my brother, but they were happy, which made me happy for her. I consoled myself with that because they were two of the most important people in my life. It must have taken so much for her to ask me. Fuck. I feel like a real douche for shutting her down so quickly.

"I just...I'm not ready."

No, of course she's not. She's never gotten over Alec. He was and still is the love of her life. Wait, what is that in her eyes? What is it she's not telling me? I'm about to ask when the microwave beeps.

"Did you get to see your parents tonight?"

I love how they come to all my home games. Raising me wasn't the easiest of jobs, but my whole family was there for me—Alec included. Which makes what Dani is asking me all that much stranger. "Yeah."

"They were bursting with pride as usual." If I hadn't forced Alec to come home that day two years ago, they'd probably have two sons to be proud of, but no, now they only have one.

"Oh, I just remembered. Rylee wants us to come to dinner tomorrow." Her eyes widen. "I mean, if you're free. If you're not, I totally get it."

Jesus, what's it going to take for her to realize I like her company and don't want to be bedding a different bunny every night?

"Yeah, I'm free."

Her eyes widen and when she shakes her head, I can only guess she's revisiting our bunny conversation—and how I should be out screwing them all. "Conner—"

"Dani." Her gaze jerks to mine, and my heart pounds a little faster. I don't want to give her hope that I'll do this favor for her. That's just cruel, because when it comes right down to it, I can't do this. I won't. Bad things come in threes and if I mess up our friendship and lose her or even the baby, well, that would be the worst thing that could happen to me. I open my mouth to tell her exactly that, when the words, "Can I think about it?" spills from my lips.

Kill me fucking now.

DANI

"If you ask me one more time, I'm going to dump this salad over your head." Conner holds up the mixed garden salad and threatens me with it. I know he won't do it, but I get it...stop asking him if dinner with my sister is keeping him from something or someone.

I hold my hands up, palms out. "Okay, sorry. I won't ask again." I eye him, my gaze searching his face because maybe I do need to hear it one more time, or even a million times, before I believe it. For the life of me, I can't understand why he prefers hanging out with me when he could be out with any other woman in the world. Just look at the man. Tall. Dark. Handsome. Everything any woman could want, and believe me, they do want.

"Dani—"

"Grab the raspberry vinaigrette from the fridge. Rylee never has my favorite kind." He hands me the salad—more like shoves it at me in warning—and bends to get my dressing out of the fridge. Holy, those jeans look good on him, and the last thing I should be doing is staring at his perfect backside. I'm sure I'm only admiring his physique because my body is on hyperdrive from all the hormones the doctor had me taking. With that excuse, I continue to stare...and compare. While Conner and Alec were brothers, they couldn't have been more different, really.

Alec was athletic in his own way—heck, he became a hockey scout for Harvard—but he never excelled at anything in particular. He was also the valedictorian, graduating at the top of his class, whereas Conner barely scraped by and acted up to get out of class. I used to try to tutor him, but he hated it, and sometimes I think I might have made him feel stupid. Not on purpose, of course.

He sets the dressing on the counter and I put it in my canvas bag. "Do you need to stop at your place for anything?" I ask.

Last night he slept in my spare room, which isn't unusual. He even keeps clothes here. When he gets tired, he crashes, and he could barely keep his eyes open after we talked last night —after he told me he'd think about it. A little bubble of excitement wells up inside me. I can't believe he's actually considering the colossal favor I'm asking. But then, that excitement is replaced by nervousness and maybe even a bout of nausea.

I have to sleep with Conner.

The old-fashioned way...like Grandpa and Grandma did.

Oh, God, what have I gotten myself into?

"Are you okay?"

"What, yeah, why?" I ask and blink rapidly. Did I say any of that out loud?

He puts his big palm on my cheek, which feels rough and warm. "You kind of went a bit pale there."

"It's the run," I explain. "I shouldn't have been trying to keep up with you earlier." After we woke up this morning, we ate, lounged, spent some time on our devices scrolling and reading, and after lunch, when he was getting ready for his run, I decided to go with him. I have no idea what I was thinking.

Sympathy moves over his face. "I told you I could slow down."

"I run after dogs all day. I'm fine." Talk about backtracking, and yeah, that doesn't explain why I'm suddenly pale. He looks like he's about to press. "I have to stop at the Airbnb after dinner. We have a couple of overnighters, and I always just like to check in on their well-being." Airbnb meaning Air Bark and Breakfast, of course. I remember when Conner told me I was a clever girl when I came up with it.

"I thought you did that with your app."

"I do, but Marley is new and I want to bring her a coffee and some snacks, just to make sure she feels comfortable."

He closes one eye in thought. "Marley being…"

"Animal care attendant. Not one of the dogs. Although I'm sure they'd love some snacks too."

He grins. "That's nice of you. I'll come with you."

I give a fast shake of my head. "You don't have to do that."

"It's Saturday night, and we just won the cup, so my schedule is pretty free." I open my mouth and his eyes go wide, stopping me before I tell him what he should be doing with his schedule. That's when another thought hits. If he does decide to help a girl out, I really don't want him sleeping with other women. It has nothing to do with jealousy. Hell no. I just need his sperm strong and abundant.

"Okay, we should get going." Conner takes the salad and we head outside. The warm sun beats down on us and I lift my face to the sky as Conner locks up behind us. Neighbors wave as we walk to the car and I grin. Conner is a superstar even in his own backyard. "What are you grinning about?" he asks.

I laugh. "Nothing." Honestly, I like how he takes it all in stride. He always has and while I admire that, I think Alec might have been a bit jealous of his kid-brother's successes. I'd never tell Conner that. He adored his big brother.

He puts the salad on the back seat and I slide into the passenger seat. As we back out, he glances at my bus parked beside the house. "I still can't believe you drive a bus." He laughs. "Actually, I think it's kind of cute."

He grins at me, and it does weird things to my insides. I take a fast breath and remind myself that he's not flirting or hitting on me. He never has and never will. We don't have that kind of relationship.

He goes quiet, too quiet, and I glance at him, noting the way his grip is tight on the steering wheel. I sink into my seat to leave him with his thoughts, because I know exactly what he's thinking about and I don't want to sway him. If he wants to do this, it has to be his decision.

He flicks the signal, turns right and his gaze slides my way, worry in his eyes. "Dani."

"Yeah?"

"I'm sorry in-vitro didn't work. I know you were really excited about being a mom."

"Yeah, I spent a small fortune only for it to fail."

"If it's money—"

"Honestly, Conner. I want my baby to know its father. Someday down the road, I want to be able to tell him or her about their father, and how awesome he is."

"Wait, if I do this, you make it sound like I'm not going to be in the picture." The lines around his eyes deepen as fear moves over his face and my heart jumps. "Are we not going to be friends anymore? If that's the case—"

I put my hand on his arm. "No, Conner. That's not what I'm saying." I swallow. How do I say this? "It's just...you don't have to be involved. The child never even needs to know." He clenches and the muscles along his jaw ripple. Oh, great. That didn't come out right, and now he's upset.

"You think I'm going to have a baby and then have nothing to do with it?"

From the look on his face, it's clear he's more hurt than angry. "Conner, what I'm saying is how much involvement you have is up to you. I know you always talked about a family of your own when we were younger. I'm not certain you want that anymore..." I pause when the muscles along his jaw clench. What happened to change his mind? I don't ask, but instead I continue with, "I don't want you to feel pressured into taking any kind of responsibility if you don't want it."

"What if I want to feel responsibility? What if I want to be in the child's life?"

"Then we figure it out."

Something dark, and worrisome crosses his face. "You know...

my DNA is not Alec's DNA. I don't…I'm not smart like he was and I'm always losing things. You know that."

Oh God, he can't think he's stupid, can he? "You just weren't book smart in school, Conner. That doesn't mean you're not smart. You're one of the smartest guys I know and everyone loses things." I wink at him. "Some just more than others." I do remember him losing all the things he loved most. He was always active and on the go, but I have to admit, he did misplace things a lot.

He rubs the back of his neck and there's something there in the depths of his eyes, something he's not telling me as he forces a laugh. "You're just saying that because you're trying to get into my pants."

I laugh at that. "I would never lie to you and you are smart." A beat of silence, and in a soft voice I begin again. "Conner, just know I don't ever want you to do something you're not comfortable doing. It's okay to say no. I promise I'll understand and I promise nothing is ever going to come between us."

He nods, and his brow is furrowed when he asks, "You don't want to date again?"

"Have you seen what's out there?" I huff out. I haven't really been looking, to be honest. At least not on the apps, and the guys I do encounter at the grocery store—the only place I really go anymore—are shopping for their families.

He laughs. "I guess once you've had the love of your life, everything else pales, huh?" He glances at me, and I turn to look out my passenger window. I mumble my agreement under my breath, and push down the unease creeping up my neck.

It's not like I can tell him that I started dating Alec simply because he paid attention to me. He was popular and smart and every girl wanted him, yet he wanted me. For the first time in my life, I felt special and this all happened shortly after Conner ignored the heartfelt letter I left on his bed. I might have been a bit broken at the time and Alec's attention helped put the pieces back together.

"Dani?"

A little embarrassed and a whole lot flustered, because I can feel his eyes drilling into the back of my head at my non-answer, and evasiveness, I blurt out, "Maybe my body only liked Alec's sperm." Oh, my God, what the hell am I saying?

"Ah, okay."

"I mean all that in-vitro. It didn't work. I'm just saying that Alec and I didn't have a lot of sex. So, I was surprised that I got pregnant when it was so infrequent, and I have an ovulation app and have been taking hormones to help me get pregnant, and yet it's not happening." Okay, now I'm rambling, and Conner knows me well enough to know I ramble when I'm uncomfortable.

A long moment of silence and then. "You didn't have a lot of sex."

"I shouldn't have said that." He nods in understanding, and because I feel the need to explain, I continue. "When we met in high school, he was busy keeping his grades high and then college and then his busy job, and there was never much time. Anyway, that's why I said my body must have liked Alec's sperm, because although we didn't have much sex, I got pregnant when we did." He nods, and now it's his turn to avert his gaze. Does he know something I don't? A burst of unease worms its way through my blood.

"So, I guess the good news is we probably won't have to have sex too many times."

His gaze jerks my way. "What?"

"DNA. Sperm. With any luck we'll be one and done."

"One and done," he mutters absently.

"I mean, if you decide to do this." I grip my purse and twist the strap around my hand, working to shut down my brain and zip my mouth. "No pressure, Conner. It's a big decision, for sure."

"I'm actually surprised Alec wanted kids," he says quietly. "He always just seemed so focused on his career." He gives me a smile. "I guess marrying an amazing woman has a way of making people change their minds."

"I was actually surprised that he wanted kids so fast. We never really talked about it a whole lot and then I brought it up after we were married..." I pause and think about that. "Actually, it came up because of you."

"Me?"

I laugh. "Yeah. I remember when you were dating Summer, and she said she never wanted kids."

"I don't ever remember her saying that."

"It was girl talk. Anyway, I had mentioned to Alec that maybe you two weren't right for each other, because I knew you liked kids." He frowns and goes quiet. I fall silent too, as I take a painful trip down memory lane. We round the corner and I point. "My sister's place is right there."

"Not my first time here, Dani."

Of course it's not. What the heck am I even saying? Conner's been here numerous times with me and my sister's kids call him Uncle Conner. I guess I just needed a change in conversation. He eases the car into her driveway, and I reach for the door handle, needing to make an exit before I say anything else stupid. I tug open the back door and grab the salad. Laughter comes from around the back of their two-story home in suburbia, and I double my steps to get there. Conner is tight on my heels and I plaster on a smile when I circle the house and find Jared at the grill, five-year-old Ava and three-year-old Jack playing on the swing set, and little baby Brynn nursing in my sister's arms.

I stop instantly, my maternal instincts flaring at the perfect scene playing out before my eyes. This, right here. This is all I've ever wanted, and I almost had it with the only man who ever showed romantic interest in me—a man I loved, of course. But was I ever really in love with him?

"Aunt Dani, Uncle Conner." Ava jumps from the swing and comes running over. She wraps her arms around my legs and then throws herself at Conner, who picks her up.

"Congratulations," she yells, cupping his cheeks and squeezing before she kisses him on the nose. "Did you bring the cup?"

He laughs. "No, I don't have it with me."

"Did you kiss it?" she asks and makes a face like that's the weirdest thing in the world. "Daddy says you kiss the cup."

"I kissed the cup," he admits and stretches out an arm. "It's this big and some people even drink out of it."

"Silly, that's what cups are for."

"Do you know one guy once made a big cheesy dip and filled the cup with it at a party." He laughs like he's remembering. "Phil Prichard, the keeper of the cup loves to tell all the stories. "Lots of guys even put their babies in it for pictures."

"That's weird." She wiggles out of his arms, runs over to the table, grabs her plastic cup and takes a big drink. "See. Cups are for drinking."

We all laugh and Rylee says, "Leave your uncle alone. He just got here."

I eye him. "Is that true?"

"It's true."

"People are weird," I agree with Ava. Conner nods in agreement as he walks over to Jared. Ava runs back to Jack, who's far too interested in whatever it is crawling in the grass to greet us. God, boys are so different from girls. That makes me smile. I want one of each. I quickly look at Conner, who's clinking bottles with Jared. Look at me getting greedy when he hasn't even agreed to the first one yet.

"Drink?" Rylee asks me. "Please say yes, so I can live vicariously through you."

"Then yes." She pours me a glass of chilled white wine and I take a big sip. "Mmm, delicious." I lick my bottom lip and when I do, I notice Conner watching me. When my gaze meets his, he quickly looks away. Okay, that was odd.

"What's going on?" Rylee asks, leaning in conspiratorially.

"Nothing, what are you talking about? I should put this salad in the fridge." Her hand closes over mine, stopping me, and she has a mischievous grin on her face.

"Did you give him a hug and kiss?"

"No," I snap far too loud, considering both guys are now looking at us.

"Shame." She leans back and adjusts Brynn on her breast as she gulps milk and my body aches a little.

I work to change the subject. "Someone is hungry."

"You know, I always thought you two would make a good couple."

Relentless, that's what my sister is. "Yeah, well, he's my brother-in-law, so no that's not going to happen." I don't dare tell her that I asked him to help me make a baby. Her head would no doubt spin all the way around, and that would just freak everyone out. I guess if he does agree, and I end up with a big belly, she's going to figure it out. Until then... silence. Brynn finishes and Rylee puts her over her shoulder to burp her.

Conner comes over, bends and gives Rylee a kiss on the cheek. "How's the little one doing?" he asks.

"She's great and we're so proud of you, Conner."

He arches a brow when she yawns. "How are you doing?"

"I'll sleep when they're teenagers. Hey, when are you going to settle down and make one of these yourself?"

I am going to freaking kill my sister.

He laughs, but his gaze quickly slides to mine, like we share a secret, and my sister is so goddamn astute I'm sure I'm going to get grilled about this later. Jack comes running onto the deck, jumping from one foot to the other and I'm happy for the distraction. "Mommy, I dropped my fart," he yells as he holds the back of his soiled pants, and Rylee stands. "Would you mind holding her for a second? She needs to burp."

Conner's eyes go wide. "I don't know—"

"It'll be good experience for when you have your own." Rylee puts Brynn in Conner's arms. "Just do what I was doing." Looking a bit like a deer in the headlights, he puts Brynn over his shoulder and starts lightly tapping her back—and boom, just like that, I'm pregnant. Honestly, if it were only that easy.

Rylee takes Jack's hand. "Let's go, little man."

Ava hurries to me and tugs on my hand. "Aunt Dani, come swing with me."

"Are you okay?" I ask Conner.

He shrugs like he's not sure. "I...don't know." Brynn lets loose a loud wet burp, which drips down Conner's back. He winces.

"Oh no," I reach for Brynn. "Let me help you." I take little Brynn from him, holding her tiny little body to mine. I breathe in her freshly washed skin, and briefly close my eyes as my heart beats a little faster. Tears press against my eyes, and emotions flood me. When I open my eyes again, Conner is watching me, warmth, wonderment and a great deal of tenderness on his face. What is going on with him?

I'm about to ask, but he asks first. "Are you okay?"

"Hormones," I admit, although that's not the only thing contributing to my tears. "From in-vitro. They're still messing with me. In so many ways," I add with a laugh. His brows raise, when he realizes I'm so much as admitting that my libido is on hyperdrive.

Brynn decides it's a good time to projectile vomit all over me. I hold her out. "Oh, God." Acting quickly, Conner grabs the blanket from the bassinette and begins dabbing my shirt, soaking up the wet milk.

"Now you're worse than me." All he's managing to do is rub the milk in. He gestures with a nod. "Why don't you go clean up first?"

"Check with Rylee," Jared says. "She'll have clothes you can borrow." I hand Brynn to Conner and he begins to rock with her, like it's instinct for him. "She can go in her bassinette now," Jared informs us.

"I'll see if Rylee has clothes you can borrow." I hurry into the house, and find the bathroom on the main level. It's empty so I step in, peel off my shirt and begin to soak it in the sink. "Rylee, can you bring me a T-shirt," I call out. "Brynn soaked mine. Conner needs a shirt too."

"Hey."

I turn at the sound of Conner's soft voice and find him standing in the doorway, shoulders tight, face grim. I'm pretty sure I've never seen such seriousness about him. He opens his mouth and everything inside me tightens, because I already know what he's about to say to me. Honestly, what was I thinking, bringing him here today of all days? After seeing exactly how messy and hard and exhausting raising a child really is, there is no way he's going to agree to be my baby daddy now, right?

It's been a week, one full week since I agreed to be Dani's baby daddy. What the hell was I thinking? Honestly, I'm not sure I was. Seeing her holding little Brynn, the way her eyes closed with love and longing, it did something to me, fucked me over in ways that had me telling her I'd give her a baby, even though it terrifies me.

The truth is, I don't have the right DNA for that, and call me superstitious, but bad things happen in threes. I can't lose anyone else in my life. I might have misplaced trading cards, games and my favorite toys growing up—although the doctor said that had nothing to do with dyslexia—at the end of the day, they were just belongings. When it comes to the people most important to me, I can't risk it.

I take a deep breath to pull myself together. I need to get my game hat on and step out of the role of baby daddy and back into the role of the cup champion. This afternoon, a few of the guys and I are taking a downtown trolley, and hopping on and off so we can showcase the cup to crowds of cheering fans. While that's fun and exciting, and I love our fans, I can't keep my focus off the text that Dani sent me earlier, the text that said two simple words: I'm ovulating.

Tonight I'm going to have sex with my best friend…my sister-in-law. Yeah, okay, maybe I thought about that back in high school. Maybe I wanted that, but I stopped thinking about it when she hooked up with my brother.

Did you though, Conner?

Yes, I fucking did. Mostly. Christ, kill me now. I open the door leading to the back of my house, and step outside to breathe in the fresh air. My yard is a bit neglected, and I need to take the cover off the pool and get it cleaned up.

For a brief second, I wonder if Rylee and Jared might like to bring the kids for a swim. But that thought brings on another. If Dani gets pregnant, this backyard won't feel so empty anymore. No, we'll be putting up a swing set like Rylee and Jared have, and we'll have to safety proof the pool more than it already is. I put my hand on my stomach, unsure if I'm frightened or excited.

Dani said my level of involvement with the child is up to me, but I think we need to have a talk to set some ground rules. What if she finds a guy and gets married and he wants to adopt our child? What if he doesn't want me in my child's life? Goddammit, no way am I going to be shoved out the back door. Not again.

I check the time and walk back inside, locking the door behind me. I grab my baseball cap and car keys and make my way to my car. I drive the short distance to where I'm meeting with my teammates, the Boston residents and the ones who stayed for the parade. Most of the guys are headed out tomorrow or the next day to wait in their hometown for their turn hosting the cup.

I spot a crowd around the trolley, and find a parking spot, which isn't easy. The second I exit my car, I'm swarmed, and that's okay. I'm here for the fans, but I do find myself searching the crowd for Dani. She told me she'd try to make it. One of the dogs she has overnight hasn't been feeling the best, and she was going to check on her to make sure she's okay. She thinks it's home sickness, but she wants to make sure.

I sign notepads and sweaters and hats, and finally I make my way to the trolley. Jesse is standing with Noah, Ash, Theodore, Brady—who doesn't appear to be taking the cup home to his small fishing village in Newfoundland—Tanner, Elias, Tuck and Jaxon. I love those guys like family. Just then Phil saunters up to us with the cup. Jesse takes it, holds the cup above his head and the crowd cheers.

"Stop hogging the cup," I joke and take it from Jesse. More cheering fills the street and as we form a line and pass it down, I once again scan the crowd. I really hope I don't see her. If I do, I'll be thinking about what's going to happen tonight. Sporting a boner while showcasing the cup probably isn't a great idea.

Tanner hands the cup back to Phil, and we all pile on the trolleys. Music blares from the speakers as we drive through town, stopping at different locations to meet and greet the crowds and give our autographs. It's nearing dinner time when we're finally back at our starting point, and fortunately, the crowd has dwindled.

"You guys want to grab a beer?" Elias asks as he adjusts his ballcap. Most of the guys nod in agreement, and I hesitate.

"Uh, sorry. Can't tonight."

"What's this?" Tuck teases throwing his arm over my shoulder. "Looks like Wood is going to be sporting wood tonight," he teases, using the nickname they've given me. "Wait," he jokes, "Maybe that's not an image I want in my brain." Everyone laughs and I do too. The guys don't know how derogatory that nickname was in my childhood and they don't need to know. When they say it, it's full of love and affection.

"Not your business," I say and for some reason a stupid, guilty grin crosses my face and for the life of me I can't seem to wipe it away.

Ash makes a fist and nudges my chin. "About fucking time."

"Who is she?" Elias asks, and when I don't answer, he presses. "Do we know her?"

"No," I blurt out so fast they laugh.

"Seems like we do know her," Jaxon says.

My phone pings, and I steal a fast glance at it to see that it's Dani, apologizing for not making the cup parade, before I tuck it away.

"I just hope it's Dani," Tuck says with a snort. "We can all feel the tension between you two from a million miles away." What the hell? Is he serious? There's no sexual tension between us. Okay, well... I mean, I like her. I've always liked her, but to her I'm just a friend. Soon to be a friend with benefits and maybe, eventually, her baby daddy. "It's about fucking time you guys got a room," Tuck adds.

I want to blurt out that it's not Dani, but I'm sure any kind of protest will simply raise suspicions. "You guys have fun at the pub, and I'll be thinking about you..." I pause. "Wait, no." I shake my head as they laugh. "I won't be thinking about you."

The last thing I'll be thinking about are my teammates when I get Dani alone in bed. I'll be thinking about her and only her, and I pray to fucking God, it's me she's thinking about, not my late brother.

How fucked up is that?

I walk back to my car, jump in and head home. My stomach grumbles as I step into the shower and consider what to wear to our baby-making session. I wash quickly, and thoroughly, and head back to my bedroom to dress. My phone buzzes on my nightstand and I pick it up to see a message from Dani, letting me know she has some steaks to put on the grill. I really don't want her going through the trouble and message back that I can pick us up some food, but no, she insists on cooking, like it's the least she can do in return. Again, how fucked up is this?

Thirty minutes later, I pull into her driveway and smile when I see the big dog bus. She really does have a fun job and the dogs all love her. What's not to love? Not that I love her. Okay, I mean I do. I love her as a friend.

Shut up, Conner.

I step from the car, my pulse pounding in my neck. Jesus, I've had sex before. I've just never been this nervous in the past. I walk up to the door, and I'm about to use my key when it opens and I find Dani standing before me, wearing a pretty floral dress.

"You look beautiful."

"Oh, this old thing." It's a lie. It's new and if I had to guess, she bought it today. She does a weird swirly thing, and knowing she's as nervous as I am, puts me at ease. As I feel a shift inside me, I realize I'm the one who's going to have to take charge here. I'm the one who's going to have to put her at ease, and make this good. With those thoughts racing around my brain, the last of my unease fades, and I lean into her and give her a kiss on the cheek, like I usually do. Later, however, it won't be her cheek I'm kissing.

"You look nice too," she murmurs.

"Oh, this old thing." I mimic her swirl, and it pulls a laugh from her. Good. I want her relaxed, and hey, we might as well enjoy ourselves, right?

"Hungry?"

I rub my stomach. "Starved."

She pouts before turning to head down the hall to her kitchen. "Sorry I couldn't be there today. I really wanted to be, but we ended up calling in a vet for Buster. He wasn't eating, and it turns out he has a bad tooth. I had to call his owners, who are on vacation in the Bahamas, and see if they wanted it pulled, and they did so I had to take him to the vet clinic and wait, and now he's going to be staying the night the clinic, because there were a few complications."

"Poor Buster."

"I'll check in tomorrow morning."

"I'll come with you."

She opens her mouth like she's going to protest, but aren't we past this by now? She glances down, and I touch her chin and lift her eyes to mine. "Here's the deal, Dani." She frowns, and blinks dark lashes over even darker eyes. God, she's so beautiful. "If we're doing this, it's you and me. No other men. No other women." A grin tugs at the corner of her mouth. I realize she hasn't been with a man in a long time and it's not on her agenda, but I want her to know that the rules apply both ways and that if she put herself out there, men would be falling all over her. "No waving your cat all over the place. You know, like from that Queen song." She bursts out laughing and I angle my head. "What's so funny?"

"That's not quite how the lyrics go and I don't think ·they mean what you think they mean."

"Really?"

"No, it's *kicking* your *can* all over the place."

I scratch my head. "What does that even mean?"

"I don't really know."

Wood. Dumb as a stump. I give her a cheeky grin and try to hide my insecurities with humor. "I never was the brightest bulb in the pack."

"Don't say that," she snaps. "You just misunderstood the lyrics."

"Anyway, no waving your cat. Neither one of us."

"Okay, and if we're still talking about the song, I guess what you're trying to tell me is, you're going to rock me."

I slide my palm to the side of her face and dip my head. A little gasp sounds in her throat when I don't speak, but instead press my lips to hers. Heaven. Holy fucking hell! A moan I have no control over crawls out of my throat as I taste her mouth. And her lips, Jesus, they're so soft and pliable as I kiss her with a hunger that has been simmering for far too many years, letting me know that what we're about to do later might be a little risky for my heart.

I break the kiss, and we're both left a little shaken, as we stare at each other. "Okay, so that's a yes," she finally manages to say and I grin. "I uh, should get the steaks on."

"One more thing." I touch her arm, and she goes still. "I don't know what is going to happen down the road. We can't predict that, but I will always be in your life, and our child's, okay? Tell me you'll never take that away from me."

"Never," she answers quickly, with authority and confidence. She must have been thinking about this too. "You're the best man I know, Conner. I want you involved if that's what you want."

Best man she knows. I could probably debate that, considering I've been lusting after my brother's wife for years, from way before she was Alec's wife, and I'm about to attempt to put a baby in her because her husband is no longer with us. She moves away, and I watch the sway of her dress as my gaze drops to take in her gorgeous, shapely legs. And now—fuck— now all I can think about is what they're going to feel like wrapped around me.

6

DANI

I am so damn nervous I can barely eat. Not only is my mouth not working right, my stomach is so tight, it's making it hard to keep anything down. But something tells me I'm going to need all my energy. Conner did, after all, tell me he was going to rock my world. Not that I would know what that's like. I've only had one lover and that was my husband, and I don't want to say anything negative about him, but my world...was never rocked.

I stab my fork into a cucumber, and as I bring it to my mouth, my gaze strays to the other side of the table. My God, just look at Conner. Chowing down on his steak with hunger and vigor, like we're not about to go upstairs and have sex for the very first time. He's calm, collected, totally in control of himself, like he knows exactly how to take care of me, and I think I might like that. Oh God, I do. I do like that.

I take a breath, and as I let it out, it releases a bit of the tension inside me. He puts his last bite of steak into his mouth and moans. The sound reverberates through my body, and I set my fork down. His eyes lift, meeting mine, and as they do, my sex quivers in heated anticipation.

"That was delicious, Dani." He licks his lips, and as his gaze drops to the vee in my dress, I'm suddenly not sure exactly what it is he's savoring. Is he going to eat me with that same kind of vigor? Oh God, I hope so. I really do.

"Merci."

He chuckles. "Do you know any other French?"

"Oui, bien sûr. Which means, of course I do. I just don't have anyone to practice it on and it would be nice to have someone to converse with."

"That accent is kind of sexy, you know, and you can practice on me. I can listen, I just can't respond."

I arch a playful brow and point my finger. "I could say anything I want and you'd never know."

"Nope, I wouldn't. Maybe I should take classes too."

"Actually, I've been thinking about taking courses again." I quit just about everything after Alec died. It's only recently I started the book club with Josie and her friends. They're all so smart and educated, I sometimes feel inferior, though.

"Why French?" he asks.

"I lived in Montreal and found the language interesting," I explain, not telling him the real reason. "Or maybe it's because it's a sexy language."

He sets his fork on his plate, his eyes dark and lustful. "Be careful waving that accent around. It's very seductive."

On that note, I jump up and walk across the room on shaky legs. I set my plate in the sink, which is full of bubbly water.

"Coffee?" I ask, and the next thing I know, his body is pressed against mine.

Heat warms my neck as his mouth hovers near my ear. "No."

That one word races through my body and settles between my legs. He touches my hair, moves it away from my neck and with the lightest of touches, presses his lips to my flesh. Oh God, this is happening. It's really happening.

"Tea?"

"No." This time that one word comes out like a growl.

"Me?" I squeak out. Catching me by surprise, he turns my body, and pins me between his hips and the counter.

He touches my chin, his gaze roaming my face as he answers with, "Yes."

His lips find mine, and I nearly melt to the floor as he kisses me with heat and hunger. I have never been kissed like this in my life. I might not be his type, but he's giving it his all, totally committing and everything about that makes me feel like I'm special, and for that I'm grateful. A weird sound catches in my throat.

"Nervous?" he asks, and inches back. He studies me as I give a tight nod. He lightly brushes his thumb over my cheek, a great deal of tenderness about him, but there's something else there, something brewing just below the surface. "What are you thinking about?"

It's an innocent question, but I get the sense it's a loaded one. I put myself in his shoes and consider what we're doing, what I'm asking of him, and what might actually be going through his mind. I was married to his brother, which complicates this a lot. Does he think I chose him as a stand-in for Alec because I'm trying to recreate what we had? He'd be wrong, and honestly when I talked about DNA, it's *this* man's DNA I wanted and he needs to know that he's the man I want in my bed tonight. How do I do that?

Never in my life have I talked dirty—sure, I've read some hot books through book club, but right now, this could be our first and last night together, and dammit, I'm going to let him know exactly what and who I'm thinking about. I move my body against his, and his big cock presses against me, giving me the courage to call on the brazen heroine in the last book I read.

"I'm thinking about you, and how your cock is going to feel inside me." He goes still. Like completely still. Is he even breathing? Oh God, did I ruin this? Did my attempt at dirty talk turn him off? Did I mess up our friendship? Is he going to run for the hills? I open my mouth to tell him I was kidding, but his lips come down on mine. Hard. Possessive. A man with a fierce hunger I'm pretty sure I don't have what it takes to sate. But dammit, I'm going to try.

He runs his hands down my bare arms, leaving goosebumps as his fingers go lower and move to my hips. He bunches up my dress, tugging it a bit higher until the hem is hovering just below my sex.

"If you ask me, I'd say it's going to feel pretty damn awesome," he murmurs.

"You think?" God, I sound so breathless.

"Yeah, but thinking is overrated."

"Conner," I murmur as he moves his body, shifting until his cock is against my side, his hands close to the needy spot that is craving his touch—has been craving it for a long time now, if I'm being honest.

"Why don't we go to your room, so I can put my cock inside you and you can see for yourself just how good this is going to be?"

"One thing," I say quickly.

"What?"

"This is just between us."

"Yeah, I'm not much into threesomes, Dani."

I laugh. "What I'm saying is I don't really want the guys or anyone else to know. Not yet, anyway. Obviously if I get pregnant, we'll have to tell them. But if I don't get pregnant..."

"It's no one's business but our own."

"Conner," I say again for lack of anything else as he lets go of my dress, and lifts me clear off my feet. I wrap my legs around his body, and link my hands behind his head. I can barely breathe as he backs up, turns around and heads for the stairs. The man has been in my house numerous times, and I think the only time he's been in my bedroom was the day he helped us move. When he stays over, he sleeps in the spare bedroom, which has always been known as Conner's room. With determined steps, he carries me up the stairs, walks by my room and takes me into his.

"I want you in my bed," he growls into my ear. "I want you naked, and your legs spread for me, so I can fill you with my hard cock."

Oh. My. God.

Does he talk like this to all women he's about to fuck? Wait, that's not something I want to know.

"Tell me you want that too," he growls.

"I want that," I breathe out. "I really, really want that." Way to sound eager, Dani. Then again, who cares. Conner knows it's been a long time since I've been touched.

"But first, I'm going to need to look at you for a while." He sets me down next to the bed, and a measure of unease creeps through me.

I point with a shaky finger. "I...the lights." He cocks his head, his eyes full of heat and questions. "I don't normally...and you know, this is just to make a baby." I actually need the lights out, because if he sees what's really in my eyes, he might conclude that this is more to me, and I don't want him to get the wrong idea...or the right idea. Ugh.

"You want me to just do the technical stuff, Dani?"

I gulp. How do I answer that? "I...I..."

When I can't find my words, he reaches out, and lightly touches my hair. "Yes, this is about making a baby, but tonight, you're under my care, and we're going to do things a bit differently if that's okay with you." I give a tight nod, and his eyes drop. A loud growl full of pleasure cuts through the silence. "I have been dying to see you naked..." He runs one hand over my hips, shaping my curves. Another growl rumbles in his throat. "You are so fucking sexy."

Sexy.

God, I don't think any man has ever called me that before, and I never felt it...until now.

"I need to see you when I put my mouth and hands on you." I gulp air. He slides a hand between my legs, and I'm so wet it's almost embarrassing. "I need to see this sweet pussy before I devour it."

There's going to be pussy devouring?

"Oh, yes." I clamp my mouth shut after those two desperate words slip from my lips. But something in his grin tells me he likes that this isn't going to be all technical.

"You like that, huh? You like the idea of me devouring your pussy?"

"Yes."

"You don't mind if I look my fill first?"

I gulp, and even though sex with the lights on is out of my comfort zone, I find myself saying, "No, as long as I can look my fill too." That brings a smile to his face as he backs up, reaches over his shoulder, and tugs his shirt off.

Oh my...

"That's a good start," I tell him, and his grin widens.

I've seen him walk around shirtless before, but the hot image before me never gets old, and when I did see him half-dressed, I was always careful not to stare. I didn't want to give him or anyone else the wrong idea. Which was probably the right idea. Am I even making sense? God, how could I be when I'm staring at utter perfection?

His chest rises and falls as I tentatively reach out. "Dani," he murmurs, his muscles clenching. I lift my gaze to his and the intensity about him is as frightening as it is exciting.

"Yeah."

"Touch me," he breathes out, and I place my hand on his chest, splaying my finger. "Fuck, yeah."

Okay, I know I'm not this man's type, but holy, I don't think this kind of arousal can be faked. A burst of excitement races through me, and his big hand closes over mine, moving it over his body, and taking it lower and lower until my palm is pressed against his hard cock and he's cursing under his breath.

"How the fuck am I going to last?" he mumbles, and I'm not sure if he realizes he said that out loud. He backs up and our hands fall apart. Mine drops to my side, and his gaze goes up and down the length of me again, drinking me in. The hunger in him gives me a new kind of courage, and I grip the hem of my dress.

His gaze flashes back to mine, his breath coming fast as I lift my dress and pull it over my head. "You are so fucking beautiful," he murmurs, as he takes in my matching bra and panties, something else I bought today, because yeah, maybe I didn't want this to be technical either. His throat gurgles as he swallows. "I can't believe I get to touch you."

I reach behind my back and unhook my bra and the moan of appreciation boosts my confidence.

"Oh la la," he says and I laugh, the tensions easing inside me. He grins. "That's all the French I know." He cocks his head. "Was it sexy?"

"Très sexy."

"I'll take that as a yes." He licks his lips, his eyes watching my every move.

Honestly, I can hardly believe I'm undressing myself in front of this man, and feeling confident in my curvy body. My God, he looks like a predator about to attack his prey.

With that thought in mind, I slide my fingers into my panties, and his nostrils flare like a wild animal ready to pounce. "You can rip them from my body, if you want."

"Oh, I fucking want," he answers without an ounce of hesitation. Two steps has him standing before me, his hands bunching the thin lace. A quick tug later, he has the lace in his palms, balling it up and breathing in my scent. My sex muscles clench at the display of heat, hunger and primitiveness radiating from him.

Conner unleashed.

I like it a lot, and make a mental note to try out more of the brazen things that happen in my romance books. Because yeah, I want more of this savagery. His fingers touch my inner thighs, and all coherent thought packs a bag and heads south. He's right, thinking is overrated. With the lightest of touches, he runs his fingers over my quivering flesh, his fingers going higher and higher, until he's a hair's breadth away from my sex.

"Conner..."

"Yeah."

"Touch me," I moan. He grins, and runs his finger over my slit, opening my folds to dip into my warm heat. I grip his shoulders. "God, yes." With the last of my inhibitions ebbing away, I move my hips forward, trying to force his finger inside and he growls. "Please," I beg.

He drags his finger down the length of my sex, and then slowly, torturously inches back upward toward my throbbing clit. "The hormones are doing a number on you huh?"

"No," I admit. "You are."

He goes still again, deadly still, his finger hovering over my clit. "You want me, Dani."

"Yes, Conner."

With that he slides a thick finger inside me and my muscles clench around it. "Fuck, you are so hot and wet." Under his breath, in an almost mystified voice, he murmurs, "For me."

Why the hell does that surprise him so much? Has he not looked at himself lately? It's not just his face and body that's attractive to women. He's a great guy. I can't believe he's still single.

I press my lips to his bare chest and breathe in his scent as he moves his finger in and out of my pussy. I haven't been touched in so long, my orgasm is going to hit fast and that's going to be damn embarrassing. I touch his chest, explore his muscles, and run my lips over his nipple as he flattens his palm and presses it against my clit.

"Conner," I gasp, lifting my face to his. "I...I..." I don't remember it ever feeling this good, and that's probably because it was always a little hurried with Alec.

"I know. Let's take the edge off, babe, and then I can spend the rest of the night taking my sweet time with you."

He wants to spend the rest of the night taking his sweet time with me? I must be dreaming. Yeah, I have to be because why would he want to make this so great for me, when our end goal is his orgasm? But mine is important to him too.

I whimper my response and he slowly eases another finger in, filling me up more than I've felt in a very long time. As he presses his lips to mine, he moans into my mouth and my sex muscles begin to clench around him. I grip his shoulders as my orgasm takes shape and when I let go, the amount of liquid heat that drips over his hands and down my thighs fills my face with heat and embarrassment.

"Nice," he murmurs into my mouth. "Next one is going to be with my mouth on you, because I can't fucking wait to taste you on my tongue."

Oh God, my muscles clench harder at that, and he eases off my clit, keeping his fingers inside me as I ride out the powerful waves of pleasure. When my body stops spasming, I back up, and his fingers slide from my body. I put my hand on his chest and give a little push.

"That's going to have to wait."

His eyes narrow, like he's worried he did something wrong, like I'm putting an end to things. "Dani...what...what's going on..." He runs a shaky hand through his hair and before he can say anything else, I drop to my knees and pop the button on his pants.

I tug his zipper down. "What's going on is that I need to taste you first."

"Oh, fuck..."

7

CONNER

As she tugs my pants down and widens her lips to accommodate my girth, pre-cum spills from my slit, and goddammit, I'm terrified that I'm going to shoot down her throat the second I feel those lush lips around me. I can't do that. She needs my cum inside her body, not in her mouth. I should stop her. I want to stop her, but dammit, I also need her mouth on me.

"Dani," I moan as she takes me between her sweet lips, her warm heat blanketing my cock in an utterly mind-fucking way. I grip her hair and move it to the side so I can watch her work her mouth around the length of me, because I'm obviously some kind of masochist.

She moans as she continues to take me deep, and I move my hand with the motion of her head. Her eyes lift and there's a brightness to them when they meet mine. She knows exactly how much I like this, and she likes doing it for me.

"Fuck, Dani."

She inches back and takes my cock into her hands, running her warm palms up and down the length of me as I thicken even more. "I guess now I know why they call you wood." I groan as she sticks her tongue out to taste the pre-cum and in that moment, I realize I won't be putting my mouth on her tonight. That will have to wait because I need to be inside her before I lose my fucking load.

I inch back and she whimpers as my cock falls from her hands. Reaching down, I grip her arm and pull her to her feet. "On the bed, legs wide open," I command in a rough voice.

A fine quiver goes through her and as she backs up, climbs onto the bed on all fours and points her sweet ass my way. She crawls to the middle, and drops to her back. The welcoming view has me kicking off my pants and boxers. I'm about to grab a condom, like I always do when I remember what it is we're doing here. I have never had sex without a condom before, and the thoughts of skin-on-skin contact with this incredible woman...well, if I thought I was going to come fast before, I now suspect I'm going to break a world land and speed record.

I climb onto the bed and shift on my knees until I'm between her legs, which aren't spread at all. Is she having a moment of shyness with me? That won't do. I grip her legs and slide them open, and moan when I glimpse her gorgeous pink pussy. My cock jumps and I take it into my hands. She bites her lip and moans as I stroke myself.

I tug hard, and groan. "This is what you do to me."

Her breathing changes, and her nipples quiver as her chest rises and falls rapidly. Her face is the prettiest shade of pink I've ever seen. I lightly stroke her pussy and find her so damn wet for me.

"Conner, please."

I angle my head, and I'm stalling slightly because I am desperately trying to keep it together. "You want my cock in here?" I ask and slide a finger into her warm, waiting core. She quivers around me and I'm happy that she's close again. Lasting long is not on the horizon for either of us, but hey, that doesn't mean I can't keep my promise and devour her later. There's no saying I'm going to impregnate her first time around.

As my one working brain cell chews on that, I fall over her, and take one of her nipples into my mouth. I moan as her fingers race through my hair and I shift my body, until my crown is pressed against her tight opening. This is going to be fucking epic. Honestly, I can't even wrap my brain around the fact that it's happening. She was my teenage wet dream for years.

I power my hips forward and push all the way into her, burying every inch of myself in her warm lush body. I go still, letting her get used to the fullness because it's been a while for her and I don't ever want to do anything to hurt her. I cup her face, push her hair back and kiss her mouth with years of pent-up need and hunger.

She kisses me back and moans as our tongues tangle. "You good, Dani?" I manage to get out, between kisses.

"I'm so good," she responds and moves her hips, letting me know she wants me to fuck her. Fuck her, I will. I inch out, and our groans mingle as I slide back into her again, stretching her tight walls as they hug my thick cock. She's so damn wet, I easily slide in and out. Her legs wrap around my back and she pulls me to her. My chest presses against her, and her hard nipples practically score my skin as I pump in and out of her.

I grind my pelvis against her swollen clit, and her eyes nearly roll back in her head. I love learning her body like this, and yeah, skin on skin is way better than I ever could have imagined.

"So good," I murmur.

"Yes," she agrees, her breath coming faster now, and I pick up the pace, a detriment to me lasting very long, but she looks like she needs to come again and I want that for her. I shift, go back on my knees and lift her hips, partly because I want to watch my cock disappearing inside of her, and partly because I want to give her clit the attention it needs.

"God, Conner," she hisses as I fuck her and apply pressure to her clit. "That...that...why does that feel so good?"

For me, it's because it's with her, and with no barriers. She's had sex with no barriers before, so maybe it's because it's with me. I can't think like that, though. She still loves my brother so much that she wants my DNA for her child. That thought is for another time, when I'm not pounding into her sweet pussy like a man drunk on lust, and she's not chanting my name over and over. I must say, I do love hearing it on her tongue, though.

She lets loose a loud groan as she squeezes my cock and a second later, I'm soaked from her hot release and I fucking love it. "Dani, fuck yeah."

She whimpers and I let go of her clit and grab both hips for leverage. I pull her to me and start pistoning in and out of her. "Yes, yes," she cries out, as her hot release singes my skin and brings on my own climax. I drive deep, holding her hips tight as my body gives in and spurts seed deep into her body.

"Fuck," I groan, throwing my head back and pinching my eyes shut as pleasure like I've never felt before zings through my entire body. I hold her tight, my dick inside her, until I give her every last drop.

When I finally open my eyes, she goes up on her elbows, her gaze lingering on her sex as I remain buried deep. "I feel you...I feel everything."

I slowly inch out of her and climb over her body. I move in beside her and cover us with the blankets, even though the room is hot. She stays on her back and I'm not sure if that's what one is supposed to do to help the sperm find an egg. I shift to my side and lightly touch her hair.

When she stays quiet, for too long, worry niggles at me. "We good?"

She gives me a big smile and my heart jumps. "We're great," she says, and rolls into me, and I think maybe she's right. I wasn't sure what to expect after sex. Maybe a measure of awkwardness, but there's none. There's contentment and bliss and a whole lot of love between us—the friendship kind.

She cups my face. Her lips find mine for a soft, grateful kiss. "Thank you for making that so amazing."

I chuckle. "My mother always told me if you're going to do something, do it right."

She chuckles. "You definitely did it right. But conner, there's a time and place for your mother...and this absolutely isn't one of them."

I laugh at her teasing. "You think…" I drag my hand down her body and touch her stomach. "…we did it?"

Her smile falters. "I…I don't know." She blinks and tries for another smile. "Let's hope so. I mean, I got pregnant fast with Alec, especially when we didn't do it a lot. Hopefully it'll be one and done and you won't have to do this again."

I frown, because I'm pretty sure she had as much fun in this bed as I had, and if I'm not mistaken, it might have actually even brought us closer, made us better friends. Or that could be my post orgasmic bliss speaking. "Do you not want to do it again?"

"If we have to, yeah."

Have to? What about if we want to? Should I ask that? "Do we have to wait until next month to see if you're pregnant before we do this again?"

"No, I mean I can get pregnant up to five days before ovulation and one day after. But today is my ovulation day according to my app. I didn't want to ask too much of you."

I think about that for a second. "Okay, so to optimize your chances of getting pregnant, we can and should do it tomorrow, right? Or maybe even again later tonight?"

"Yeah, that sounds about right."

"Math and calculations aren't my strong suit as you know, but if we go into next month, we should utilize those five days prior to ovulation. Doesn't that make sense?" Way to twist this and make it all about fertilization when the truth is, I want more.

She nibbles on her bottom lip. "If you don't mind. I don't want to put you out."

I give her a wink. "You asked me to give you a baby. Isn't that all about putting out?" She laughs and whacks me. "Besides, I already told you I won't be shaking my cat all over the place, so hey, I need to get my sex somewhere, right? And why shouldn't you have a few orgasms of your own while we're doing this?"

"I think all that makes sense. We can't have you sperming all over the place. We need those swimmers strong and abundant."

"Sperming all over the place? Wait, maybe those are the lyrics."

"They're not."

Her laugh fills me with such happiness, I roll on top of her and press my lips to hers. I kiss her deeply, and when I pull back and find confusion on her face, I realize what I've done. We agreed on sex and orgasms, but those intimacies are for when we're trying to make a baby. "That was practice," I tell her.

She runs her tongue over her bottom lip like she's savoring the taste of me. "I see."

"We're allowed to practice, right?"

"I think practice is good."

"That makes me think in the weeks before ovulation, we could have some practice runs. I can't help but think that will make us experts when you do ovulate."

"Yeah, that might not be a bad idea. My mother always said practice makes perfect."

"Mothers give the best advice," I agree and flop onto my

back, pulling her to me until her head rests against my still racing heart.

I get to have lots more sex with Dani.

Is that a good thing or a bad thing, dude?

Ignoring that inner voice, I quiver as her hot breath tickles my flesh. She snuggles in tight and exhales a contented sigh. Her body is warm pressed against mine, and as I think about all the sex we're going to have, my damn dick starts getting hard again.

"Dani?"

"Hmmm?"

"Is it later?"

"**W**hy are you looking at me like that?" As I sit on my big bus, I glance at Conner in the through my peripheral vision on the right. He's in the first seat by the door, which is Trixie's usual seat. Good thing I'm not picking her up today, or she'd probably bark her face off at him until he moved.

A cute grin curls up his lips as it taunts the well-sated but still hungry spot between my legs. "Like what?"

"I don't know, like you're amused by something."

"Maybe I'm just in a good mood from last night."

Now it's my turn to grin as I think about all the sex we had, last night and again this morning. I'm almost afraid to look down because I think there might be flames between my legs. We were definitely burning it up between the sheets, having sex like we'd discovered something no one else in the world knew about.

It was crazy, fun and I'm far too happy that we get to do it again. I know what I'm asking of him is a bit crazy, but he's going to be the best dad out there, and when he finds true love and gets married and has a family of his own, I know he'll still be the best daddy to our child—and to his own. But thinking about him being married leaves a hollow in the pit of my stomach. It's not like we can ever be more. He loves me like a best friend. Now, however, we're best friends with benefits.

"So that's it?" I ask and adjust the rearview mirror to see him better. "You're in a good mood because we had sex."

"Yeah, and you just look so damn cute driving this big-ass bus. It's kind of making me hard."

I laugh at his foolishness. "I think I handle big things just fine." As soon as the words leave my mouth, Conner bursts out laughing and so do I. I have no idea where the hell that even came from. I don't normally make jokes, and especially not sexual ones. Maybe all that sex dislodged something in my brain.

He grabs the pole and shifts in his seat, like he might actually be sporting a boner. "Who are you and what have you done with my Dani?"

My Dani.

It's insane how much I like when he says things like that. Like when I fed him the mozzarella stick the night at the pub after the big win and he said *at least someone loves me.* I have no idea why I have this deep need to feel important. It's one of the reasons I started dating Alec. To have a guy like that pay attention to me was such a huge ego boost for a girl who had no game and no boyfriends up to that point in life.

"I have to pick up Buster, and I always pick the dogs up in the bus."

"It's one dog, we could have taken the car."

"No, he's used to this and he's under enough stress as it is, so I want to make sure he's as comfortable as can be. Plus, he's a St. Bernard coming in at around one hundred and fifty pounds."

"That's a big boy."

"That he is," I agree, although I'm not exactly talking about Buster. I really have no idea what's come over me lately. Must be from the hormone injections.

Grinning back, Conner shakes his head and smiles at me. "You're going to be a great mom." My heart flutters at the thought and I almost want to make a quick stop at the drug store to pick up a pregnancy test, but it's far too soon, and maybe there's a part of me that doesn't want to know. If I don't know, we can keep on having sex. While that's good for my libido, I'm honestly not sure how great that is for my heart. I can't get involved emotionally with Conner. He told me long ago, with zero words, that we—us—were never going to happen.

"Wait," he begins. "You love dogs, and take care of everyone else's dog, but you don't have one. I never thought about that before."

"Yeah." I flick on my signal and take a left at the lights.

"Want to elaborate?"

I shrug. "When Alec and I got married, and I got pregnant, I really wanted a dog but he didn't want one."

His muscles tighten and he gives me a look that suggests I have no idea who his brother is. He could be right. There were times in our marriage I wondered who he was too...and wondered where he was when he came home late, or didn't come home at all.

"You could get one now."

"I'm going to. Just not yet." I give him a fast glance and crinkle my nose.

"Why not?"

"It's just...do you remember Bear?"

He grins. "Yeah, I loved Bear."

Unfortunately, he only knew my chihuahua for one year. We moved to Boston when I was sixteen and Bear died the next year. It was so damn hard, but Conner was there to help me get through it, just like he was there when we lost Alec. Once again my stomach cramps, guilt making it tight. He's adamant that he wants to be around me, likes hanging out, but there is still a part of me that thinks I'm holding him back.

"Bear was the best."

I smile, my thoughts going back to my dog. He really was the best, and so protective of me. He might have been small, but he was mighty, and I think the only guy he liked was Conner. A couple of times when Alec came to the house to find his brother, Bear nearly took out his ankles.

"Mom and Dad got Bear when they were pregnant with me. Bear and I grew up together. He was my best friend in the whole world." When Conner pouts, I laugh. "Besides you, of course. But Bear was always there for me. We moved a lot because of Dad's career, and making friends was never easy."

"A chihuahua named Bear. It was fitting considering he was small but fierce." He toys with his phone in his hand when it lights up, but he doesn't check the message. "You want to wait until you're pregnant."

"I kind of do."

"That makes sense. You want another chihuahua?"

"Actually, no. I've been thinking about getting a big dog this time. I just haven't made up my mind yet."

"A baby and a dog at the same time. Here I thought I was the masochist."

"What?"

He gulps. "Oh, nothing. It's just going to be a lot of work."

I flick on my signal and ease my bus into the parking lot at the vet. Conner is right, it is a big bus, but I've gotten used to driving it. "I'll just be a minute." I open the door, and Conner stands.

"I'm coming." I shrug and he continues, "What if you have to lift him?"

I feign offense. "Are you saying I'm weak or something?"

"Nope, but if you're pregnant, I don't want you lifting heavy things. We are not taking any chances, and if you fight me on this, no more cock for you."

I laugh at that. "You're going to hold out on me?"

He lifts his chin. "Maybe."

"That means no sex for you too right. You do understand that?"

His shoulders slump. "Oh yeah..."

He looks so adorable, I can't help but cup his cheeks and kiss him. Surprise moves over his face, and I quickly say, "Practice."

"Right." He gives a curt nod. "Anyway, no lifting. Okay?"

I'm about to protest, but he's so damn serious, I just go with it. Clearly, he's going to be very overprotective and I secretly like that. In my marriage, I did everything, from cooking and cleaning, to lifting, even when I was pregnant. It was the life I chose, and I'm not going to think anything bad about my marriage. All I'm saying is if I ever get married again, I'd want things to be different. Not that I'm ever getting married again. *And why is it you're never marrying again, Dani?* I exit the bus and turn to find Conner behind me. My heart skips a beat, because yeah, the guy behind me could be the very reason I'll stay single for the rest of my life.

Maybe I should put an end to this baby-making plan right now.

He angles his head and he must misread whatever it is I'm showcasing on my face, because he says, "I'm not going to let anything happen to you." He puts his hand on the small of my back and guides me toward the building. I like his touch so much, the caring way he holds me, that even if I wanted to end this—knowing it was for the best—I'm not sure I have the strength to do it.

We make our way inside, and the receptionist gives me a big smile, but that smile turns to shock and excitement as her gaze strays to Conner.

She stares, her mouth open and then she finally blurts out. "You're Conner Birch."

He laughs and I try not to let jealousy invade my body. I'm used to women throwing themselves at this man, and why wouldn't they. It's probably all the hormones making me feel more protective. Or maybe it's because he was inside me last night and this morning. Oh boy. Once again, I question if we should be doing this or not.

"Yes. Dani and I are here to pick up Buster."

"Right, of course." She stands so fast her chair spins backward and a few files on the desk fall to the floor. She runs to the back office, and a giggle spills from her throat. I note the way Conner frowns.

I put my hand on his arm and he flinches. Whoa. I tug it away fast. "Are you okay?"

"Yeah." He takes my hand and gives it an apologetic squeeze. Clearly, he wasn't himself there for a moment. "Sorry, I was uh, a million miles away for a second there."

I take in the deep lines on his forehead, the way he's avoiding my gaze. "Do you know her?"

"No, I don't." He scratches his head like he's remembering something. "Forgot to wear my ballcap."

He always wears his ballcap when he doesn't want to be recognized. There seems to be something else going on with him at the moment though, something he has no intention of telling me, and I'm not about to ask if he doesn't want to share. Here I thought we didn't have secrets. Maybe that's not true at all.

I'm snapped out of my thoughts at the sound of Buster barking. He comes from the back room, his tail wagging madly. "Buster," I call out and drop to my knees. He comes barreling toward me, drool spilling the whole way. "How are you feeling, boy?"

The vet comes out behind him. "He's great now. He had some swelling in his jaw and under his eyes. The tooth was pretty infected. No toys or dental chews for a couple of days and soft foods only."

"Ice cream?" Conner asks and I turn and smile at him.

"For the dog or you?" the vet asks, and then her eyes go wide. "You're Conner Birch."

He grins and nods. "That's me, and I was thinking for both of us."

Her demeanor changes, her professionalism morphing into flirtation. "I'm a fan."

"Kat, this is Conner. Conner, this is Kat. Kat takes great care of my dogs. I don't know what I'd do without her."

Kat's eyes narrow, her gaze going from Conner, to me, back to Conner. There's confusion in her eyes, and I get it. What would a guy like Conner be doing with a dog caregiver, plain Jane like me?

"Are you two...I didn't know."

"No, no," I correct quickly as the receptionist giggles nervously again, and Conner's gaze strays her way. "We're friends. We go way back. I was actually married to Conner's brother."

"Oh yes, that explains it," Kat responds, a new kind of interest in her eyes. What the hell? That explains it? I get it that guys like Conner don't date girls like me, but that's just rude. But more importantly, can the man go nowhere without being hit on? Maybe I should have told her we're more than friends. But one, I'm not that brazen, and two I don't want to make things uncomfortable for Conner.

"In that case." She takes off her gloves and holds a hand out. Conner takes it in his palm. "I'm off at three if you want to get that ice cream."

My head rears back, and I push to my feet as she aims a come-hither smile Conner's way. Wow, brazen. Which is fine. I'm not jealous. Much. Seriously though, I wish I had her confidence. Maybe if I looked like her. Tall, blonde, completely put together, I'd be bold too.

It was you who was in Conner's bed last night, not Kat.

Yeah, but only because he's trying to put a baby in me.

Conner gives an easy laugh. "Actually," he begins and puts an arm around me. "We're more than friends. Dani's just so used to telling people she used to be married to my brother, it seems to slip out easily now." He kisses the side of my head. "When the truth is, we're more than friends." When Kat's eyes go wide, he pulls me in tighter. "In fact, we're friends with benefits." He wags his brows. "How lucky am I, huh?"

Oh. My. God.

My gaze flies to Conner's and I take in the mischievous grin on his face. Damned if he doesn't look proud of himself. I gulp, and nearly swallow my tongue as his words once again race around inside my brain. What the hell is he doing? I wanted to keep this thing between us a secret and then he goes and says we're friends with benefits.

"Anyway, we should get Buster to the park for ice cream," he says and Kat hands me a pamphlet.

"All his instructions are in here," she explains, returning to professional mode.

"Thanks," I manage to get out. We walk outside, and I turn to Conner. "What the hell was that, Conner?" I glare at him, but there's a little bubble of happiness inside of me. I love the protective way he acted.

"What, I didn't say anything that wasn't true?"

I glance over my shoulder to make sure she's not at the door listening. "Now she thinks...we're..."

"We are, Dani." He shrugs. "I've given this some thought, and soon enough, you're going to have to explain why you're pregnant, so maybe we should pretend to be dating. It might make the whole explanation thing simpler and we have that whole no waving your cat all over the place deal, and I don't always enjoy being hit on, you know. Especially when I'm out with you."

"What does that mean?" Why do women just assume we're not an item? I sigh, my stomach turning. What am I even thinking? Of course, they do. I stick out like a sore thumb in his crowd.

"She was rude, Dani. Which is why I went for the shock value. Friends with benefits. Did you see her face?" He laughs and it wraps around me and squeezes so tightly—in a nice way.

"Yeah, but I told her we weren't together. That's why she asked you out and I sounded like a liar."

"I covered it well." He bends and starts patting Buster, and jumps back up when Buster shakes his head, getting drool all over his clothes.

"I don't know about that."

"Look," he begins, and faces me, putting his hands on my shoulders. "We're going to have to explain it when you get pregnant. This way, we can pretend to be in a relationship and stage a breakup."

"What, like we're a romantic comedy or something?"

"Or something."

Did Kat think a girl like me with a guy like him could be nothing more than a comedy? I guess her response as to why we were together was rude. "There was a moment when I admired her." He arches a brow. "She's a woman who goes for what she wants and I admire boldness."

"Why admire her for that? You're a woman who goes for what she wants too. You're bold as fuck, Dani," he says matter-of-factly.

"Hardly."

He snorts out a laugh, puts an arm around me and drags me to him. He dips his head and his mouth is right there. All I have to do is go up on my toes and kiss him if I want to. But I don't have to do that, because he bends down farther and presses his mouth to mine and whispers, "Did you not ask me to put a baby in you? That's pretty fucking bold, babe."

Babe...God, when he calls me that. But seriously, I feel like he's asking me a question here, wanting clarification on what we're going to tell people.

"You're saying you want to go cash in on some benefits," I ask, needing a moment to think about things. We have his family, my family, and our friends to consider here. I don't want to lie to them but it sure would be easier to explain down the road.

"Yeah."

"Let's drop Buster off and head home." He holds his arms out, and shakes off the drool.

"I thought you wanted ice cream."

He makes a disgusted face. "I'm kind of wet."

Oh, he's not the only one. I decide to keep that to myself.

"I need to get out of these clothes," he informs me and I kind of like the idea of that, but poor Buster needs a treat. Conner leans in, and lightly swipes his tongue over my bottom lip. "We'll grab Buster a treat first, but no worries, babe." He wags his eyebrows. "There's something I'm definitely wanting to lick."

DANI

A bang inside the house wakes me and as I stretch out my tired limbs, I turn to find the other side of my bed empty. I reach across and the sheets are cold. How long has Conner been up? I glance at the clock and note that it's nearing noon. I jackknife up and take in the bright sunshine seeping in through the cracks in the curtains.

How did I sleep in so long? I guess it's been a busy week at work, with Marley, my nighttime animal care attendant, off sick. I had to pull off a few night shifts, and while I have a whole very nice bedroom set up at the Airbnb, I don't usually sleep all that well—especially with a two-hundred-pound man in a twin-size bed beside me. Yes, he insisted on staying with me. I make a mental note to switch it to a double bed. Then again, it's been two weeks since our sex fest, and if I am pregnant, this whole thing between us will be over.

Or maybe it won't be. We've been having so much fun, spending all our time together, and we get along so well. Don't even get me started on how amazing the sex is, or how attentive he is to my needs inside the bedroom and out. A girl could get used to that. I briefly close my eyes and imagine what it would be like if one of us sold our house, and we lived together, like a real family. My heart misses a beat, as I envision it. The thing is, it's something I thought about back in high school, before he ignored the letter I gave him.

But now, things are different. Maybe we do have a chance at a future. We agreed on a pretend relationship. Not that we had to play that card. We've been holed up in my place baby-making. Soon enough we'll have to go outside and people will start asking questions. Maybe the relationship doesn't have to be fake, though. Is that something he might want? I know I'm sure as hell not going to leave a note asking, and truth be told, I'm afraid to bring anything of the kind up. I don't want to ruin what we have, what is budding between us. Or maybe it's all my imagination.

I hear a bang again, and I kick the covers off as my stomach cramps. That could either be a good thing or a bad thing. Last time I got pregnant, I had a lot of cramps early on. I do have that pregnancy test in the bathroom, and was planning on using it today. I push to my feet and pull on my pink fluffy robe. Here goes nothing.

In the bathroom, I find Conner sitting on the floor, a list in his hands. His eyes are narrowed, like he's having a hell of a time figuring something out.

"What are you doing?"

His head lifts, and the lines in his forehead smooth out as his soft gaze settles on mine. "I got this baby proofing list from the store."

I look at the list in his hand, although I'm thinking about his frown. Was he frowning because this is all real to him now, and he's having second thoughts? Because he really looks upset about something. He holds a sheet out to me and I take it, giving it a quick read.

"You were out already?"

"Some of us don't sleep until noon," he teases. "I even got a run in and I picked up some of your favorite bagels and that..." He pauses to make a face like he'd just eaten something vile. "...vegetable cream cheese that tastes like dirty feet."

"It's delicious and how do you know what dirty feet taste like?" He arches a brow and I shake my head. "Never mind." I fold my arms and lean against the wall. "Seriously though, you did a lot this morning and now I feel like a lazy oaf."

He winks at me. "Your body is busy making a baby. You need to be lazy."

A measure of unease grips me as I get another cramp, because I suddenly think I'm going to disappoint the man who was reluctant to get involved in my crazy hairbrained scheme. Maybe I should have left him out of this because dammit, he's really committing to the job.

I glance at the baby proofing list again. "It's a bit early for this."

He shrugs. "Maybe, but once the season starts again in the fall, I'll be on the road a lot and I just want to make sure this is all done."

He almost looks a little sad that I'm not all that happy about this. I squat down, cup his face and kiss him. "This was really sweet." He shrugs like it's nothing, but I know it's not. I'm just a bit worried that I'll never be able to get pregnant, and now that I've involved him, this isn't just about me anymore.

Why didn't I consider that? Dammit, how could I have been so selfish?

"Conner, it might not happen."

"Yeah, I know but I like to be prepared just in case." He jumps to his feet, opens the cabinet and produces the pregnancy test, and I'm a little surprised—although I shouldn't be—that he remembered today was testing day. "And there is only one way to find out if it did happen."

I take it from him, and that's when I notice the plastic pieces on the floor. "What were you doing down there anyway?"

"Trying to put the safety lock on the cabinet."

I bend and pick up the plastic lock and instructions, giving them a quick read. "This doesn't seem too hard." He goes quiet, something troubling on his mind, judging by his frown. "Conner?"

He puts one hand on the counter, and glances at the cabinet doors. "What if...my DNA isn't up to snuff with my brother's?"

"Conner," I begin quickly. "You are an NHL superstar. Any child would be so lucky to have your DNA." He glances at the instructions as I set them on the counter, and that's when I realize he was having trouble with them. "I know how to do this because I helped my sister baby-proof her house years ago."

He nods. "I just don't want our child to have a hard time, or get picked on."

"A hard time with school, you mean?" What is it he's not telling me?

"Yeah." He forces a smile.

"I had a hard time in school too, you know."

His brow bunches. "You did?"

I nod, and continue. "One of the reasons I started learning a new language was because it came easy to me, and I wanted something to make me feel more educated. All the people we hang out with, they're all so educated and I just take care of dogs."

He touches my face. "It's a very important job."

"Don't get me wrong, I love what I do. I just knew college wasn't for me, and no one has ever made me feel inferior, but sometimes I just feel less than when I'm around highly educated people who seem like they're good at everything. So instead of letting those feelings overtake me, I embraced them and try to conquer them by learning a new language. It gives me confidence. Does that sound silly?"

"Not at all, and I didn't know that, Dani." I wait for him to tell me what's going on inside his brain. He finally opens his mouth and asks, "Do you want me to leave while you pee on that stick?"

Clearly, he doesn't want to talk about what's really upsetting him. "Why don't you go put a bagel in the toaster for me, and I'm sure we'll have the results when it pops."

"Okay." He bends and gives me a soft kiss. Even though it seemed like he wanted to stay, I'm going to need a minute with the results, no matter what they are.

"Wait, can I have your phone? I need the time."

"Sure." He unlocks his phone and hands it to me. "Meet me downstairs." He leaves and that's when I see that the messages on his phone are open. I'm about to slide my finger across the screen to close them, only to stop when I see Alec's name. My heart lurches. Was Conner re-reading old messages from Alec. For the briefest of seconds, I think about reading the exchange, but stop. That's an invasion of privacy. What was said between brothers should stay between brothers. It does make me wonder if whatever was bothering him had something to do with Alec.

I pull up his clock app, and take the stick out of the package. I've done enough tests to know how they work, so I don't bother with the instructions. I pee on the stick, and set the timer. Honest to God, these are always the longest minutes of my life. I wash my hands and brush my teeth, and try not to stare at the timer. When it finally goes off, I take a big breath and pick up the stick. My chest deflates when I see that it's negative. I wasn't sure I expected it to happen this fast, and while I'm disappointed, I can't deny that I'm looking forward to spending more intimate time with Conner.

I drop the stick into the trash can, and without bothering to dress, I tighten the belt on my robe and make my way downstairs. Conner is leaning against the counter, a cup of coffee in his hand when I enter. His body is tight and I'm not even sure he's breathing. I slowly shake my head no, and he sets the cup down, quickly closes the distance between us and pulls me into his arms.

"I'm sorry, babe."

He hugs me tight and I melt into his warmth and comfort. I always loved the way this man held me. "Are you okay?"

"I am." A beat and then, "Are you?"

He inches back, cups my face. "I am, and hey, on the bright side, we get to have more sex."

"I was thinking the same thing."

He guides me to a chair. "Sit, let me get your bagel ready and then I want you to tell me what I can do today to make you happy."

I laugh as he grabs the cup of coffee he was holding earlier and hands it to me. I take a much-needed sip and moan my appreciation. He grabs the cream cheese from the fridge and I say, "This isn't all about me."

"Of course, it's all about you, Dani." He drops the tub of cheese onto the counter, and turns back to me, his eyes narrowed in deep concern. "This is all you've ever wanted."

I gulp and try to hide my disappointment. He's right. This is all about me. How could I ever have thought it wasn't? That I let all this playing house go to my head, like something real was happening between us. Stupid. Stupid. Stupid.

"We don't need to do anything special. Not for me."

He takes the bagel from the toaster, drops it onto a plate and coats it with cream cheese. "Fine, if you're leaving it with me, then we're going to the park, having ice cream and doing some bird watching. I know you like that."

Okay, so he's not going to let it go. Why is he so incredibly good to me? He places a bagel with a generous amount of cream cheese in front of me.

He crinkles up his nose. "After you enjoy eating your stinky feet, we'll go."

I laugh, my chest loosening. "What is it about this cream cheese that you don't like?" I swipe my finger through it, put it into my mouth and moan out loud. "Delicious."

He backs up a bit, and adjusts his jeans. That's when I realize what I've done. I dip my finger back in, and put it back in my mouth. "Oh my God, so good, Conner. You have no idea what you're missing."

"Actually, I do."

"Oh?"

"Change of plans for the afternoon."

Taking me by surprise, he lifts me clear from my chair, and carries me to the island in the middle of the kitchen. He sets me on it, grips my thighs and widens them. My bare sex warms in sweet anticipation. "If you're going to put something in your mouth and moan like that, I am too." With that, he lowers his head, plants his mouth on my pussy and moans as he eats me like a man starved. His head lifts, his eyes on mine. "Now this." He lightly rubs his finger over my throbbing clit. "Delicious." I moan, putting my hand on the back of his head and his chuckle fills the air as I guide his mouth back to where it belongs. I let loose a moan of pleasure.

Yeah, a girl could really get used to this.

CONNER

The sun is cresting the horizon as I just about finish my run. I take off my shirt and wipe the sweat from my forehead. Tanner Bang has the cup at his place tonight, and he's having a big get together. It will be the first time Dani and I have been out with anyone since we started having sex, and now, we're going to tell everyone that we're dating. I'm not sure how they're going to react. Maybe they won't be surprised. We do, after all, spend a lot of time together. Still, she used to be my brother's wife and that can make things a bit awkward.

I head inside the house, and even though it's a workday for Dani, it's still early and she doesn't have to be up just yet. I've been helping her out at the Airbnb, but soon enough, once school lets out at the end of June, just a week away, I'll be busy helping with the hockey camps. I love helping out the younger players and giving back to the community. A lot of the guys who live in the local area like to help out too.

I tiptoe up the stairs and make my way to the shower. I pass by my room, and glance in to find Dani sound asleep. My heart squeezes tight at the adorable sight and while I'd like to climb back into bed with her, I'm too sweaty. She's not ovulating until next week, but that hasn't kept us from ravishing each other. I pass by her bedroom, and my chest tightens. I don't want to sleep in my brother's bed, which is why we're always in the spare room.

What if you become a real family, Conner?

I step into the bathroom and tear off my shorts and socks as that thought bangs around inside my brain. Dani hasn't even cleaned the place out yet. It's pretty much the same as it was when my brother was alive. I don't even think she's emptied his side of the closet. I realize it's because she still loves him, but when does one move on, and will she ever be able to love another?

Will she ever be able to love me?

Fuck, that's what I want, what I've always wanted, and if it's never going to happen having a baby with her isn't my smartest move. Not that anyone ever considered me smart. But that could lead to hurt and pain...loss. I gulp, because I can't lose Dani. I can't even consider what my life would look like without her in it in some capacity.

I turn on the rain shower nozzle and step into the big open shower. I tilt my head back, and try not to let panic overtake me as I let the hot spray fall over my tired body. A good run is supposed to help clear the head, not mess it up.

"Need a hand?"

I open my eyes and find a sleepy-looking Dani gazing at my naked body. My cock instantly thickens at the deep desire in her eyes and it's in that moment, as I look at her, the fear subsides and I think maybe things will be different this time.

"Did I wake you?" I hold my hand out to her, and she unties her fluffy pink robe, letting it fall to the floor. My cock jumps at the gorgeous sight and I can't help but think how quickly she's became comfortable in her own skin around me. It was just three weeks ago that she wanted to have sex with the lights off, which is ludicrous. She has a body that needs to be admired. Did my brother allow her to leave the lights off, or worse, not pay her the attention she deserved? Jesus, I hate to think that, but the more time I spend with her, the more apparent that becomes.

She takes my hand, and mine swallows hers whole as I guide her in, and pull her against my body. "No, but I wish you would have."

"I was probably going to, after I showered," I confess.

"Didn't you know I like my men hot and sweaty?"

I laugh at that. "I somehow doubt that."

She squirts soap into her hand and starts washing my chest. "I also like when they smell like grapefruit."

I moan. "Yeah, it's such a manly smell."

She breathes me in and I cup her chin, lifting her face to mine. I bend my head and kiss her deeply, and her moan of pleasure curls around me and tugs at my balls.

She runs her hands over my cock, massaging the length of me and I groan. "Shower sex is the best."

Her hand stills for a second and that's when I realize what I said. Of course, she doesn't want to be thinking about shower sex with my brother, and I know I sure as hell don't want to be thinking about it either.

"I'm sorry, Dani."

She blinks up at me. "For what?"

"Memories," is all I say. "They're not easy. I know."

She groans and glances down, her hands still on my cock, still caressing me. She stares at my length, and I'm not sure I even want to know what's going through her head. I'm about to pull out of her hand when she speaks.

"I've never had shower sex before, Conner."

What the fuck.

"Dani." Her head lifts, and eyes full of sadness meet mine. What the fuck was wrong with my brother? How was he not having sex with this amazing woman all the time, all over his house. "I'm your first?" I ask. She nods and averts her gaze, like she's embarrassed about that, but it's not her who should feel shameful. My brother didn't do right by her. But goddammit, I sure as hell am going to. Then another thought hits. "Do you want to have shower sex?" I ask.

She nods eagerly. "I do," she admits eagerly and honestly, which prompts me to tell a small truth, too.

I push her damp hair back, my gaze moving over her flushed face. "I like having a first with you."

She grins, and teases, "I woke up so needy." A small laugh bubbles out of her throat. "My hormones are all over the place."

Her words are a reminder that we're not a couple, a family. We're friends having sex and while we're enjoying it, there's an end purpose. She rubs my cock a little faster, and blood drains from my brain. What was I just thinking about?

No longer able to remember or care, I squirt soap into my hands, and run them down her back, wanting to make her first time having shower sex spectacular for her. I cup her ass and give it a small squeeze and she chuckles as she continues to stroke my hard cock. If she keeps that up, this will be over before it begins.

I move her so she's positioned under the warm spray and I run my hands over her breasts, taking time with her pert nipples. Her body sways and I slide one hand lower, brushing her inner thighs.

"Conner," she murmurs, and reaches down, taking my hand and putting it on her sex. I do love a girl who knows what she wants.

"Need something, babe?"

"Yes," she groans, and I slide a finger into her. Her muscles clamp around me, and I curse under my breath. She really did wake up needy. I move my finger in and out of her slick heat, and her hands move to my balls.

"Fuck yeah."

"Seems like you need something, too," she teases.

"I do." I pull my fingers from her hot sex, grip her shoulders, and turn her. She gasps as I take her hands and put them on the back wall. With my mouth close to her ear, I whisper, "Keep them there."

She gasps again, a quiver racking her body as I put my foot between hers to widen her legs. "Conner," she whimpers, the pleasure in her voice teasing pre-cum from my crown.

I grip her hips and tug until her ass is in the air, her body opened for me. Pistoning forward, my tip breaches her tight opening, and in one quick thrust, I'm all the way inside her, my cock hitting her cervix. She calls out my name as she gasps and claws at the wall, her muscles quivering around my dick. Jesus, that feels incredible.

I grip her hips and hold tight as I pull out and drive back in again. I am never, *ever* going to get enough of this woman. Her breathing changes and I fuck her for a few more minutes. Her hot juices coat my cock, and I easily slick in and out of her. As her body quivers, chasing an orgasm, I fall over her, taking one breast into my palm while I slip my other hand between her legs to tease her clit.

The second I touch her, her heat explodes around my cock and I groan as I press hot, open-mouthed kisses to the wet flesh of her back. I circle her sensitive clit as she rides out the waves, and once her tremors subside, I grip her hips again.

"Conner, so good," she breathes out, her voice soft and sated.

I drive in and out of her, her muscles squeezing me tight. After three thrusts, I drive deep, and stay there as I deplete myself in her, filling her body with my cum. "Fuck yeah."

She whimpers and moves her body, milking every last drop out of me. I fall over her again and breathe against her back as my heart pounds against her. I run my hands down her legs, knowing they're probably unsteady.

I hold her to me, and when we both catch our breaths, I stand and pull her up. With her back pressed against my chest, I move her hair to the side and lightly kiss her neck. She moans, and sags against me, and the intimacy in the way our bodies meld tugs at my heart.

After a moment, she breaks the quiet. "Shower sex is pretty amazing."

I chuckle against her ear. "It's pretty amazing based on who you're having it with."

"We're going to be doing that again."

"For sure." I get the sense that Dani has only ever had bedroom sex, and dammit, I want to broaden her horizons. "But did you also know sex on the kitchen table, in front of a mirror, against the window, or even outside under the stars is just as amazing?"

I turn her in my arms and her half-lidded eyes meet mine. "Really?"

"Yeah, we can try all those things."

She tugs her bottom lip between her teeth. "I'd like that. But my neighbors..."

I shrug. "My place is pretty private." I like the idea of us being in my house, in my own bed, where memories aren't haunting either of us. "No one can see into my windows or my backyard."

Her eyes go wide. "Ooh, pool sex."

"You want that?" She nods and I kiss her. "How about tonight, after the party?"

She chuckles and reaches between our bodies. "Will you be up for it?"

"Babe, I'm just about ready for round two right here in the shower."

She grins. "While that sounds nice, I have to get to work. I don't want to be late picking up my pups."

"Right." I move her again until she's under the spray, which is beginning to get cold, so we both shower quickly. Once done, we dress, have coffee and breakfast, and thirty minutes later, we're on her bus. I get great joy watching her face light up as she picks up the dogs, and they truly love her as much as she loves them. Honestly, what's not to love? I knew how loveable she was when I first met her in high school. But I was worried about our friendship and then my brother stepped in. I couldn't help but think she went for the right brother. I barely made it through high school. At least I was good at hockey and channeled all my frustration at my inability to learn into scoring.

Once all the dogs are picked up, we head to the Airbnb, and she opens the gate. After closing it behind her, she opens the doors to the bus and the dogs all jump off and start running around the fenced-in grass area.

I shake my head and grin. "You have the best job."

She laughs. "I love what I do." She stands and I pull her into my arms, needing my mouth on hers. "Can't wait for tonight," I whisper when I break the kiss.

She nods and is about to get off the bus, but stops and calls, "Conner."

"Yeah?"

"I liked having a first with you too."

DANI

I cast a fast glance at Conner in the driver's seat as we head to Tanner and Maeve's place. I smooth my hands over my dress, and hope the little black number I'm wearing is appropriate. I wasn't really sure what to wear, but this is the dress Conner said he wanted to see me in and take off me later. We'll be moving to his place tonight, and I can definitely understand why he prefers that. I guess after I get pregnant, we'll both be going back to our own places, our own beds, alone. Well, I'll be alone. He can date whoever he wants. I push down that unpleasant thought as his hand reaches out and takes mine.

"Are you okay?"

"I am." I sink back into the seat, trying to appear comfortable. "I was just thinking about tonight."

He wags his brows. "Me too."

"Thanks for coming to work with me today." I laugh when I think about Ranger, the big goofy lab, and how he nearly knocked Conner over when he ran at him. Conner is a big guy, and it takes a lot to knock him off balance. Although I'm pretty sure he was off balance when he took me in the shower. God, just thinking about that is turning me on again. "The dogs really love you."

"Yeah, well. I love them too." He sticks his tongue out and makes a face as he pulls what appears to be fur from his mouth. "I just don't like eating all their fur."

"They do shed. When a breeder says a dog only sheds twice a year, what they really mean is January to June, and July to December."

He laughs at that and I open my phone, pulling up the app to do a quick check on the dogs. I know they're in good hands, but Penny seemed to have a bit of a cough and I want to make sure she's sleeping soundly.

"That app is such a great idea," Conner says and taps his head. "Smart girl."

"The owners really love it."

"I do too."

I crinkle my nose. "Why would you love it?"

"Because when I'm missing you, I watch you on the app." He grins looking completely proud of himself.

My jaw drops. "Are you serious?"

He gives a non-committal shrug. "Maybe."

"Conner, that's creepy." I fold my arms, but I'm not mad.

"Totally creepy. I like it."

I fake anger, because I really think he's just messing with me. "You want me to get Buster to take a bite out of you?"

"No, but when we get home, I'd like to take a bite out of you."

My heart jumps and deep between my legs, my sex comes to life. This man is turning me into a hormonal nympho. I've never had so much sex in my life. You'd think I'd be sated, but no, I want more. "Ah, the benefits of friends with benefits," I tease.

He arches a brow, "It's also the benefit part of a fake relationship, right?"

I read into his question and understand he's asking me if we're going to tell our friends we're in a relationship, albeit fake to us. "It is," I tell him and he nods, a small smile touching his mouth as I let him know that yes, we're going with the relationship scenario. I study him in the dim dashboard light, taking in his firm jaw and the nice button-down shirt he's wearing. The man is a catch and I once again wonder why he doesn't have a ring on his finger.

"Stare much?" he teases.

"You're one to talk. You're creeping on me when I'm at work, when I don't even know about it." Who am I to talk? When I wake up before him, I take my time admiring the hard body next to me.

He taps the steering wheel, like he's in deep thought. "You know, I think you should get audio for your app."

"Why?"

"So, I can say all kinds of dirty things to you."

I fold my arms, and glare at him, and while I like the idea of him talking dirty to me, I shoot back, "You will not say dirty things and corrupt my dogs."

He laughs. "Okay, I'll say dirty things to you later, though." I angle my head, my eyes questioning, and he grins. "Like how much I want to devour your pussy and put my cock inside you."

I groan and shift in the seat, suddenly too warm between my legs. "Great, how am I supposed to make conversation when I'm aroused?"

"Just talk to them in French."

I laugh at that. "Right, because I don't stick out enough as it is."

"Hey, babe. You don't stick out." There's warmth and sympathy in his voice when he adds, "They all love you as much as I do."

He turns his head quickly, staring at the road as I focus on the word love. He means it in a friendship way, I get that, but is there something more there or is it just my hormones messing with my brain?

We finally reach Tanner's big house, and Conner parks on the street behind Noah and Brighton's SUV. I might stick out, but all these wonderful people make me feel like I'm part of the family. I do love them for that. We exit the car and I grab the dip I made and Conner tucks the champagne under his arm. I'm not pregnant yet, so at least I get to have a glass... and I get to have more sex.

He puts his arm around me and tugs me to him. We've touched and joked around in public before, but this is different. Now we're pretending to be a couple, and with the way he's holding me, it's easy to tell he's committed to the role. Yeah, we're a real walking rom com.

We reach the door, and Conner doesn't bother knocking. There's laughter and music inside and no one would hear it anyway. We let ourselves in and we're instantly greeted with hugs and handshakes. The place is lively, everyone in a good mood. Conner puts his arm back around me and I notice a few looks as he guides me into the kitchen. We run into Gina, who is good friends with Melanie. I've gotten to know her a bit and really like her. She's a single mom and she runs a café in town. It was so kind of her to have a big party for Melanie when Mel finished her exam last year.

"Gina," I say and give her a hug.

"I was just refilling the wine." She reaches for another glass and sets it on the counter. "Red or white?" she asks.

"You serve all day. Let me pour the wine and serve you."

"Nah, I don't mind at all."

I think about her situation and then my own. One of these days, I'll be a single mom too, so to speak, with a lot on my plate. But unlike her little girl Zoe, my child will have a father who helps out. Who's helping her out? Does she ever get a break?

An idea hits. "Fine, you pour, and next weekend, I'll take Zoe overnight." I glance at Conner. Maybe I should have checked with him first. But he's nodding in agreement. Maybe he too knows Gina needs a break and it could be good for us to see what it's like to have a child for the night.

"We can take her to the resort for a swim," he says. "I'm sure Camryn and Tate would love that."

"You guys are the sweetest." I point to the red wine and Gina pours me a huge glass. She exhales like she's been holding it all together by herself for far too long. "I'm sure Zoe would love that, and honestly, I could use a night to myself, but I don't want to put you guys out."

"Not putting us out at all," I assure her.

Just then Melanie and Josie come into the kitchen, debating on what book to read for next month's book club.

"Oh, yeah," Melanie says. "But I heard the hero is a real alphahole."

"Oh, alphahole," Gina mutters, almost longingly, as they approach the island.

"You like alphaholes?" I ask.

"In fiction, only. I wouldn't want a guy like that in real life. I like the man whore character, though. I like when he starts caring about the heroine. That's hot."

"Uh, on that note..." Conner says, and snatches a beer from the fridge. "I'll leave you guys to discuss alphaholes. What-ever that is." He's about to leave but stops. "Wait, what exactly is an alphahole?"

"Ash," both Melanie and Josie say in unison, and I don't miss Gina's fast breath as she takes a sip of wine. What the heck is that all about? Oh wait...

"Ash?" Conner asks.

"Yeah, Ash is an alphahole. Actually, he's a man whore, which falls under the umbrella of alphahole. Which I guess makes him an Ash-hole," Melanie explains as everyone laughs. "Think about what he's like when he's not on the ice."

Josie clicks her tongue. "One day he's going to find a woman who takes him to his knees."

Conner thinks about that for a moment. "Do you women classify all us men?"

"Mostly," Gina tells him with a laugh.

"What am I...wait, nope." He holds one hand up. "I don't want to know."

We all laugh, but it dies an abrupt death when Conner leans in and presses his lips to mine, like it's the most natural thing in the world, like he's not even pretending. He pulls back and when he first realizes what he's done, there's surprise in his eyes, but it morphs into mindfulness.

The ruse is on.

He leaves the room and I slowly turn to take in the three sets of eyes watching me. "I...um..."

"What the heck, Dani," Brighton shrieks, a big smile on her face. I relax a bit. Okay, she's not judging me, and she's not upset.

"We...uh...we're trying this thing."

"I bet you're trying a thing," Gina laughs. "Heck, if I were you, I'd be trying that thing too." She points in the direction of Conner and everyone cracks up.

I take a much-needed sip of wine. "You guys don't think..."

I don't finish the sentence. I don't need to. Brighton takes my hand. "Dani, first of all, it doesn't matter what we think, but if you do want to know..." She glances around, getting a consensus from our friends. "We're all damn excited for you." She actually starts squealing in joy a bit. "We have been waiting for you two to figure things out for a while, but we know there are past histories and complications..."

"What she's trying to say," Melanie, who has her master's in psychology, interrupts. "Is that we're all happy for you. That guy has had it bad for you for a long time." She snaps her fingers. "Get it, girl."

I laugh at that, and almost under my breath, I whisper, "Oh, I'm getting it." Although I don't think she's right about Conner having it bad for me.

This time they all squeal and Melanie continues, "Good, now give us all the details and don't leave anything out."

Gina picks up her wine for us to salute. "Here's to getting it and maybe I don't want to hear the details. While I'm happy for you, Dani, deets on your sex life will just depress me. I'm not looking for any sort of relationship, but casual sex once in a while would be nice." She moans in delight at that thought. "But I've given up on getting some and that's probably for the best with Zoe to consider."

"Getting some what?" Ash asks as he saunters into the kitchen. I take in his broad shoulders and the way his button-down shirt showcases his body. He's definitely tall, dark and problematic. That's when I notice I'm not the only one admiring this male specimen, not that I think he compares to Conner, but a girl can recognize beauty when she sees it. She can also recognize a guy she might be attracted to but should stay away from.

"Nothing," Gina answers quickly, that pink flush back on her cheeks. She looks both aroused and mortified that he might have heard her.

He snatches two beers from the fridge. "Tanner and Maeve have an announcement to make. They're waiting for everyone in the living room."

We all follow Ash, but his big body blocks the entire view of the hall. In the living room, I spot Conner talking to Elias. I'm about to make my way over, only to stop when Tanner stands and holds up his glass. Everyone goes quiet and lifts theirs.

"To the team, and the trophy," he salutes and points to the big cup in the room. "To the support of our wives, girlfriends, and friends," he adds and lifts his glass a little higher. We're all about to take a drink. "Wait." Our hands still as he glances at Maeve and pulls her to her feet. "We have one more thing to drink to." He winks at his wife, who is holding a glass of water. "At least, some of us get to drink." Gasps sound in the room, because we all know where he's going with this. "To my wife." He touches her stomach, and the love shining in their eyes brings tears to mine. "And to our little one, who I can't wait to meet. We're pregnant!"

We all shout our congratulations and when they drink from their cups, we all drink from ours. Tanner glances around the room and makes eye contact with everyone, and that's when I see the way Conner is watching me. "One by one, we're all getting married and having kids," Tanner adds, holding his glass up.

Maeve holds up her glass. "Must be something in the water." She searches the room, looking at the players. "I wonder which one of you guys will be next."

Ash, as well as a few of the other single guys, mumble protests under their breath, which makes us all laugh. I take in the young pretty girl who Ash has his arm around. He probably doesn't even remember her name. Yeah, it's best for Gina to stay away from him. Or is it... They would make an interesting couple.

My gaze strays to Conner again, and his eyes remain locked on me. I am in so much trouble here. Why did I ever think having a baby with my best friend, my brother-in-law, the guy I've been in love with for far too long now, was a good idea?

What we're doing here is pretending. He's helping a girl out. Nothing can come from that, and now we're trying to bring a baby into the mix. My mind races back to what Melanie said in the kitchen. Could she be right? Does Conner have it bad for me? What if I ask, and I have it all wrong? That could so easily come between us, and I promised that would never happen.

Gina nudges me. "Hey, are you okay?"

Under my breath, I mumble, "I think I need a glass of water."

12

CONNER

I flick on my signal, take a right turn and glance at Dani in the passenger seat. She's smiling as she checks on the dogs at the Airbnb. "It's crazy that no one at the party last weekend thought it was odd that you and I were 'dating'." I do air quotes around the word dating.

"I know. I mean we hang out a lot so I guess they thought that was just a natural progression of our friendship and no one cared that I used to be married to Alec."

"Yeah, I got congrats from all the guys. They all said we make a good couple."

"Really?" She scrunches up her nose.

"Why so surprised?"

She snorts out a laugh. "Let's face it. I don't look like the girls you normally date."

What is she even talking about? I haven't dated in years, and haven't really felt like I missed out on anything. "Puck bunnies," I explain. "You can't tell one from the other."

She nods. "The girls wanted all the details."

"I swear women are worse than men when talking about sex."

"Are you telling me stories aren't shared in the locker room?"

"No."

She laughs at that. "But I think you might be right, and no, I didn't tell them you were amazing in the bedroom."

I grin at her. "Amazing, huh?" She rolls her eyes at me. "Oh, I was talking to Noah, and they're not going to their summer home until tomorrow."

She sets her phone down. "They don't mind staying home?"

"No, Camryn and Tate are looking forward to hanging out with Zoe, and it's a long weekend so they'll go to their summer home on Sunday. Besides, it's Noah's weekend with the cup, and he wants to have everyone over."

Frowning, she glances at her lap. "I didn't realize it was going to be a party." She nibbles her lip, concern on her face.

I capture her hand. "I'm sorry. I didn't think you'd mind."

She snaps back to her perky self quickly. "No, it's okay."

What the heck is going through her head? Did she want quiet time with Zoe and me? "Tonight, we'll make popcorn and watch a movie with Zoe."

She gives me a big smile. "I'd like that." A beat of silence and then, "Are you going to have a party when it's your turn with the cup?"

"I don't know. I wasn't really going to." I groan. "All that work and clean up." I eye her. Is that disappointment on her face? "Do you want to have a party?"

"I think it could be fun. I can't remember the last time I had a party." She chuckles. "I think it might have been my wedding. Alec never wanted to have anyone over."

"I can't remember the last time I had a party either." Maybe a party would be a good idea, a way for us to move on after... well, after Alec. I'm pretty sure Dani has just been going through the motions, right up until she asked me to be her baby daddy. How could I say no when she needs this so much, when it was her first big step in creating a new life?

"I was thinking," she says quietly, a little too seriously.

"About me naked?"

That makes her smile. "Always," she teases. "But seriously. I was thinking if we're going to baby proof my place, maybe it's time I did a bit of remodeling. Some new furniture, and maybe clean out some closets and boxes, and a new bed."

My heart tightens and I squeeze her hand. "Yeah?" She nods, attempting a smile as she wrings her hands together. There are so many stages of grief and clearing out her place of old memories so she can make new ones in an effort to move on is not going to be easy on her. "I can help with all that."

"No, that's okay. I wasn't asking that."

Maybe she really doesn't want me there, so she can be alone with her memories of Alec. She's definitely still in love with him. "It's going to be hard, Dani," I point out quietly.

"It's going to be hard for you too, Conner."

I nod in agreement. "Then let's do hard together, okay?"

She gives me a grateful smile that tugs at my heart. "I was online looking at some new furniture, and a new bed. Mine is getting kind of lumpy."

"A new bed is a good idea." I take another turn. "Seems kind of crazy that we both have such big houses, and we're the only ones living in them."

She laughs. "Yeah, we could probably share one and not even bump into each other for days."

Is she suggesting what I think she's suggesting? Would cohabitating be such a bad idea if we had a child? I guess it would be if she continues to move on and eventually find a husband.

"We'll have to baby proof my place too," I inform her. "Our little one will be at my place too."

"Right, and again, if we shared a place, we wouldn't have to do double the work."

Maybe she really is hinting at the idea of living together, but again, is that a good idea? Maybe if I did have her under one roof all the time she might see just how good we are for each other before she found a husband.

It was your brother she chose, dude.

Yeah, but it was me she chose to have a baby with.

It was your DNA she wants, remember?

Fuck off.

"My place or yours?" I tease.

"You have the pool."

Okay, she really has been thinking about this. Probably because she wants what's best for the baby. But before we make any decisions, she has to get pregnant first. "You're staying with me now while we work on getting you pregnant, and if you're going to be doing some remodeling, and buying new furniture, you'll need a place to stay until it's done."

She smiles like she likes that idea. I pass by Gina's café and look for a spot to park. The city is busy on Saturday. I finally find one and ease into the tight space. Dani sits up a little straighter, excited to be taking Zoe for the night. She's going to be an amazing mother, and knowing that eases some of my anxiety. If our child has troubles like I did in school, I'm sure she'll know what to do, and I suppose I eventually have to tell her about my dyslexia. I can't have her guessing what might be wrong with our child. Hell, I was in high school before anyone figured it out, and those early years were hell. Thank God I had a big brother who scared the shit out of my tormentors. And, if I hadn't acted out all the time, my parents might not have put me in hockey so I could take my aggressions out in a different way. It's funny how things work out.

That thought makes me think of Alec, and how I'm with Dani today because he died, and a huge knot tightens in my stomach, as a sound catches in my throat. I cough to cover it and reach for the door. I step out and circle the car to meet Dani on the sidewalk. I put my hand on her back and tug her to me.

We stop outside the café, and note the closed sign on the door. I turn to Dani who is frowning. "What's going on?"

"I don't know. She's always open on the weekend. Let me text her."

I put my face to the glass and glance in. "The place is empty."

"I hope nothing is wrong." She shoots off a text and a moment later, her phone buzzes. "She's inside and on her way to let us in."

The door opens and we find a very frazzled Gina standing in front of us, a bit of grease on her face, and sheets of paper in her hand. Honestly, she looks adorable, and I'm not blind. I've noticed the way the guys on the team watch her, but she has a child and maybe that scares them off.

Dani touches Gina's arm. "Gina, what's wrong?"

"Something's wrong with my commercial fridge, and the damn air conditioner is on the fritz again. I'm beginning to wonder if my uncle liked me when he left me this place." She waves the papers as she holds a screw in the other hand. "I had to close because the food all spoiled and I was googling how to fix it, because I can't get anyone in to repair it until next week. I found this screw on the floor so it might have something to do with it."

Dani takes the papers from her, and looks them over. She shows them to me, but they might as well be written in Greek. "Do you know anything about refrigeration?" Dani asks.

"Only that it keeps my food cold." I pull my phone from my pocket. "But I do know someone who does."

"Really," Gina says, her eyes wide with relief and gratitude. "Do you think they could come by today?"

"I'm going to check." I call up my contacts and call my buddy. He answers on the second ring. "Hey, you busy?" I hear his TV blaring in the background and know he's watching old games.

"Nah, just hanging, and heading over to Noah's for the party later." He mutes his TV.

"What's up?"

"I'm at the Nook with Dani. Gina's fridge is broken. She can't get anyone in to fix it for a week. Can you help her out?"

A moment of hesitation and then, "Yeah, sure. What seems to be the problem?"

I glance at the screw in Gina's hand. "We're not sure. It might just be a loose screw. Gina found one on the floor. Hopefully it won't take you long. We're taking Zoe for overnight, but we'll wait until you get here."

"Okay, be there shortly."

He doesn't live too far, so that won't take long and hopefully I'm not setting him up for a whole afternoon of work. "Thanks, buddy. I owe you."

"Yeah, you do," he teases.

I end the call, and Gina throws her arms around me. "Thank you." She turns to Dani and winks. "Cinnamon roll, told you."

Dani grins and they exchange a look that I know nothing about. "I'll have a cinnamon roll," I say.

"Come in. Zoe is upstairs with the sitter. I sent the staff home today because I couldn't open. But I do have coffee and cinnamon rolls."

We head inside, and the smell of fresh coffee reaches my nose. "Have a seat." Gina wipes her forehead and I tug on my shirt, the warmth of the place a bit unbearable. "You should have him check out the air conditioning too."

"I hate to ask too much."

"If he can, he can, if he can't, he can't. He won't mind."

"If you're sure." I nod and she smiles. "Okay, I'll get the coffee."

"I'll help," Dani says and they disappear into the back. Feet pound on the set of stairs behind me, and I turn to see Zoe coming my way.

"Hey kiddo."

"Conner," she squeals. "I can't wait to go swimming." A teenage girl comes down behind her, and her eyes are wide when they see me. "Hey."

"You're Conner Birch."

I grin. I always find it funny when people tell me who I am. "I am."

"Can I have an autograph?"

"Of course." I pick up a napkin. "This okay?" She giggles, and it tugs at something deep in my brain, something that reminds me of the day my brother died. I search the tables for a pen and try to push down the unease. Dani and Gina come from the kitchen, and I turn toward them as Zoe squeals, so happy to see Dani.

"You wouldn't happen to have a pen, would you?" I ask Gina. She sets the coffee down and pulls a pen from her apron. I scribble my name on the napkin and hand it to the girl.

"Thank you," she says, and giggles some more. She glances at Gina. "Do you need me for anything else?"

"No, we're all good. Same time next week, though?"

She nods, and gives a little wave as she heads out the front door. "Someone's a fan," Dani teases as she slides a cinnamon roll across the table.

"Dani, are you going to swim with me?" Zoe asks.

The smile falls from Dani's face. "Would you like me to?" Zoe nods emphatically as Gina shares a cinnamon roll with her.

"Mommy, are you going to be okay with me not here?"

Gina laughs. "I will miss you, but you don't have to worry about me, and you are going to have so much fun with Dani and Conner and Camryn and Tate."

"A lot of the other guys are coming with their families too, so there's going to be plenty of kids." Dani looks down, picking at her cinnamon roll. She has that concerned look on her face again. I know she likes the guys on my team and their families, so I'm not really sure what's bothering her.

"Do you have a favorite movie, Zoe?" I ask.

She throws her arms out. "I love Wish."

"That's streaming?" I ask Gina, and she nods. "How about we watch that with popcorn tonight after swimming?"

"Yes," she practically screeches.

"Inside voice, Zoe." Just then the front door opens and a little squeak, much lower than Zoe's crawls out of Gina's throat when Ash walks in. She sets her cup down, and if I'm not mistaken, her cheeks are turning a light shade of pink.

I stand and slap Ash on the back. "Thanks for coming."

Gina pushes back in her chair. "You called Ash to help with my fridge?"

"Yeah, sorry. Didn't I tell you?"

"No, you just said you were calling a friend." Gina stands, and smooths her hands over her apron. "You know how to fix fridges?"

"You seem surprised," he mentions.

"No, I mean yes...I guess I am surprised."

"This guy can fix anything," I tell her. "His dad was a handyman, and he made sure his son learned the skills."

"Oh, okay. Great. I really appreciate it, and I'll pay you for your time of course."

"Hi Ash," Zoe says. "Do you want a bite of my cinnamon roll?"

He glances at Zoe and backs up, like he's terrified of the little girl.

He holds his hand up, palm out. "No, I'm good." Zoe shrugs and finishes off the roll, and Ash looks past Gina's shoulders. "Do you have that screw?"

"What?" Gina says, the pink intensified in her cheeks.

"Screw." Ash looks a bit flustered himself. "You got a screw loose."

Gina almost looks offended. "I don't have a screw loose."

"No, I'm mean." He holds up his metal toolbox. "I brought all my tools. I wasn't sure what tool you might need."

I bite back a chuckle, because this is coming out all wrong.

"He's not insulting you, Gina. He's asking about the screw you had in your hand earlier," I explain, coming to their rescue. "Do you have it?"

"Oh, yeah, right." Blinking rapidly, her chest rising and falling rapidly like she'd been running, she reaches into her apron and produces it. "Screw."

I pick up Zoe's small backpack. "You got everything you

need?" She nods, and I help her put it on her back. "Okay, see you at the pool later, Ash."

Ash grumbles something under his breath, as I turn back and spot Dani wagging her eyebrows and mouthing something to Gina, something that looks like, "Tell him what tool you need."

13

DANI

I t's a beautiful sunny day and as I glance out the passenger side window and as Conner drives Zoe and me to the resort, I almost wish it would rain. Not that I want to ruin the pool party for everyone, or Noah's turn with the cup, but a bunch of the guys and their wives are here and while I like them all, I don't like the idea of being in my bathing suit in front of them. I will not, however, be a party pooper and ruin this day for Zoe, or for Conner.

"Are you going to tell me what you said to Gina?"

My eyes go wide and I put my hand over my mouth. "You heard me?"

"No, I saw you mouth something to her, and I think it was about Ash's tools."

I work to bite back a chuckle, but it bubbles from my throat. "Don't say anything, but I'm pretty sure Gina likes him."

"Why?" He keeps his voice low so Zoe, in the back seat, can't hear. "Didn't you all call him a womanizer? Why would she want to be with a guy like that? Don't get me wrong. I love the guy. He's just not ready to settle down and I'm pretty sure he's terrified of Zoe. Did you see the way he backed up?"

"I know, it's hilarious, really. A big defenseman like him, a guy who takes down two-hundred-pound men, looking like he was about to run for the hills when she offered him a bit of her cinnamon roll. But to answer your question, he's really good looking and is in great shape." He frowns like he might be jealous, but I'm sure he's just kidding. "Besides, who says she wants anything more? From what I know about Gina, she is not looking for a man in her life. Maybe her bed, but not her life."

I glance into the back seat to make sure Zoe hadn't heard anything over the show she's watching on her children's tablet, and she begins to sing along, very badly. But good for her for having the confidence to belt out lyrics. I glance at Conner, and he winces. I chuckle, and join in. No, I can't carry a tune either, but I love everything about this. I love that I can be my goofy self with Conner, and I love how he makes me feel comfortable inside the bedroom and out.

I put my hand on my stomach, desperately wanting a child and family of my own. As I glance at Conner, I can't help but think he wants that too. There's something there, though, something holding him back and I'm not exactly sure what it is. Is it the fact that I was married to his brother, or maybe it's just the fact that we're friends and he doesn't feel anything more?

But when we're in bed, and he's taking such good care of my body, it makes me question everything. What do I know though, really? I've only been with one man, and Conner has been with lots of women. He probably worships them all between the sheets.

The song ends and Zoe yells, "Are we there yet?"

"Just about," Conner answers and flicks on his signal.

"Yay!" Zoe squeals and starts bouncing in her seat. "Can I get that drink with the umbrella in it?"

"I'm sure you can," I tell her, thinking I might need something a bit stronger to give me liquid courage.

Conner eases into the parking spot, and when I open my door, music and laughter from the rooftop pool reaches my ears. I open the back door and Zoe unbuckles herself, getting out of her booster seat. I take her hand in the busy parking lot as Conner grabs her backpack as well as our bag.

"Do you need to get changed?" I ask as she jumps from one foot to the other, so excited.

"I already have my suit on." She lifts her shirt to show me her pretty pink bathing suit. Conner follows behind with the bags as I lead her to the stairs. We hurry up them and when we reach the top, we're greeted with hugs.

"Zoe, come in," Camryn yells from the pool.

She starts stripping off her clothes, and I help when she gets her shirt all twisted up in the excitement. "You need your water wings first," I say.

"Are you getting in too?" Melanie asks me as she comes over to greet us. Conner pulls Zoe's water wings from the bag and blows them up.

A couple of the guys at the bar call Conner over.

"I am. Can you watch her so I can get changed?"

"I can get in with her," Conner tells me.

"Yeah, but go have a drink with the guys first. They seem eager to tell you something. I'm going to get changed and get in. I'm hot."

He leans in and kisses me. "Yeah, you are," he murmurs and everything in the way he's looking at me makes me feel a little bit less self-conscious.

"I got her," Melanie assures me as Zoe holds her arms out. Once Zoe has her wings on, Melanie calls her over, and Zoe jumps into her arms. I take my bag and make my way to the change room. I undress, pull on my swimsuit, and wrap myself in my coverup. Knox, who's the new rookie on the team, has his head down as he exits the men's change room and bumps into me.

"Sorry," he says quickly and puts his hands on my arms to stabilize me before I fall over.

"I'm good."

He smiles as his eyes meet mine. I don't know Knox very well. I only know that he played hockey at the university level here in Boston. He seems nice enough, and a bit quiet. I guess he's still finding his place amongst the guys.

"Want to cannon ball?" he asks me, and I laugh.

"I'm going to pass."

He looks around his gaze settling on Conner, who is watching us carefully. "You and Wood, huh?"

"Yeah, me and Wood." I scan the rooftop. "Are you here with anyone?"

"Yeah, she just ran back to the car. She forgot her sunglasses."

"I look forward to meeting her."

"I think you'll like her. I'll introduce you when she comes back. She's a professional dancer. Well, not yet anyway, she's still in college." He holds his hands up. "Don't go there, she's not as young as you think. She had to take some time off for personal reasons."

It sounds like he really likes her and he looks hopeful that we'll be friends. Wait, were the other WAGs not friendly? I seriously doubt that. That's not how things are done with this group.

"Dani, come on in!" Zoe yells.

"I am being summoned. I'll catch up with you guys later." He walks away, and I move to the end of the pool. I sit and take off my wrap, sliding right into the water. Melanie comes swimming over with Zoe.

"Did you meet Knox's girlfriend?" I ask, my conversation with Knox leaving me curious.

"No, I was in the water. I only saw her for a second. Why?"

"I don't know. He just really wanted me to like her."

"I'm sure she's lovely."

I spot Noah tossing Camryn into the air. "Toss me, Dani. Toss me like that."

"I don't think I can," I say, and that's when Conner gets into the pool and swims up to me. "I'll toss you."

I take one look at his face, and instantly sense something is wrong. Surely to God he wasn't jealous that I was talking to Knox. He gathers Zoe and lightly tosses her. She surfaces and he picks her up again. He slicks his hair off his face, and my heart does a little flutter. He is so damn handsome, and as far as I'm concerned, the best-looking guy here.

Brighton comes swimming over as Noah climbs from the pool. "Who wants a drink?" he asks, as the bartender starts pouring some kind of punch into the cup. I laugh as Noah starts handing out straws.

"Let's go drink," I suggest, and as I swim to the side of the pool, my gaze goes to the stairs, to the woman opening the gate. Knox walks over to the pretty blonde and puts his arm around her back. He says something to her, and she looks my way, her smile dissolving when she sees me, and the man standing close to me. Is this why the guys called him over? I spin around to see Conner.

"It's fine," he says quickly. "The guys gave me the heads up."

"Are you sure you're fine?" He actually looks a bit shocked to see Summer, his ex-girlfriend, with Knox.

He shrugs. "I just haven't seen her in a couple of years. She just disappeared from my life after...Alec. I can't blame her. I was in a bad place." She must have been in a bad place, when Conner just sort of deserted her, so lost in taking care of me after Alec. That must be why she missed a year or so of college. Damn, I really hope she's okay. "I'm happy she's with Knox. He's a good guy."

It's clear he's over her. There's nothing in his words or his expression to suggest anything else. Either that or he's a great actor.

I help Zoe from the water. "We should say hi."

"Who are we saying hi to?" Zoe asks.

"An old friend." I quickly tug on my cover up and grab a towel for Zoe. I wipe her face, and dry her off. Conner doesn't bother with a towel. Instead, he lets the sun warm his body.

Knox comes our way. He opens his mouth, to no doubt introduce Summer, but she speaks first.

"Conner." She glances at me. "Dani. Nice to see you both again."

Knox's gaze goes back and forth between the three of us. "You guys know each other?"

"Yes," Conner answers. "Nice to see you too, Summer."

"Hi," Zoe chirps.

Summer frowns as she glances at Zoe. "Is she...wait...no...unless..."

Summer was still dating Conner when I lost my baby, and I can see she's struggling to put it all together. "We're babysitting for a friend. This is Zoe."

"Hi Zoe." After greeting sweet Zoe, Summer's head lifts and her gaze moves over us, a careful assessment. I consider what she sees: the close way Conner is standing beside me, the warmth between us, and likely the little sparks my body gives off whenever his fingers brush against me. While we might be pretending, faking a real relationship, there is nothing fake in the way this man affects me. Can everyone see that? Is this why everyone thinks we're good together?

Her eyes narrow and she doesn't at all look surprised as she waves a finger between Conner and me. "So, you two..."

Conner puts his arm around me. "Yes."

An unexpected, almost hurt laugh bubbles in her throat and she quickly gets control of it. Her eyes seem to hold a hint of pain as she averts her gaze. "Always wanting what the other has," she murmurs under her breath. At least I think that's what she said.

"I'm sorry. What was that?" I ask as Conner's brow knits together, like he's searching for a response at her unexpected reaction.

"Oh, we should go get a straw and get a drink," Summer says quietly, a sadness about her as she loops her arm in Knox's. He has a worried look on his face. I guess he thought things would go down differently.

"I want to drink from the big cup, Dani," Zoe says as Summer and Knox walk away, Knox saying something into Summer's ear. Something he doesn't want anyone else to hear. I'm not sure how long that relationship is going to last. Come to think of it, I really never was much of a Summer fan. I think Conner dodged a bullet there. But people change and grow, and she's likely a different person than she was two years ago.

With his arm still around me, and his eyes on me, not his ex, who happens to be showcasing her entire backside in a thong —yes, she looks gorgeous, just ask any of the single guys ogling her—Conner reaches for my hand.

"Drink?"

Noah hands straws to the kids. "Preferably one with alcohol."

"Agreed," he says. "But we do need to drink from the cup first."

"Is that even sanitary?"

He laughs. "No, but we do what the cup holder wants us to do."

"What are you going to do when it's your turn?"

"I'll probably just take it over to Mom and Dad's for a picture. I bet your folks would like a picture too."

"They would love that, Conner. That's so thoughtful. Although." He eyes me. "Dad might want to do something weird with it."

"Weird?"

"Yeah, you know he's huge into fishing these days and I can only imagine he'd want to make a fishbowl."

"That would be fine."

"Really?"

"Sure, one for the records because I'm sure no one has used it as a fishbowl before. We'll ask Phil later, he'd know."

I'm laughing by the time we reach the bar, and the tension inside me has eased. Honestly, why should I give Summer's presence here another thought? We don't mean anything to each other anymore. Why then is she staring at Conner, with a new kind of interest in her eyes? Dammit.

"That smells so good," Zoe says, as she runs around the kitchen, excited after an afternoon of swimming, eating and hanging with friends. I have to say having her has been a blast, and has helped make this big old house feel less huge and homier.

"Do you want to carry it?"

She nods and I put the big bowl into her small arms. "Careful. I'll get our drinks." I pour wine into two stemmed glasses, and apple juice into the other. Zoe asked if she could have her juice like that and I don't see the harm.

I carry the glasses into the room, and my heart does a little thump when I see Zoe snuggled beside Dani, leaving space for me on the other side, so she can be between us. She shoves a handful of popcorn into her mouth.

"Hey, save some for me." She chuckles and Dani picks up a kernel and tosses it at me, like they're conspiring. I couldn't love this more.

I set the drinks down and slide in next to Zoe. She smiles up at me, and as I ruffle her hair, I can't help but think this little girl could use a little male influence in her life. Gina's not interested in bringing a man into her life and that I can understand, but I hate the thoughts of this sweet girl missing out on having a dad. When my child is born, I plan to be there for them no matter what.

I lift my head and find Dani smiling at me. "All set?"

I nod, and she reaches for the remote and hits play. For the next hour and a half, we eat popcorn, have our drinks, and stop the movie for a couple of bathroom breaks. Just before it's over, I feel a nudge on my arm, and glance down. My heart pinches tight when I see Zoe slumped against me, sleeping. It's a good thing we had her brush her teeth earlier. I should say, it's a good thing Dani had her brush her teeth earlier. I'm guessing she saw this coming, and it once again reminds me she's going to be such a great mom.

"I better carry her up."

"She had a busy day." Dani yawns and stretches as she pushes off the sofa.

"Looks like you're ready for bed too."

"Oh, did you want to stay up longer?" she asks, her lids half closed.

I give her a playful smile. "Nope." I ease from the sofa and scoop up Zoe. "We've had far too many late nights."

"I don't know if I'd say far too many," she responds sleepily, her eyes warm, sated, and full of happiness. I'm not sure I remember seeing Dani this happy. Was she ever this happy with Alec? Would she hate me if she knew the secret I was keeping, and that I was the reason he was dead?

Pushing those hard thoughts to the back of my mind, I follow Dani to the stairs. We head up and she goes into the spare room and pulls down the covers. Zoe had been to Dani's house, just never mine. In fact, it's been a long time since I've had anyone in my place. I sort of stopped living after my brother's death. But we showed her around earlier, and let her know where our room was if she needed us.

Dani tucks her in and turns on the nightlight she picked up when we knew we were taking Zoe. She stops at the door, and the longing in her is palpable as she stares at the sweet, sleeping child. My God, it makes me want to put a baby in her all the more.

We make our way across the hall and after we brush our teeth and wash our faces, I tug off my clothes, turn the lamp on and climb into bed. Dani leaves on her T-shirt and panties and crawls in beside me.

She rolls into me, and as I breathe in the scent of her hair my mind goes back to this afternoon. "Did you enjoy getting in the pool today?"

"It was fun," she murmurs, and I don't miss the hitch in her voice.

"Hey," I inch away to see her and she angles her head to see me. "Did you just want it to be us and Noah's family? You seemed upset when I told you the guys were coming."

"It's just…"

I pull her to me. "What?"

"I told you before that I don't always feel like I fit in. I'm not…like the other women."

"No, you're not." She looks down, and I continue. "Which is why you're in this bed and they're not."

She gives an almost hysterical laugh. "I'm in this bed because we're trying to make a baby."

"What if I told you otherwise? That you're in this bed because out of all the women at the pool today, you're the one I like best."

"Summer was there, you know that, right? She was the girl you asked out. She's not the one who asked you for a favor. You picked her."

I'd actually picked Dani first, all those years ago. I just didn't think I was good enough for her, and then when my big brother, who always watched out for me, swooped in, that was that.

Under her breath she adds, "I'm not tall and thin and gorgeous like the other women."

"For the record, not every man likes tall and thin, and also for the record, you're fucking gorgeous. I've thought that since the first time I laid eyes on you." She rolls her eyes like she doesn't believe that and I slide my hand over her hip. "You're sexy as hell, Dani, and you speak French, now that is a real turn on." She grins, her mood shifting. "Do you have any idea how much I wanted to sink my teeth into these curves today when you were out there in your bathing suit?"

"Really?"

This time she sounds like she might half believe me. "Yes, really." I go quiet for a second, guilt eating at me. I can't tell her everything but she needs to know some things—even if this could change everything, but it's the right thing to do and a chance I have to take.

Since we're being completely honest with each other, I begin. "I don't always feel like I fit in either."

Her head rears back. "What are you talking about?"

"I had a hard time growing up." I shrug but the memories are still painful. "I couldn't learn like other kids."

"You had some struggles." Her voice is soft, and gentle, and it wraps around me and squeezes tight. "Everyone has struggles in different areas, Conner."

I swallow against a painful lump. "What if our child..." I really don't want to pass down my struggles.

"What if our child, what?"

"I know you want my DNA." I shift in the bed, uncomfortably warm now. "I understand why, but what if my DNA is flawed?"

She sits up, crosses her legs and faces me. "You are not flawed in any way."

"I...I have a learning disability. Dyslexia, actually. It didn't get diagnosed until high school. That's why I had such a hard time in school and that's why my parents put me in hockey when I was young. I didn't get my brother's brains." I lift my eyes to find loving concern on her face, which prompts me to continue. "I have a hard time reading and learning. I don't want our child to suffer like I did. I realize I should have told you that before. I find it hard to talk about."

"You haven't told anyone?"

I put my arm behind my head. "No."

"It's nothing to be embarrassed about, Conner."

I snort out a humorless laugh. "Kids were cruel."

"Yeah, kids can be cruel," she agrees, as she frowns and glances down. "Teens are cruel too."

Is she remembering something from her past? Or maybe she has a secret of her own that she's not telling me. "I understand if you don't want to have a child with me. I should have told you. I want to help you, Dani. I just don't talk about my learning disorder, but you should have had all that information before we began this...I understand if you don't want—"

She puts her finger on my lips to stop me. "Conner. You were having a hard time reading the instructions."

"What?"

"When you were baby proofing the bathroom." She gives a small laugh of relief. "I thought you were having second thoughts, but that wasn't it at all."

"I was having a hard time," I admit. "Actually, my learning disorder was a big part of my hesitation when you asked me for a favor."

"What is the other part?"

I frown and reach for her hand. "I didn't want anything to ruin our friendship. We both know things can be taken away from you pretty quickly." My gaze moves over her face, gauging her reactions as I wait... Wait for what? Do I really expect her to say she wants to be more than friends? She asked for my DNA, not marriage. She still loves her late husband. Besides, how could we ever be together? The secret I'm keeping would make me insane, because I think about it whenever I see her, and if I ever told her, to get it off my chest, it would gut her and she'd never forgive me.

"I was thinking," she murmurs. "You said you have a hard time reading instructions."

"Yeah."

She smiles at me, her eyes tired. I'm about to tell her we should get some sleep, when she says, "You know what you don't have a hard time reading."

"What?"

"Me, my body. What I want and need." She moves to straddle me. Falling forward, she takes my hands and weaves her fingers through mine. Her mouth finds mine for a soft, gentle kiss full of want, need and passion, and it curls around my heart and hugs tight, momentarily making me forget what's happening between us is just to make a baby. When she breaks the kiss, she grins. "Did you read anything into that?"

"Hell yeah, I did."

I put my arms around her back and roll her, until I have her pressed beneath me. I move her hair from her face, the softness in her eyes seeping under my skin and pulling every emotion from my darkest corners.

"Conner," she murmurs, like she's feeling something very different here too.

I don't answer. I know what she's asking. I kiss a slow path down her neck, zero urgency in us tonight, probably because we're both so tired, or maybe it's something else. My brain isn't really working at top speed at the moment.

I moan against her skin and kiss her breasts through her shirt. She wiggles beneath me, and my cock presses against her leg. My fingers connect with soft skin as I lift her shirt, and moan in sheer delight when I'm gifted with a view of her beautiful pert nipples. With a gentle touch, I lightly trace one with the tip of my finger, and slide my tongue around the other.

"Yes, Conner." She arches her body, her fingers raking through my hair. I spend a long time on her nipples as my cock aches for release, but I ignore it for the moment, because I simply want to savor every minute, every taste of this incredible woman.

Her moans are soft, breathy, and when her hands move to my shoulders and back, her touch is slow and thorough as they feather over my muscles. I eventually tear my mouth away from her luscious breasts and start a slow path downward until I reach her panties. I grip them with my teeth and tug them down. Her fingers fall from my back, no longer able to reach me and she moans with displeasure.

"I love touching you," she murmurs, and I glance up to see her go up on her elbows to watch me. That moan of displeasure turns to one of delight as I remove her panties and bury my face between her legs, and the second I taste her, I honestly don't know which of us is experiencing more pleasure.

With the soft blade of my tongue, I swirl through her liquid heat—I do love how excited she gets when she's with me. She softly chants my name as I turn my focus to her perfectly aroused clit.

I rub it with my finger. "So beautiful."

She whimpers and moves her body, and I cover her swollen nub with my mouth, and suck her in. Her whimpers grow louder and I slip a thick finger inside her channel. As I torture her with my mouth and hands, her breathing changes and in no time at all, she tumbles into a sweet orgasm.

"That's my girl." Keeping my finger inside, giving her something to clench on to, I ease the pressure on her sensitive clit and glance up at her. I take in her flushed cheeks, the way her eyes are locked on mine, the look of happiness and stupor on her beautiful face. There is nothing I'd like more than to make this woman come every single day.

Will there ever come a time that I can do that?

15

DANI

It's just after lunch time as I toss a ball for Buster, and okay, even though I'm not supposed to have favorites, I'm super fond of the big St. Bernard. As I walk around the big playroom at the Airbnb, Buster runs for the ball. The second he's gone, Chester, a small King Charles Cavalier spaniel comes rushing over for a rub.

I smile happily as I play with all the dogs. It's been busy as we pick up more pups in the summer with people going on vacation. Honestly, I can hardly believe how quickly the days are passing. Time has been flying by. I guess that old saying is true: time flies when you're having fun. Conner and I have been having fun, and now that school is out, he's gearing up for his hockey camps at the rink.

We've been having sex like randy bunnies—when I'm ovulating and even when I'm not. Conner has been keeping fit by running, and exercising, and I've been busy with the dogs, and buying new furniture and renovating.

He likes to help when he can, and I always enjoy when he comes along with me. I honestly have never been happier, which scares me. I'm not superstitious like Conner, but sometimes I do believe when things are too good to be true, they are. I know how fast you can lose everything. I'm not sure I could ever go down that road again. Soon enough we'll be taking another pregnancy test, and while I want a child, I'm very conflicted, because I don't want things to end.

My phone pings and I pull it from my back pocket and grin when I see the message from Conner. Did he sense me thinking about him?

Conner: I see you.

I laugh and glance up at the camera.

Me: Creeper.

Conner: Haha. Are we still taking Buster to the nursing home?

I walk over to the camera, and adjust it. Being a tease, because it's fun, I toy with the top button on my blouse. Anyone else watching wouldn't take what I'm doing as sexual, and in fact it looks like I might be checking out the camera to make sure it's working.

Conner: Oh la la.

I laugh out loud at his French. He's been taking lessons with me one night a week these last couple of weeks, but he still has a long way to go. I'm happy he's trying, though, and it would be fun to teach our child a new language if I ever get pregnant. I'm actually starting to worry about it. After losing a baby, and failed in-vitro, I didn't expect it to happen overnight, but I've been through a couple of cycles already and nothing. I do believe in nature knowing what's right and maybe, unlike with Alec, this isn't meant to be. That's kind of strange when you think about it. I loved Alec, but was never in love with him like I am with Conner.

Me: Like what you see?

Over the past month, I've gotten even more comfortable with my body. The way Conner worships me, touches me…I sigh. It fills me with confidence. Heck, I feel so good about myself, I could probably join one of those dating sites. Not that I want to. The truth is, I don't want what I'm doing with Conner ever to end.

Conner: Want to see more of it. (Peach emoji)

Me: (eggplant emoji)

I smile into the camera, and really wish I could see his reaction.

Conner: I'll be by shortly.

Me: See you soon.

I turn from the camera, and walk over to the sink to refill the bowls. Jessica comes in for her shift, and the dogs run to her. I grin as she greets them. I really hired good staff and I'm very fortunate to have this place. Conner was right. What I do is important.

"Hey Jess," I say, and wash my hands. "I'm heading out with Buster."

"Oh, Buster. You are such a good boy." She gives him lots of love and he soaks it up. It's no wonder he's a great therapy dog. Someday, I'd like to have a therapy dog too.

I head to the lunchroom and grab my bag and keys, and leash Buster up. He prances out the front door with me, and I wave to the front staff, who all get a kick out of the way this big male dog prances like he's a prince or something. I guess he knows his value.

I take him to the fenced-in grassy area as we wait for Conner, and when he arrives, he climbs from the car with a big coffee in his hand. He walks up to me, kisses me like we're long-time lovers, and hands me the coffee.

"You're too sweet." He really is the most thoughtful man I know and later, when I finally do talk to him about something that's been on my mind for a while now, I hope he doesn't get upset with me.

"I know what my girl needs," he says with a grin, and I walk Buster over to the bus. We all climb on, and I take a big sip of my coffee before starting the engine.

"How was your morning?" I ask, and set my cup into the holder. I start the bus and glance at him sitting in Trixie's seat. Buster, who's so incredibly smart, takes his seat and before I back out of the parking lot, I toss him a biscuit.

"Got a run in, talked to the guys about our drills for hockey camp, and flipped through that book on your nightstand."

My mouth drops open. "You did not."

He grins. "I'm pretty sure some of the things I read in that book aren't possible. No one is that twisty, Dani."

I laugh at his use of the word twisty. "You have to suspend reality." I glance into the side mirrors and back from my spot.

"I can only suspend it so much. I think those things should be tested before going into a book."

I laugh out loud. "Oh, I get it. You want to try out some of the positions."

"I mean, for research, right. Did you once say you wanted to write a book? If you do, you need the facts right."

"I never once said I wanted to write a book." Now I'm laughing so hard at the sheepish look on his face, tears are welling up in my eyes.

"Damn, I was pretty sure you said that."

I reach into the doggy bowl, pick up a biscuit and toss it at him. It hits him in the forehead and he feigns hurt. Buster barks, and Conner picks up the treat and tosses it to him. "That's going to leave a bruise."

"I'll write that into my book."

His phone pings, and he's chuckling as he pulls it from his pocket. He reads through a message and I concentrate on the road as I drive. He texts back before shoving his phone into his back pocket, not bothering to tell me who he was messaging with and it's not really my business.

"Oh, I meant to tell you. My new bed, table and chairs and sofa are coming tonight." I flick on my signal. "I wanted to repaint before everything arrived but time has somehow gotten away from me."

He nods, and looks out the side window, like he has something on his mind. When he glances back at me, that melancholy look is gone, and he says, "We can pick out paint after the nursing home. I can work on it when I'm not at hockey camp."

"You don't have to do that."

He shrugs. "I don't mind."

"I really think new paint and furniture will really help spruce the place up." What I'm trying to say is I think it will help Conner feel more comfortable in my place, sleeping in the main bedroom with me when we're at my place. My stomach cramps, because what am I even thinking? We're sleeping at his place now, and he's already started baby proofing it. If and when I have a baby, I'll be moving home and when he comes over, he won't be sleeping in my bed.

Buster starts barking when we go over the speed bump. "I think he knows where he's going."

"He does. He loves it here and I love taking him."

I park the bus, and clap my hands. "Ready, boy?"

He jumps from his seat and comes barreling toward me. It's crazy how big and goofy he can be, but the minute I put the vest on him, he goes into gentle mode. He kind of reminds me of Conner on ice and in bed. Will our child grow up to be athletic like him, or more of a couch potato like me?

I fit him with his vest, and we exit the bus. Buster begins sniffing around, anxious to get inside to see his friends.

"Beware of Marta the receptionist," I tease and Conner gives me a curious look. "She's a man eater."

Conner steps ahead and pulls open the door and we stop at the receptionist desk. Marta, the elderly lady who has been working here as long as I've been coming, squeals and comes hurrying around the corner, bending to pat Buster, who takes it all in stride.

"You're such a good boy," she says and pulls a treat from her pocket. She always has one ready on visit day. She waves toward the hall. "You can head on into the lounge." Her head lifts and her cloudy eyes go wide when they land on Conner. "I didn't realize you'd be bringing a friend." She gives him a once over...twice. "I'll have to register him. Do you want to step up to the counter and give me your name and number."

"Number?" I blurt out with a laugh. "Really, Marta, can you be any more obvious?" I tease. From the rumor mill inside the nursing home, Marta dates a different man every weekend, as she should. Get it, girl.

Marta blushes and waves me away. "Oh you."

"Marta, my love." Conner begins, his voice playful as he puts his hand over his heart. "As much as I'd like to wine and dine you, you're way out of my league."

She laughs, her eyes bright and shiny, loving the attention from the famous hockey player. She waves us off. "Go. I know who you are, but feel free to stop by later and give me your number."

He puts his arm around me. "I think my girl here would be jealous."

Marta's smile widens and she gets a devilish look in her eyes. "Mmm, mmm. Good for you, girlfriend."

We all laugh at that, and Conner asks, "On that note, where's the lounge?"

I give him a nudge. "This way."

As Marta watches us walk away, her eyes no doubt peeled to Conner's perfect backside, he shakes his head at me. "You could have warned me."

"I thought I did." He laughs. "She's something, huh?"

"Yeah, I like her."

"Well, she did say you could drop her your number."

"I still might," he teases and lifts his chin an inch.

"Yeah, well good luck with that."

He throws his arm around me again and pulls me against his body and I really love when he does that. Buster walks gently, even though he's excited to get into the lounge to see all his beloved elderly friends.

We reach the door, and step in, and when Mrs. Fraser sees Buster and holds open her arms, we walk over. "Buster, my buddy. I've been waiting for you all day." Buster, being the best boy, lays his head on her lap, and she pets him. "Is he allowed a treat?" she asks.

"Of course."

I glance at Conner, who's smiling as he watches the encounter, and it really does make me feel like I'm doing important work. He can do important work too, if he's open to the idea. I'm just not sure how or when to broach the subject. Maybe I will tonight. I have the brochures at home, and we'll be there because the furniture is going to be delivered.

"Stop hogging Buster," a male voice calls out from the other side of the room and I look over to find Mr. Johnson sitting there snarling. He's always grumpy and while not even Buster can put a smile on his face, I know Mr. Johnson loves the visits.

"Want to go see Mr. Johnson?" I ask Buster, and he starts toward the elderly man with his arms open, a treat in his hand.

As we approach, out in the hall, a woman chuckles. It carries through the room and when I turn back, not feeling Conner behind me, I see him standing perfectly still, his face paling as he angles his ear toward the door. What the hell is going on? Does he know the woman who is laughing? If so, why does he look like he just saw a ghost?

16

CONNER

"Did you have to buy the biggest, heaviest sofa in the store?" I ask as I lift the end to put it in position.

"It's not that bad."

"Says the girl who's not lifting it."

"Here let me help."

I shoo her away. "No, you could be pregnant, and I'm not going to risk you straining yourself and hurting the baby."

She rolls her eyes. "You're going to have me on bedrest for nine months, aren't you?"

"If that's what it takes."

She puts her hands on her curvy hips, looking so damn adorable I want to rip her clothes off and christen this sofa. We did, after all, talk about all the fun places to have sex, and I think new furniture might be the best.

"I have a job, you know. I can't just lay in bed for nine months. I'd go insane."

"You can if I tie you there, and you won't go insane because I'd entertain you." A little gasp catches in her throat and her cheeks flush. "Oh, you like the idea of that, do you?" I put the sofa down, pull her to me and kiss her lush mouth.

"I never said that."

"Not in words, no." I break the kiss and she crinkles her nose. "What, you didn't like the kiss?"

"No, I liked it." She points to the sofa. "I'm just not convinced that's the right spot for the sofa. Maybe over by the window."

I throw myself down on it. "Come here. Try it out."

She walks over and sits beside me. Catching her by surprise, I flip her until she's beneath me, and I kiss her with heat and fervor as I dry hump her like two teenagers indulging in a make-out session before their parents get home.

"How's it working for you now?" I sit up, and she takes a couple of deep breaths as she looks up.

She crinkles her nose. "I think I need to paint the ceiling."

I laugh at that. "Does the sofa stay here or not?"

She sits up and glances around. "I'll try it here for a few days, and see if I like it."

"Fine, even though you'll be staying with me at my place for the next few days, or months, or for however long it takes to get you pregnant, and until this place is painted, and put back together." I glance around. "What's next?"

"Table and chairs, then the bed." I nod and head toward the kitchen. She sold the old table and sofa set online, but we do need to tear down her bed and move it to the garage until heavy garbage pickup day.

In the kitchen, we go to work on taking the plastic and foam off the chair and table legs, and once we're done, I position the table in the corner where her old table was, and admire the oak surface. "This is really nice." I drop into a chair. "Comfy too."

"Should we try it out?"

"You want to eat?"

She laughs. "Not what I had in mind..." She puckers her lips and straddles me.

"Oh, yeah, this is definitely the best way to try it out." I slide my hand up her back until my fingers are at her neck. I pull her toward me and a moan catches in her throat when our lips meet. After a moment, she leans back. "What do you think? And I don't want to hear about anything needing paint."

She chuckles. "I think this set is going to work just fine."

"The position?"

She wiggles. "I have zero complaints about this position."

I whack her sweet backside. "You know what I mean."

She grins, and climbs off me, standing back to look at the table. "It's a bit smaller than my last one. Maybe we can pull it out."

I jokingly reach for the button on my pants. "I can pull it out if you want to."

She laughs and whacks me. "I mean pull the table out from the wall."

I laugh, stand and do as she asks. She taps her chin. "I like it."

"Good." I gesture to the stairs. "Now on to the bed, but first I need a glass of water." I walk over to the sink and pull down a glass. I fill it, and my gaze strays to a stack of brochures. "What's this?" I take a drink, hand the glass to Dani, and pick up the brochure. I slowly read: Speak up for Dyslexia." Dani takes a big gulp of the water, her eyes wide, almost worried. "What is this, Dani?"

"I've been wanting to talk to you about your dyslexia." She hands the water back and I finish it before setting the cup in the sink. "I know you don't like to talk about it, but I was thinking you should be doing the exact opposite."

"What, you think I should talk about it?" What is going on here? I don't talk about it because I was teased relentlessly.

She backs up and leans against the big island, a new kind of seriousness about her. "You're a well-known hockey player with a platform, Conner." I eye her, waiting for her to say more. "You were picked on." I nod. "Lots of kids are picked on when they're different." I nod again. "What if you could show kids that kids aren't different simply because they have dyslexia?"

I flip the brochure over and search for answers. "What are you getting at?"

"If you opened up about your learning disorder, and went to schools and did talks to bring awareness to it, it could help those who have it, help them see themselves in you, and that dyslexia is not something that should ever hold them back.

Look at you, a famous hockey player. I actually think it would be beneficial to you too, Conner."

I frown as I reach for another brochure. "You've been looking into this without even asking me?

She swallows, and grips the counter. "I only gathered the brochures. I didn't go behind your back and talk to the schools or anything."

"The world can be so tough on you if you're different," I say under my breath. What would I have done without Alec there to protect me? I was a scrawny kid, which is probably why I was fast on the ice.

"I know, and I just think kids need to know they're not alone. I'm sure you felt you were the only one having a hard time reading and learning. Lecturing in schools can make a world of difference, and a lecture by the great Conner Birch will show these kids how they can succeed."

I drop the brochures as I listen to her reasoning. She stares at me through worried eyes, because yes, she knows she's touching on a sore spot. "I can't believe you did this."

"I just thought... You're a smart guy, Conner. A very fast thinker. Which is why you're such a great hockey player. I know how much you love to give back to the community, and I also think if you open up, get it off your chest, and share your stories, not only will it be good for you to stop hiding it, it will be good for the kids who need help."

I angle my head. "Why do I get the sense you're talking from experience? Is there something you want to get off your chest, Dani?"

She shakes her head fast. "No. I'm just saying you could be an advocate. Do something positive with a disorder that you've always kept hidden. We're all adults now, no one is going to call you names or look down on you and you can make a difference for the next generation. Plus, it's good karma."

"You believe in karma?" I ask.

"Yeah, I do. Do you?"

I nod. "I could use some good karma." My brother is gone because of me, and that's some pretty bad fucking karma right there.

"We all could, and I think you players are all pretty superstitious too."

She's right we are, and I believe bad things come in threes and here I still am, wondering waiting for the shoe to drop. "We are."

"I think becoming an advocate is a win-win, Conner."

"Do you now?" I take a step toward her and her body tightens, concern all over her face. Does she think I'm mad?

"I'm sorry if you thought I went behind your back." She holds her hands out to me, wanting me close and I want that too. "I only have your best interests at heart."

I reach her, put my hands on her waist and lift her onto the island. I push her legs apart and slide between them. "How do you know what my best interests are?"

She brushes my hair from my forehead. "Because I know you, Conner."

"What do you know?" My gaze drops to her perfect lips. I once again wonder why my brother was getting his sex elsewhere, from a girl who giggles no less, when he could have been getting it from his wife, a woman who is the epitome of perfection.

"I know that you're a great guy with a big heart that had some hurts in the past. I know you offered to help a friend have a baby, even though you were battling a few demons about bringing a child into this world."

"Go on."

I laugh. "Now you're just fishing. Maybe you should be called Coddy, like your Newfoundland fishing teammate Brady, instead of Wood."

"Hey," I say quietly and she falls silent. I press my forehead to hers. "I think that was very nice of you."

She exhales. "I was worried that you were going to be upset."

"How could I be upset when you only have my best interests at heart, and the best interests of the next generation of kids? Becoming an advocate and making change is exactly what I should be doing, instead of hiding it because I was picked on. I'm a grown-ass man. Let someone try to pick on me now."

She squeezes my bicep. "You don't need Alec fighting your battles anymore." At the mention of Alec, my thoughts race back to the nursing home and that laugh I heard in the hallway. I left the lounge quickly, in search of the woman who made it but she was already gone. I briefly close my eyes. That sound has haunted me for two long years.

"Conner?"

I open my eyes and blink. "Yeah."

"Where did you go there?"

I shake my head. "Nowhere. We should get working on the bed." I pick her up and set her on the floor.

"You actually had that same look on your face at the nursing home, when we heard that laugh. Was it someone you knew?"

"I don't know…I don't think so." I check the time. "It's getting late. We should get the bed done, and get some sleep." I playfully wave my eyebrows. "Tomorrow is ovulation day, so we're going to be busy."

She looks like she wants to say more, and maybe there are things I can't answer, so I turn and head toward the stairs. She's right about getting things off my chest, but there is one thing I know about Alec that I'll never tell her, for her own good. He's gone now and there's no need for me to hurt her and I can't have her hating me because I'm the reason he's gone.

She follows me up the stairs and the hall is filled with a huge new mattress and the base and headboard. I stop outside the main room. I glance in, barely able to make my legs move. I eye the bed she shared with my brother. The bedding has been stripped, and all that's left is to remove the mattress and disassemble the base.

"I'm going to need one of the guys to help me get this down the stairs. I don't want you lifting anything. I should have thought of that."

"We can ask my brother-in-law, Jared. He won't mind."

"He's busy with three kids. I can get Ash to come help tomorrow. He's handy and I can use his help putting the new frame together." I give her a half smile. "I'm not so great with instructions." She nods in agreement. "Do you want to head back to my place?"

"Yes, actually I need to grab some more clothes." She heads to her closet and opens it, pulling a few things off hangers. I spot a few boxes and things of Alec's there, and my chest constricts. "We, uh, should probably get on that."

She nods. "Yeah, I know. I bet there's things in here that I can donate. He was kind of a packrat."

"Really? I didn't know that about him."

She laughs. "Oh, yeah. All these boxes here. I don't even know what's in them. Look at this huge one. It's heavy too."

I move toward her, a deep compelling need driving my actions. I can't understand it, I only know I need to see what things were important to my brother. I never knew him to be a packrat at all. I'm beginning to believe there were a lot of things I never knew about my brother, and I have the weirdest feeling I'm not going to like what I find. I've never been intuitive, and I've always learned things the hard way, so I can't really understand why my gut is in knots.

"Can I take a look?"

Her gaze goes from me to the box, back to me and with a shrug, she agrees, "Sure."

I walk to the closet and even though it's weird to go through my brother's things, if I don't do it now, I'll have to do it eventually. I know Dani would like to donate what she can, which means we really have to open every box.

I carry the big box to the chair near the window and sit. Dani grabs a tote bag, and heads to her dresser and starts pulling things from the drawers. I guess she's not as interested as I am. I slowly peel the lid off the box, and when I look inside, my heart stops beating, like really stops beating.

I try to suck in a breath, but can't seem to get any air into my lungs as my gaze catalogues the contents of the box. I finally get air in, and a little sound escapes my throat.

"Conner?" Dani asks.

I lift my head, and as she comes toward me the room begins to close in on me. "Dani," I murmur. "This...this is all my stuff. All the things I've lost over the years."

She glances into the box. "Are you sure?"

My chest rises and falls rapidly, as hurt stings my eyes. "Why... why would he take my stuff?"

DANI

I t's been two weeks since Conner found all his missing things in a box in my closet. He's been rather quiet, confused by his brother's actions, and I have to say I am too. I always felt that Alec might harbor some jealousy, but then I would dismiss it as quickly as the thought would hit. What did he have to be jealous of? He was brilliant, the class valedictorian, popular, and had landed a great job at Harvard.

But he wasn't Conner.

Did he take those things to hurt his brother? I actually can't wrap my brain around that. When Conner was younger, Alec was always there for him. Conner adored his older brother, looked up to him. Conner told me that numerous times and never once did I hear Conner say a bad word about Alec, or vice versa. But the box...the things Conner treasured most over the years, things that he thought he'd misplaced and lost. Well, they weren't misplaced or lost at all. They were taken by Alec, and now both Conner and I are quietly, in our own heads, trying to figure out why.

I glance at the camera in the dog's playroom. I smile, not that I think Conner is watching me. He's been so quiet lately, focusing on helping me fix the house, and every time I look at him, and see the pain and confusion on his face it hurts my heart. He could barely concentrate during French lessons the other night and he loves helping at the hockey camps, but when he was getting ready to leave this morning, he didn't seem all that excited about it.

I know finding his things was odd and hurtful and confusing, but a part of me wonders if something more is going on inside his head. I don't know what, but what I do know is that tonight, I'll be taking another pregnancy test, and if it's positive, hopefully that will give him something else to concentrate on.

Tomorrow is Saturday and we're going to my parents' place for a meal, and we're going to have to tell them we're dating. Sunday his parents' are coming over. I'm a bit nervous about what they'll all think. My folks love Conner, for sure, but are they going to think this is a mistake? What about if we actually get pregnant? I know they want more grandkids, and they know I want a child of my own, but how will they react when they find out it's Conner's baby, and then we have to part ways and co-parent? How the heck are Conner's parents going to feel when we tell them on Sunday?

I take a fast breath and stop my chaotic racing thoughts. Right now, with a lot going on with Conner, I'm just going to take things one day at a time. I check the time and when Marley walks in, the dogs all run to her. She gives them love and those that are staying overnight are brought into another room while I get the others packed on the bus, for their trip home.

Most of them are tired after a long day of play as we lead them outside to the bus, but once they're on, and know they're going home to see their owners, they perk up. I wave to Marley and glance in the rearview mirror to spot Stallone trying to bite Ivy's ear in the seat in front of him.

"Stallone, mind your business, or no treats for you."

He barks and turns away to look out the window and I just laugh. Since it's Friday, I take a different route home so I can go through the drive-thru and get them pup cups. It's always a fun adventure and I usually get more on me than they get in their mouths, but I love it.

Howls start in the back when I take the turn, because they know where they're going. I reach the drive-thru and pull up to the window and Tabitha is waiting with a cardboard tray full of cups filled with whipped cream. They're free, but I always leave a big tip since I'm ordering so many. I pull the bus over, and one by one, give the dogs their treat, laughing as they slurp and soak me. Buster is the worst, though.

Once done, we make our way home, and I drop the dogs off with their owners. I'm anxious to get home to Conner. Tonight, we're painting the main bedroom, and if the pregnancy test is negative, I'm helping. I'm not incapable, and I'm excited to get a new color on the walls.

I don't know why but I feel a measure of relief when I find Conner's car in my driveway. I park the bus and climb out, wiping some drool off my sleeve. The front door opens and when I find Conner waiting for me, a sense of home and hearth wrap around my heart. I never felt that way with Alec. Not that he ever waited at home and opened the door for me.

"Hey," I murmur when I reach him and he bends to kiss me,

greeting me without words. I inch back and take in the warmth in his eyes. "How was skating camp?"

He smiles. "It was actually really fun."

That warms my heart. "I ordered a pizza, and picked up wine. Alcoholic and non-alcoholic."

I put my hand on his cheek and kiss him again. "Are you ready?"

I nod. "I'd like to shower the slobber off me first if that's okay."

"Yeah, it's okay and I'd like to help if you don't mind." He grins. "I can't promise I won't slobber all over you though."

I laugh at that and take his hand. "Come on." We both head upstairs and this time I guide him into my bedroom. It was nice of Ash to come and help him set up the bed. "You know what?" He follows me into the ensuite bathroom.

"What?"

"I just realized something." I reach into the shower and turn it on, as he starts taking his clothes off.

"Ash never made it to the party at the pool when it was Noah's turn with the cup." I tug off my shirt and drop it on the floor. Conner's eyes go to my bra as I reach around my back and unhook it. I almost laugh at how easy it is to be naked around him, how we're so damn comfortable with each other we can have a conversation as we strip. Oddly enough, Alec never wanted the lights on during sex, and we never got naked in front of each other. He might have been my first lover, and I was naïve and innocent, but something told me that wasn't the norm.

"Maybe it took longer for him to fix Gina's fridge than I thought." He kicks off his pants and boxers and is already sporting a beautiful erection. "Shit, I feel bad about that. He was looking forward to the celebration."

"You haven't talked to him since that day?" I undo the button on my pants.

"No, been kind of busy."

"Have I been keeping you from your friends?" I swallow, remembering that conversation with the girls from long ago. I know he assured me he'd rather hang with me. There was nothing about him to suggest he was being dishonest. I know that. It's just, if nothing can ever develop between us, and I'm not sure it can, he really should be out there finding someone. I know I want him but if he doesn't want me, I don't want to hold him back.

"There's nowhere else I'd rather be." He steps into me, slides his hands down my back and cups my ass.

"Oh, so you're here for the sex," I tease, loving that his mood has shifted to a playful one. I hate seeing him upset or unhappy, and honestly, we'll probably never know why his brother did what he did.

He answers with, "Let me help you with your pants."

He drops to his knees, and I admire his naked body as he unzips my pants and tugs them to my ankles. I hold his shoulders as I take turns lifting my legs, and once I'm completely naked, we step into the shower.

He pumps soap into his hands, his mouth on mine as he begins to wash me. He does my back and, tired after a long week, I just stand there and let him. Like me, he falls silent and after he washes me, he turns me to face him. I open my eyes and scan his troubled face.

"Maybe he was going to do something with them. Like...I don't know. Remember when Gunther had that cod fish mounted for Brady and Melanie?"

At first, I'm completely confused. I'm about to ask what he's talking about when I clue in that he's referring to all the things his brother took. He's putting a positive spin on it, thinking with his heart, and maybe it's the only thing he can do. The alternative, that his brother wanted to hurt him, might be too much for him to bear.

"I think you could be right. Maybe he was going to make a Conner room, and display all your stuff."

A strange noise, a half laugh sort of, catches in his throat. "A shrine to his baby brother."

"Yeah, a shrine," I agree.

A long moment of silence as he washes my shoulders and arms. There's a deep concentration about him as he continues to lather me, and I'm almost afraid to ask what he's really thinking.

"I'm not sure I knew who he was," he says, the sadness in his voice slicing through my heart like a serrated blade.

"Conner," I whisper, and put my arms on his shoulders. "He was your brother. You loved him and he loved you. You had a bond. He watched out for you. Protected you."

He frowns. "Yeah." A beat of silence and then, "You don't think he did it to hurt me in some way? If you look at it logically, without emotions, it seems like that's the only answer."

"There are more boxes," I tell him. "Maybe you can find the answers you're looking for in one of them." Or maybe he should leave well enough alone and not go searching for the truth.

His hands fall from my body and I see the fear and worry in his face. "I might do that."

"In the meantime, I think I need to put my hands on your body."

He moans and throws his head back as soon as my fingers touch his chest. My moan mingles with his, and I touch him longingly, lovingly. Yes, I love this man. I have loved him for a very long time now and my heart aches with the truth that he's never loved me back. I let my hands go lower until I'm gripping his beautiful cock and he cups my face, stares into my eyes as I stroke him. "I've been thinking about this all day," I whisper.

"What I'm hearing is you're in this for the sex too," he murmurs, as he slides his hands around my body and turns me until I'm facing the wall. More shower sex. I resist the urge to scream hallelujah. He spreads me, and a second later, his cock is inside me, stretching me as it hits all the right spots.

"Conner, yes." I claw at the wall, as he holds my hips and moves in and out of my body. My brain shuts down and I hope his does too. I want nothing more than peace for this man after his awful discovery.

He grunts and bends over me, kissing my back. "You feel so good, babe." It takes only seconds and I'm clenching around him, my orgasm fast and powerful. "Fuck."

I chuckle as he curses, my liquid heat no doubt bringing on his climax. He grunts again, drives deep and stays inside me, filling me with his hot seed. He pulls me upright and holds me against his body, his hands on my stomach, holding me with tender care.

Backing us both up, he takes us under the spray and rinses off our sated bodies. Once we're cleaned, he turns off the water, and spins me. "Ready?"

I playfully glance at his flaccid cock. "As if…"

He laughs. "For the test."

My heart jumps with excitement and nervousness. "I am."

We step from the shower and he hands me a fluffy towel. "I'll go heat the pizza. Come down when you're ready."

"Would it be weird if I asked you to stay?"

"I've been inside you a million times, Dani. Nothing is weird after that."

"Peeing on a stick might be."

He grabs the test from the drawer, opens it up and hands it to me, and my heart fills with everything I feel for this man. "Pee."

I nod and take the stick and he pulls his phone from his pocket to set the timer. I sit and pee on the stick and set it on the wrapper on the sink. I clean myself up, and sink to the floor to wait. Conner slides in next to me and takes my hand. I turn to look at him as hope wells up inside me.

"Tomorrow we're telling my folks that we're just dating, but if that test is positive, we might be elaborating on that," I say as I glance at the stick. He smiles, brings my hand to my mouth and kisses it. With that we both go quiet, lost in thought, and his gaze darts to mine when his timer goes off.

I take a deep breath, stand, and pick up the stick.

CONNER

"How do I look?"

I close the fridge as Dani comes into the kitchen, smoothing her hand over her pretty yellow sundress, her lashes blinking rapidly. It's easy to tell she's nervous. "Beautiful as always, and it's a backyard barbecue, not a dinner at the White House. We've done it a million of times so you don't have to be nervous."

She laughs. "I know, but we have never told my parents we were dating before." She's right. But she did once tell them she was dating my brother. I wasn't there to see their reaction, of course. I can only imagine they were elated, though. She landed the Birch brother with brains and a college career ahead of him. "It's not like I can tell them we're sleeping together because I asked you to be my baby daddy." Beneath the worry I catch the hint of sadness. Stepping up to her, I pull her in for a hug.

"It will happen, Dani. It's hasn't been that long, and hey we get to have more sex and I believe you said something about me being amazeballs."

She miles up at me, and I kiss the tip of her nose. "I almost feel relieved to be honest. I think we need to let our parents get used to the idea of us being together before we spring a baby on them."

"I agree, and what about the more sex part? Does that make you happy?" What am I doing? Fishing for compliments? Trying to figure out if she might want to keep this relationship going after she's pregnant. I mentally scold myself. Jesus, she wants my DNA because she's still in love with her late husband. I inch back, and before she can answer, I hold my arms out. "How do I look?"

She lets her gaze rake down the length of me. "Nice polo and khakis. Perfect for a backyard barbecue. It's almost like you didn't shower and tug on the first thing you found in your closet."

I feign offense. "I'll have you know, I agonized over the look."

She rolls her eyes at me and walks around me to get to the fridge. "I think Rylee is going to lose her mind when we tell her."

"Why's that?"

"She's been trying to get us together forever."

"No way."

She places the salad on the counter, and grabs two water bottles. "I'm not sure she ever really understood Alec and me."

"Really? I didn't know that."

To be honest, I never really understood it either. His interest in her seemed to come out of nowhere, and if they weren't having sex, what were they doing? I realize relationships aren't built on sex. Hell, Dani and I have our friendship, and it's real, truthful and deep. Although I am hiding a secret, but it's for her own good.

"I think this is going to make her happy," she says, her smile dissolving. "I just don't look forward to telling them the truth. At least they'll think the baby was created out of love, and that in the end we weren't compatible. I think that's the best way to handle it."

I nod, my stomach tight. "I'll do whatever you want, Dani."

She turns from me, and picks up the salad. "Let's go get this over with."

We walk outside into the bright sunshine, and I hit the fob on my car. She puts the salad in the back and slides into the passenger seat. Her eyes are on me as I cross the front of the car and get into the driver's seat. I back out of my driveway and turn to her.

"I was thinking about the cup party," she says.

"You want to have one?"

She gives a small shake of her head. "I think you should celebrate. I'd love to plan it, Conner."

"You're busy enough as it is, and if you get pregnant I don't want you on your feet and stressing."

She rolls her eyes at me. "I'm fine."

"Dani, last time..." I remind her gently.

Her hand reaches out to take mine. "It wasn't meant to be. I've learned that over the years. That doesn't mean it's going to happen again, but believe me, if and when I get pregnant, I'm going to be very, very careful. I really want this."

"I know you do." Heck, I want it too. I never even knew how much I wanted it until I warmed to the idea and if our child does have a learning disorder, we'll figure it out right away so he or she doesn't have a hard time in school. My heart beats a little faster, and as I look at her, I almost blurt out that I love her. "We'll get there, Dani," I tell her quietly and as her small smile wraps around my heart, love and guilt and every other emotion I've tried to keep in check for years, presses against the back of my eyes and I nearly fucking sob. I turn from her and concentrate on the road as I work to pull myself together.

"Anyway, I'd like to have a party. I'd love to get Ash and Gina in the same room again."

I shake my head no. "We are not playing matchmaker." What the women fail to realize is Ash isn't who he used to be. He's not quite the player off the ice anymore. Not since the incident. But it's not my place to talk about it, or what management is requiring of him.

Ignoring that, she hurries out with, "Oh, I forgot to tell you. Lucy passed her training. She's now a certified therapy dog. I'm so excited for her. I can now take her into the nursing homes. It's fun for the residents to see different breeds." I arch a brow and she reads the question in my eyes. "Dachshund."

I laugh. "Those are the wiener dogs, with the tiny legs."

"Yes. I'll have to lift her for the residents to see her, but she's only tiny. I was thinking about going in next week. Want to come?"

"I'd love to. What day are you thinking? I have kids hockey camp Tuesday and Thursday."

"Does Wednesday work?

"Yup." I take in her big smile. She really is so lucky to love what she does and I really hope she can get a dog of her own one of these days. It's odd that Alec didn't want a dog. Growing up, he loved our lab, Jersey. Unfortunately, Dani never got to meet her. We were all gutted when we lost her during our elementary school years. Maybe he didn't want to face that pain again.

Twenty minutes later, I pull up to the bungalow where Dani grew up, just down the street from where I grew up and my parents still live.

Dani exhales loudly and turns toward me as I kill the ignition. "Here goes nothing."

I give her a confident smile, although it defies what's going on inside my gut. This whole situation is messed up and I hope what we have to say doesn't cause any trouble. But we're all adults who are simply adulting, and I do know her parents have always supported her decisions, and they were by her side for months after Alec, especially when I was away playing and couldn't be there for her.

"Do you think they'll like me?" I tease.

She laughs. "You know they love you."

Their faces always lit up when I came over to hang with Dani back in high school, before Alec started dating her. That gives me pause. "Did they love Alec?"

Her hand stalls as she reaches for the door. "I…I assume they did." She looks off into the distance, like she's trying to drag memories from the back of her mind.

When she remains quiet, I open my door. "Okay, let's go get this over with."

We step from the car and she grabs the salad. The front door opens as we head up the walkway. "You didn't have to bring anything," her mom Beverly scolds, with a big smile on her face.

"It's Dad's favorite, so I think he might have something different to say." Dani leans in and gives her mom a hug.

"Conner, it's so good to see you." Beverly throws her arms around me. "How's your mom and dad? It's been so long since we all had a family gathering. Maybe we can do something for the upcoming long weekend?"

Mom and Dad go to my games, but they don't go out or socialize like they used to. The loss of a son will do that to you and that thought brings another pang of guilt. Alec is gone because of me.

"I'm sure they'd love that," I agree around the lump in my throat.

"I saw Darcy at the grocery store last week." She gives me a warm, motherly smile that holds so much sympathy and compassion. "She looks well."

"I'll talk to them about the long weekend."

We follow her down the hall and into the kitchen, and outside I hear laughter. Rylee and Jared and the kids are obviously all here. For a brief moment, I consider what it will be like when Dani and I add a child to the mix. The house will be filled with so much love and happiness. I want that. Honestly, I'm sure a child would help fill my parents' house with life and laughter, and they sure as hell could use that.

"You two head out. I'll get us wine," she says to Dani.

Out on the back deck, we're greeted with smiles. "Hey, Conner," Jared greets me.

"Let me get you a beer, son," her dad Calvin says. He disappears into the house, just as Beverly comes out with two glasses of wine. She slides one to Dani and drops down into the chair.

Ava comes running up to Dani. "Aunt Dani, push me on the swing."

"She will in a minute," Rylee tells her. "Let her sit for a moment, she just got here." Rylee pushes a chair out for Dani. "Sit, drink wine, and get me caught up on all the gossip." She sighs and glances at her children, everything about her alluding to the fact that she doesn't get out much anymore. "I miss gossip..." She stares at the wine as Dani takes a sip. "I miss wine."

"What you have is better than gossip and wine," Dani murmurs, a deep longing in her voice.

Rylee's eyes go wide when she realizes what she said. "I'm sorry, Dani."

"No, it's okay. I'm not...anyway." Dani waves her hand. "Let me figure out what gossip you missed." She glances at me, and takes her bottom lip between her teeth.

Ava grumbles and blinks at me. I laugh at her antics. "How about I push you in a minute?"

"Fine." She takes off down the stairs and joins her brother on the swing set.

"Any gossip you can think of, Conner?"

I wait a second, wanting her father here so we only have to announce it once. He comes out with a cold beer for me and hands it over. I take a much-needed drink of the cold liquid, and as I think about what to say, or how to say it, I realize action is better than words.

"Well..." I begin, and lean down and kiss Dani on the lips. Gasps sound around us and when I inch back and give Dani a small smile, she looks both horrified and amused. "How's that for gossip?"

Rylee jumps from her seat. "Are you kidding me?" she starts clapping and jumping up and down. "I knew it. I knew it. And it's about freaking time." I note the way Beverly and Calvin are staring at their daughter carefully. "Wait." Rylee stops clapping. "Is that gossip, or is that real?"

"We're dating," I tell them all. Silence ensues for a second which feels like an eternity, and I can only imagine—other than Rylee—they're all trying to grasp the reality of this. I take another sip of beer as my throat dries.

"Mom," Dani says. "Dad." She toys with the stem of her wine glass. "Conner and I are dating. I know this is confusing, and maybe—"

"It's wonderful," Beverly gushes, a wide smile splitting her lips as she pulls her daughter in for a hug, tears filling her eyes.

"You're okay with this?"

"More than okay with this," Calvin answers, as he too leans in to hug her. My gaze slides to Jared, and he lifts his beer bottle in salute.

He grins as he tips it toward me. "About time, dude."

I take in Dani's family, who've always been like family to me too. I'd hoped they'd be okay with us dating, but I hadn't expected them all to be looking at us like they know something we don't. Wait, do they?

DANI

"Missed a spot," I point out when I step into the living room. I take a moment to admire Conner's body as he stretches the paint roller above his head.

"Where," he asks, and I dip the brush I'd been using to edge the trim in the dining room to the pan, and tap his nose with it when he looks my way.

"Hey." He swipes at his nose. "You're going to pay for that."

I just laugh at that, because Conner never really gets mad at anything when it comes to me. There were so many times Alec was short with me, or annoyed about the littlest things. I chalked it up to his busy job, and just tried to be careful around him. It's nice not to have to walk on eggshells all the time.

We haven't talked much more about the box he found in my closet. There were times I could tell he was thinking about it, but unless he brings it up, I'm going to let him work it out himself. Besides, I don't know what to say. I can't understand his brother's actions, and have no explanation for them.

"I did a thing." I set the paint brush down, and blow my hair from my forehead.

"Oh, did you?"

"I painted your portrait." I lift my chin an inch, everything about me full of mischief. "It's not half bad."

"When did you do that?"

I gesture with a nod to the dining room. "On the wall. I had no idea I was such a talented painter." He cocks his head, his eyes full of doubt.

"We were in art class together in high school, Dani, so I know it's not half bad, it's all bad."

"Hey." I feign hurt, but can't stifle the chuckle bubbling up inside me. "That's just rude."

"Okay, show me this masterpiece."

I skip away, my heart full and happy as he follows me into the dining room.

"Jesus," he mumbles when he sees the horrible picture on the wall—a life-size painting of his naked body.

"Fantastic, right?"

"You're a regular Van Gogh."

I arch a brow, biting back a grin at the horrified look on his face. "You think?" He's wrong, I'm no Van Gogh.

"Yeah. If only you'd done this on a canvas we could put it away somewhere. My parents will be here later, we can't have them seeing this." At the mention of his parents, I consider the way mine reacted to the news. It was a surprise to say the least. "Sorry, but I have to do this." Conner lifts his roller and paints over my masterpiece.

I gasp. "Do you have any idea how much time I spent on that?"

"Five seconds."

"At least ten. Hmph." I begin to walk away, only to come to a fast stop as he captures me and drags me to him.

"The anatomy was all wrong."

"Maybe you're right. Maybe I'll have to see you naked again and do a better study."

"That can be arranged."

"I'll hold you to that. Right now, however, we need to get cleaned up before your parents arrive." All happiness from earlier dissipates. Telling my parents we were dating was one thing. Telling his, that's another thing altogether. Will they think we're disrespecting them, the memory of my late husband—their son? The last thing I want is to hurt anyone.

I start breathing a bit faster, and Conner puts his hands on my shoulders. "Hey, it'll be okay."

I swallow around the lump punching into my throat. "Maybe this is a bad idea."

"Dani, we don't have to tell them if we're not ready." I take in the dark shadows under his eyes. Has he been worried about this too, or is it what we discovered in the box that's preventing him from sleeping properly. "If you want to wait until you're pregnant, we can."

I consider it. "That might just be a double whammy if I get pregnant." I let loose an uncomfortable laugh. "Maybe I won't even get pregnant, and this is all for nothing."

He frowns, and says, "I think we should tell them then." He places a soft kiss on my forehead. "They both want what's best for us too, and with any luck, they'll react like your family did."

"They must be wondering what today is really about? They haven't been to my place in a long time. I just don't want to upset them, you know."

"I know." He gives me a soft, comforting smile. Why don't you run up and shower and get dressed. I'll clean up down here."

I stare up at the man I love as he gives me a tap on the backside to set me into motion. I go up on my toes and give him a kiss full of love.

A moment later, I'm making my way upstairs and I go to my closet and pull out a sundress. My gaze strays to the boxes on the floor. Some sealed with tape. My insides tighten, and I drop to my knees, tugging one to the front of the closet to examine it. I stare at it for a moment, my body tight, and when I pick it up, it's pretty light.

I shake it like it's a present under the tree on Christmas morning. I somehow think the contents inside won't bring a smile to my face. I debate on opening it for one whole second and then push it back like it might contain spiders, and just like our friend Noah, Conner's teammate, I hate spiders. Not that I could ever bring that up. Brighton told us gals Noah's 'spider incident' in private. To think a grown-ass man, a hockey player at that, lost his cool when he came face to face with a spider.

What if it's the letter you wrote Conner, Dani?

I gulp. Is it possible that Alec took the letter out of Conner's room and he'd never known it was there? It's awful to think I want to believe that. Maybe that's easier than to think Conner never wanted to be anything more than friends with me. If I dug into those boxes, maybe I could find the proof. If I don't find proof, however, it might just hurt all over again, and I'm not sure I want to go back to that hurtful place, when we're here now, in a better place.

The sound of tapping from downstairs, no doubt Conner putting the paint lids back on the cans reaches my ears and prompts me into action. With a knot still in my stomach, I hurry to the bathroom and have a quick shower. Once I'm done, I dress, head downstairs and find Conner in the back-yard, on his phone.

I step outside and he quickly ends the call and turns to me. "Everything okay?" I ask.

His gaze rakes the length of me. "Yup. The guys are talking about a meet-up for a game of pool Tuesday night. We want to bond with the new guys." His gaze rakes the length of me. "You look gorgeous." He pulls me to him again and kisses me deeply. "I'd better grab a shower too. Mom and Dad will be here soon."

"Steaks are marinating, and salads are ready. Your mom said she was bringing dessert."

"The only dessert I want tonight is you, my sweet thing."

I laugh and shove him. "Go." I shake my phone. "I want to check on the dogs." As he walks off, I think back to our visit to the nursing home on Wednesday. It was weird and I can't quite put my finger on it, but he was totally distracted, looking around and listening. The first time we were there, a woman's laughter seemed to throw him off. Was he searching for the person behind that laughter? Could that be what's keeping him up at night?

God, maybe all my surging hormones are making me paranoid.

His footsteps pounding on the stairs reach my ears as he hurries to the shower, and I open the app and smile as I check on my dogs. Once done, I head to the kitchen and make some iced tea. It's such a gorgeous, hot day and I'm super thirsty from painting my portrait. By the time I'm done, Conner comes downstairs and after giving me a kiss, he heads back outside. I pour him a glass of iced tea. Before I meet him on the deck, my phone pings and I receive a message from Brighton that there's a girls dinner Tuesday night, when the guys are off to play pool. Smiling, I step onto the deck and Conner ends a call.

"Brighton just messaged. The girls are meeting up for dinner Tuesday night."

He takes the iced tea. "That'll be fun."

"I think so." She didn't say who was going, and this might sound awful, because everyone was so accepting of me, but I sort of hope Summer doesn't come. She rubbed me the wrong way at the pool.

We sit and enjoy the sun as we have our drinks, and I jump up, my stomach coiling when the doorbell chimes. Conner pushes to his feet, and takes my hand. "It's going to be fine. Come on."

I follow behind him as we head to the door, and of course his parents won't think anything about the two of us hanging out.

We've been friends for years. Conner opens the door and gives his parents a hug.

"Cherry pie," his mom tells him as she hands it over. "Not as good as Beverly's, but I tried." As we laugh, Darcy turns to me and opens her arms. "Dani." Darcy pulls me into a hug. "I think the last time we saw you was the night the Bucks won the cup."

"Sorry, I've been busy."

"Yes, life is busy. I do know that." As Conner says a few words to his father, I weave my arm through Darcy's and lead her into the house. She stops and glances into the living room. "You're painting." Before I can answer, she continues with, "Are you freshening up the place to sell?"

"No." I briefly consider that foolish thought I had of Conner and I sharing one house. "I just thought it was time for a bit of redecorating." She glances down and nods, because she gets it. It's a way for me to move forward, but it doesn't mean I'm forgetting Alec. I hope she realizes that.

She smiles at me. "I love the soft gray."

"I like it too. I made iced tea, but let's go find something stronger." She laughs and we head to the kitchen. I find wine, and when Conner and Bill come in, Conner grabs a couple of beers, checking in with me as he twists the caps off.

For the next hour we sit outside, choosing our topics carefully as we chat. Eventually Conner grills the steaks and we make our way inside for a nice dinner. I note the way Conner has gone a bit quiet, thoughtful toward the end of the meal, so I work to carry the conversation.

Darcy takes her last bite of steak and sets the fork down.

"Dinner was lovely. It's so nice for us to all be together." She reaches out and squeezes my hand.

"Mom, Dad," Conner says, his voice deep and sure. "Dani and I have been dating."

The room goes silent for a moment, and then smiles spread across Darcy and Bill's face.

"Is that right?" Bill asks, and reaches over and puts his hand on Conner's shoulder.

"I know this is awkward," I begin. "It doesn't mean I don't cherish the memory of Alec or what we had."

Darcy gives me a wobbly smile. "We all loved Alec," she begins. "But you're young, Dani. You need to move on and build a life for yourself. We understand that."

"I just...Conner...me."

"I always thought you two made a lovely couple."

Her words take me by surprise. They must shock Conner too. "If you'll excuse me for a second." Conner gets up so fast, he nearly knocks his chair backward. He disappears quickly.

"Let me clear these dishes." I pick up my plate, and reach for Bill's. I'm not sure where Conner went, and I'm not sure why I have a knot in my gut. A few minutes later he comes back and drops a box down in the middle of the table, and my blood drains to my toes. My gaze darts to his. I honestly had no idea he was going to do this today. I'm not sure he knew either, judging by the uncertainty on his face.

"I...I found these things in a box in Alec's closet."

"What things?" Darcy asks, as she leans forward to look into the box. Conner pulls out some old trading cards and his mother's eyes go wide.

"Conner, you lost those years ago. I remember helping you search for hours."

"I know." He reaches in and pulls out a couple of medals he won in high school hockey and his father pushes back in his chair, his face paling.

"You found these in Alec's closet?"

Conner nods and his mom and dad quickly face each other, sharing a look I don't quite understand. Conner scratches his head as his gaze goes back and forth between the two of them.

"What?"

With a shaky hand, his mom wipes her mouth with a napkin, but I don't miss the tears in her eyes. "Should we get dessert?" She makes a move to stand.

"Conner." I reach for his arm, before this goes any further, and Darcy becomes more upset.

"No, Darcy. Stay put." Bill's touches Darcy's hand as his shoulders sag. In that brief second, he looks twenty years older. Alec's death was hard on them, but something here, something right now, is killing them just as much.

Darcy sits, and puts her hand in her lap. Bill reaches for one and brings it close.

"Dad?"

"Things haven't always been easy for you, son."

"I know," Conner responds and crinkles his brow.

"But you were always a very special boy. A very special son, and brother."

He swallows and goes still, like he's waiting for the ball to drop. "We know how much you loved and adored Alec." Bill casts a quick glance my way. "We all loved Alec."

I glance down quickly, sensing he knows the truth about me, and my love for his eldest son. "Alec was a special boy, too."

"But he wasn't you," the words burst from my mouth, and I gasp, instantly wanting to take them back as all eyes turn to me.

"That's right, Dani," Bill agrees with a heavy sigh.

Conner shakes his head. "I have no idea what's going on here. What are you talking about?"

"Your brother was jealous of you, Conner."

Darcy dabs her eyes. "We always suspected it."

"No." He gives a hard, unyielding shake of his head. "He protected me. He was always there for me. He stood up for me."

"He wanted what you had," Bill states quietly, like his low words will soften the blow of Alec's betrayal.

"I had a goddamn learning disorder that led to me getting bullied when I was a kid. No one wants that, Dad."

"You were and always have been just a little bit golden, Conner. It just took time for that light to shine, but it's always been inside of you. Your brother knew it every bit as much as the world did."

Conner drops into his chair, his shoulders falling as he tosses his high school hockey medals back into the box. "I…I don't understand. Why would he want my things?"

"He didn't want your things, son. He just didn't want you to have them."

As I glance around the room, take in three sets of tortured eyes, all cast down in pain, my heart jumps into my throat, that's when I have an epiphany.

Did Alec love me, or did he just not want his brother to have me? But wait, Conner never wanted me, right? Isn't that why he ignored the letter? Unless…

20

CONNER

I stand back and look at the freshly painted walls in the dining room. A pretty good job if I do say so myself. I grin when I glance at the spot that once held my very bad portrait, but then the smile fades from my face as my mind races back to dinner with my parents, and the thing they told me.

I didn't want to believe them at first, naturally. I don't want to think anything bad about my late brother. Yet, I can't find any other explanation for the box of my things I found in the closet. It raised so many other questions, mainly, is that why he went after Dani?

My heart jumps into my tight throat, and a tortured sound fills the air as I try to process that. Dani once said they barely had sex. Could it be because he only wanted her so I couldn't have her? Did he know I had feelings for her? Jesus, I don't want to believe that and I sure as hell hope Dani doesn't either. There's another part of me, however, and it's strange to think this... I'm so damn superstitious, believing things happen in threes. I've spent years waiting for the ball to drop, and there is this measure of relief in me to think this was it.

Finding out about my brother's betrayal, that had to be the third thing, right? I'd reasoned out the other day that I no longer have anything to worry about. My biggest fear was losing Dani in this situation, and that can't happen now. The third ball had fallen. I'm sure of it. The truth is, we've actually grown closer through all this, and I no longer fear that our relationship is at jeopardy.

I glance at my phone. After a busy day at the day camp, I didn't think I'd get this wall finished before she got home from work. Tonight, I'm headed out with the guys and she's having dinner with the girls. I need to get a shower, and get ready if I don't want to be late.

I quickly clean up, and make my way upstairs to shower. In the main bedroom, I begin to strip off my clothes. I toss my shirt onto the bed, my gaze going to the open closet door. My heart beats a little faster as my gaze settles on the boxes in the closet, and I swallow hard, a part of me wanting to tear into a box, the other part of me wanting nothing at all to do with it.

Forcing myself to turn away, I take one step toward the bathroom and stop. I stand for a good two minutes, my thoughts a chaotic mess as I consider my next move. Do I really want to dig deeper? Hasn't enough damage been done?

Walk away, Conner.

We don't ever have to open those boxes. We can clear the closet out without ever having to know what's inside. With that thought in mind, I step toward the bathroom only to spin around, take three big steps toward the closet and scoop up one of the damn boxes. It's heavy, and it's taped closed.

Shifting it in my hand, I carry it to the bed, and drop it onto the new comforter set Dani picked out. My fingers stall as I stare at it.

Nothing good can come of this...

What if something can? What if everyone is wrong and there's something very redeeming in this box. Fuck. Before I can talk myself out of it, I rip into the tape and peel it off. The cover is folded over, so I tug it free, and a measure of relief washes through me, when I find Alec's old college textbooks. Nothing about the stack of textbooks is redeeming. I'm just glad it's not more of my stuff.

I pick one of the books up, and flip through the pages. An envelope falls out, and as I bend to pick it up, and see my name on it, the room closes in on me. "What the hell," I murmur and tentatively grab the corners of the yellowed edges of the envelope. I stare at it for a long moment, the handwriting, especially the wispy curve of the C in my name, letting me know who wrote it.

The room falls silent, the only sound now reaching my ears is paper unfolding, as I open the envelope and pull out the single piece of pink paper inside. I can barely breathe, and my vision is blurry as I begin to read the words—written to me— words that I've never seen before.

The paper shakes in my hands as I read and reread, my brain registering that Dani had written this to me back in high school. Words like: best friends, don't want to ruin friendship, really like you, and meet me later at the café on Ashwood Street if you like me too, jump off the page. My heart is pounding so hard now, I'm sure I'm going to hyperventilate and pass out—because I never did meet her at the local diner that night. I didn't meet her because I had no idea about this letter. To make matters worse, I'd never even brought it up, and how horrible must that have been for her. Especially after the courage it must have taken her for her to write it.

Jesus, I have to tell her about this. I have to let her know I never laid eyes on this letter. If I had…things would have been different. But how…how do I tell her and if I do, will she simply think she's one of the things my brother never wanted, but simply didn't want me to have?

Fuck me.

Downstairs, the door opens and closes and in my moment of panic not knowing what to do, I shove the box back into the closet and fold up the note and put it in my pants. I stand in the doorway, debating my next move.

"Conner, I'm home." I go quiet, my heart pounding. "Conner, are you here?"

I swallow and try for normal. "Up here."

I back up, close her closet door, and pretend to check something on my phone as she steps into the bedroom. "Hey." I lift my head to see her, and she cocks her head, her gaze moving over my face. "Are you okay?"

I smile, and lean down to give her a kiss. "Yeah, just finished painting the dining room." Her eyes go wide. "I'm sorry, I came straight up and didn't notice."

"That's okay." I do my best to come off as playful, and nod toward the bathroom. "Join me?"

She starts unbuttoning her blouse. "I smell like wet dog."

"Oh, is that what that smell is?"

Her small palm lands on my chest. "Funny guy."

I pop the button on my jeans. If I take them off and drop them on the bed, will she see the letter? Fuck. As I struggle to figure out what to do, she goes quiet. "Conner."

"Yeah."

She walks over to the bed, and exhales as she sits, her eyes sliding to the closed closet door. For a second she looks confused. Does she remember leaving it open? Her head slowly lifts, and the lines in her forehead thicken. But the distant look in her eyes clears as she taps the bed, wanting me to join her. I close the distance and sit. She backs up, crosses her legs and I turn to face her.

She reaches for my hands and holds them. "Are you okay?"

Jesus isn't that a loaded question, and the truth is I'm not okay. I'm not okay, and it's not about me. It's about her. But she needs to know. How can I keep this from her? "Dani—"

"I'm so sorry, Conner. I'm so sorry for the things Alec did, and what you had to hear from your parents on the weekend. I know we haven't talked about it. I wanted to leave you with your own thoughts for a few days—heck, I needed to sort things out myself. I'm just as hurt and confused as you are." She puts her hand on my face. "I think we should talk about this."

She's so right about that.

"Why don't you go first," I suggest.

She briefly closes her eyes. "I have so much to say. Things I've thought about for years, and..." Her lashes flutter and big brown eyes meet mine. "I'm embarrassed."

"Hey." I shift, and cross my legs, sitting across from her. "You never have to be embarrassed with me, you know that, right?"

Her face twists. Jesus, is she holding back tears. "What is it, Dani?"

She sniffs. "I can't believe I'm even going to tell you this." My heart beats a bit faster, worried about where this is going.

"You can tell me anything, you know that."

With the bottom of her shirt, she dabs her eyes and a moment later, she begins. "Growing up, we moved a lot. It was always so hard to make friends." She glances at the closet again. "I always felt like an outsider, like I stuck out in a crowd, because I was...different."

"Different how?"

"You know. Boys just weren't into me, and I always just felt... unattractive, maybe even unlovable."

"Babe, you know that's not true, right?"

She swallows. "You make me feel special. You always have. You've always been such a good friend to me, Conner. Heck..." She glances at her pillow. "Look what you're doing for me now."

"Dani." I'm about to tell her I'm helping her have a baby because I fucking love her, but stop when a sob catches in her throat.

"Alec..." She stops and looks at me, and I clamp my mouth shut. "When he started paying attention to me, I just...I don't know. He was so popular, and older, and then...me." She snorts out a humorless laugh. "I mean why me?" She grabs a tissue and wipes her nose. "I was flattered. All that attention went to my head. For the first time I was someone, you know.

People paid attention to me, and I felt important. Not that you didn't make me feel important. We were friends, and Alec, he wanted to be more."

Oh, fuck that, she needs to know exactly who my brother was. "Dani."

"Let me just finish. My behavior…it was juvenile and embarrassing. But for the first time in my life someone loved me. Then, when your parents said those things the other day." She looks away, tears flooding her face. She cries for a long time, and I shift, lean against the headboard and pull her to me. I let her cry it out, and fuck there isn't much I can do about my own tears.

Eventually she pulls away and faces me. "He loved me, right?"

I stare at her, take in the sadness and vulnerability in her eyes, and my heart breaks into a million tiny pieces. How could Alec have done this to her? Used her as a pawn in a game of hatred of me.

"I was…loveable?"

"Of course you are, Dani."

She nods, and glances down. "I just…I thought maybe he only wanted me because…" Her words break off, and she takes a couple of deep, fueling breaths. "You heard what your parents said, and well, you and me. We were…close."

I pinch the bridge of my nose, my throat so tight, it hurts to breathe. If she knew the truth it would fucking kill her. I hate having to defend my brother's actions, but I can't hurt her, I won't.

"He loved you."

"Are you sure?"

"Dani," I whisper, wiping the tears from her face. "I know for a fact that you're loveable."

"How?" she asks, blinking up at me with big hopeful eyes.

"Because, baby, I fucking love you."

She stares at me, her body frozen, all except her eyes, which are moving rapidly over me, gauging me, searching for anything to prove that I'm not telling the truth. Jesus, life and well...my brother...have done a fucking number on her.

"I love you, Dani. Making a baby with you, a family, is what I want. I was reluctant at first. I was worried about my learning disability, and you know you were married to my brother, and that complicated things, but trust me when I tell you this. I love you. You're loveable. I promise you that."

She sobs harder because of the loss and hurt. How must it make her feel to know the man she was married to would do this to his own brother? But what I'm seeing are happy tears that fill my heart with even more love. I brush her hair back and kiss her deeply. While I'm telling her the truth that I do love her, I can't tell her that my brother never did. Nothing good can come from that and we've all been hurt enough.

"Conner...I love you too."

I pull her to me and we hold on to each other like our lives depend on it and in this very moment, I think they do. I inch back and kiss her forehead. "How about we leave the past in the past, and move on with our future?"

She nods. "I like that idea."

"Me too," I tell her, because if we leave all this in the past, it can't hurt us in the future, right?

DANI

I can't stop smiling. My heart is so full. Conner loves me. I love him. It might have taken us many years to get here, but we made it. A part of me is very sad. Alec hurt him deeply. He hurt me too. There's a part of me that's still not sure he actually loved me, and in my moment of weakness and vulnerability, Conner assured me he did. He's a good guy like that.

Did he also tell you he loved you because you were sad and broken?

No, no, no. Conner is not that guy. He'd never do something like that. He cares about me, has always been there for me. I might not have known who Alec really was deep down inside, but I know who this man is, inside and out. Lord knows I can't be wrong twice, right?

"Oh la la."

As I stand in the mirror, putting my earrings in, I spot Conner coming toward me, hunger in his eyes. My entire body heats up and my heart swells with the love I have for him. "Is that all you've learned?"

"No, but that's the perfect way to describe what I'm feeling right now." I arch a brow as he puts his hands on my hips and shapes my curves. "You look so beautiful, I think I should tear this dress from your body, toss you on that bed, and have my way with you."

"While I love that idea, I don't want to keep the girls waiting, and you..." I turn, and the second I see him, I melt a little inside. "You have a pool game and beer to get to."

"That beer won't taste nearly as good as you," he assures me.

I put my arms around him. "Funny you should say that. I was thinking no matter what I order tonight..." I slide a hand between our bodies and cup his thickening cock. "...it won't sate my appetite, like you do." He thickens in my hand and I chuckle, loving what I can do to this man. I haven't gotten pregnant yet, but knowing he loves me, knowing he isn't looking to move on with his life, takes a bit of the pressure off to get it done fast. Besides, we're both enjoying the process.

"Can't we stay in and have sex?"

He pouts and it almost makes it hard to say no. "No. That doesn't mean we can't have sex later, though." I step away from him, walk to my phone, take a boob shot, and send it to him. Honestly, I can't believe who I've become with him. He really brought me out of my shell, made me more confident in myself. His phone pings and he pulls it from his pocket.

A wide grin turns up the corners of his lips as he opens the message. "Oh la la."

I laugh hard. "That'll give you something to look forward to."

"Sporting a boner all night while with the guys isn't going to be fun."

I tap the air. "Maybe not, but what we're going to do later is."

His shoulders slump. "Babe, you're killing me."

I walk back to him, go up on my toes, and throw my arms around his shoulders. "Aww, I'm sorry." I kiss him, and he deepens it, moving his hard cock against my body. By the time we break the kiss, I'm flushed and breathless and when I take in his mischievous grin, I realize what he's doing.

"Not fair."

"Two can play your game," he tells me with a wink.

I fan my face and pick up my brush, needing the distraction. He steps up behind me and kisses the side of my neck. "Cut it out, Conner." I moan, and lean into him, my words saying one thing while my body tells an entirely different story.

His phone pings again, and he groans. "That better be another picture of you."

"Nope."

He inches back, and reads the message. I watch him in the mirror as he furrows his brow, and messages something back. "I gotta run. Ash asked if I'd pick him up."

My ears perk up. "Oh, good. Get all the deets on him and Gina."

"No, I'm not doing that."

"Come on, for me."

He groans. "I'd do just about anything for you, but we are minding our own business and not playing matchmaker." I'm about to protest. "Isn't Gina going to be there tonight? Ask her yourself."

I lift my chin. "Maybe I will."

"Good, do it." He holds his hands up. "I am not getting involved in your scheme."

I laugh, turn to him and point my brush. "Are we having our first fight?"

He grins. "It's not much of a fight." His lips land on mine. "I'll see you later. You're good getting to the restaurant?"

"Yes, you go have fun with the guys, and we'll have fun talking about all you guys."

He laughs as he walks out of the room, and I stare at his cute buttocks. When it comes to personalities, the man is a cinnamon roll. Not that there's anything soft about him or his butt, but his backside is sweet, like him. How the heck did I get so lucky to have this man in my life for so long?

I listen to his footsteps on the stairs, and the downstairs door opens and closes. I lean against the dresser and glance around his bedroom. He might be a bachelor, yet everything about his place is cozy. Will we live together someday? Raise a baby together? Heck, if you have love, you have everything, right? I'd much prefer to stay here, where old memories didn't haunt us and we can make new ones. Am I getting ahead of myself? I mean, love is love and that's great. There's no talk of marriage, and yeah, okay, I am getting ahead of myself. I've just never been so happy or giddy before.

The bed sheets are still a bit mussed from earlier, when we were snuggling, and I walk over and fix them. As I trail my fingers over the pillows, I imagine all the ways we'll mess the bed up tonight.

With that in mind, I head downstairs, grab my purse and walk outside. I jump into my car and drive to the downtown restaurant and as I approach, I once again hope Summer isn't joining us. Is that awful? Ugh, it probably is. Everyone took me in and accepted me, and I should do the same for her.

After parking, I hurry into the restaurant and quickly glance around. I spot Brighton, and scan the table as the hostess comes up to me. "I'm with them." I point to the WAGs at the big table. Will I be a real WAG someday? *God, girl, get it together.*

"Dani." Brighton jumps up and gives me a hug. "I'm so glad you could come out tonight. I know it's a work night, but if the guys are having fun, we should be having fun too."

I drop down next to Brighton and glance around the table. I greet Melanie, Josie, Gina, Maeve, and Harper, who is Korbin's wife and doesn't get out much because she has so many kids at home. "Is everyone here?" I ask as my gaze lands on the empty chair.

"I invited Summer. She wasn't sure she could make it, though."

"Oh, okay."

She nudges me. "Hey, you look really happy."

I can't stop a big smile from spreading across my face. "I am."

"I wasn't sure whether to invite Summer or not. I know she and Conner have a history. Everyone seemed okay at the pool party, and I hate to leave anyone out."

"Oh, it's fine." Actually, it is fine. I'm secure in myself now, and I believe in Conner.

"Good, because you don't have anything to worry about. Conner is totally into you, believe me."

"You think?" God, why am I fishing for compliments and information. I'm completely secure in our relationship.

Ah, but there's a small part of you that wonders, isn't there, Dani?

Ugh, I hate that it's true. I hate that I'm still not sure Alec actually really loved me and that Conner might have been holding back the truth to spare my feelings.

Stop.

I take a fast breath and push that thought out of my head. I do not want to go there. I am going to focus on the future and the future only.

"Of course I think," she says as the server comes to take our drink order. Since I'm driving, I only order a water with lime, and the pregnant and nursing women at the table go non-alcoholic too.

The server leaves and Maeve, who announced her pregnancy at her party, grins as she picks up her menu. "Does someone have news?"

Since I'm sure she's not talking to me, I open my menu and scan it. Maeve clears her throat and I glance up to find her looking at me, her brows raised in question.

"What?" I ask, and note the way all eyes are on me.

"You ordered water with lime. Is there a reason you're not having alcohol?" She rubs her belly and that's when I get a clue.

"Oh." I laugh. "No, no. It's just that I'm driving, and I'm a lightweight."

Brighton laughs and nudges me. "I thought you might have been joining the SUV team."

When I don't say anything, Brighton reads into it. "Ohmigod, are you trying?"

I close the menu and take a breath. I don't want to lie to these women, although haven't Conner and I been doing that all along with our fake dating? That turned out to be real so if I tell them, will it jinx it or will it happen? Could I possibly overthink this anymore than I already am?

"You don't have to tell us anything you don't want to," Josie pipes in and reaches across the table to give my hand a squeeze.

I've always felt a part of this group, but more so now than ever, and they've all accepted me, which is probably why I find myself saying, "We're trying." Claps and cheers and smiles erupt around the table. "We're keeping it low key, though. I've had complications in the past, so we're keeping this quiet, and trying not to make a big deal out of it."

"Of course." Brighton gives my arm a squeeze.

Gina sets her wine down. "Okay let's talk about all this *trying*, and *big* deal."

Everyone laughs and when it dies down, Brighton glances at Gina, compassion in her eyes. "Are you still on a dry spell?"

Gina glances down, her lashes shading her eyes, and I can't help but grin. Oh, that girl is definitely getting some and I'm pretty sure I know who's giving it to her.

She lifts her head slightly, a playful grin on her mouth. "I thought we were talking about Dani."

"Oh, hell girl, we want all the deets," Melanie blurts out, all attention turning to Gina and her sex life and I'm grateful all eyes are off me. I probably shouldn't have said anything about trying. That wasn't fair to Conner. I'm going to have to speak to him about this. I don't want to be telling secrets behind his back, and while I asked for this to be between us girls, I know they're going to tell their husbands. It's what married couples do.

The server comes back with our drinks and we put in our orders. We talk about work and books and upcoming vacations. The night is lively, the conversation interesting, and I'm so happy to be a part of this amazing group of women.

By the time we're done eating and the dishes are cleared, Brighton looks at us all, a gleam in her eyes. "What do you say we crash the boys party and beat them at a few games of pool?"

I laugh. "I don't know much about playing pool."

"Oh, don't worry about that." Josie winks at me. "We have the goods..." She stops talking and fixes her blouse around her breasts. "To throw them off their game enough that we don't need to be good."

I cock my head. "Isn't that cheating?"

"Damn right it is," Maeve agrees and drops her napkin. "Let's go bust some balls, so to speak."

Laughing, we all stand, pay our bills and head outdoors. Since I came alone, I hurry to my car and hop in, a sense of giddiness inside me. I drive the short distance to the bar, and we all meet up at the door.

"Ready?" Melanie asks, and pushes open the door like she owns the place, and I do love the woman's confidence. Squaring my shoulders, I walk in full of confidence too. The guys all turn our way as we storm the castle, and I look for Conner, but don't instantly see him. Perhaps he made a trip to the little boys room. I glance down the hall, and find it empty. Scanning the room my gaze zeroes in on the blonde making a fast exit, and that's when I see Conner coming my way.

But the blonde is the one holding my attention. Was that...Summer?

I pull in behind Dani at my place and kill the ignition. I was thrilled to see her and the girls tonight. I love that they crashed the party and won the rest of the pool games. Honestly, we were all ready to call it a night when they came, but stayed a little longer to have fun with our women.

She steps from her car and I hurry from mine to catch up to her. She stifles a yawn. Maybe that's why she was quiet tonight. I realize it's a work night, and she doesn't usually go out for dinner when she has to get up early, but I'm glad she joined the women tonight. Although I do think it wore her out. Then again, she was worn out before she left. I've been keeping her up too late at night.

"Hey." I put my arm around her when I reach her and give her a kiss on the top of the head. "You tired?"

"I am." She stifles another yawn. "I'm not usually out this late on a work night."

"Then let's get you to bed."

She smiles, and we head to the front door. I unlock it and usher her inside. She quickly kicks off her heels and moans in delight. Her job doesn't require heels and she sure looks happy to be out of them.

She walks up the stairs ahead of me, her body tight, and I can't help but think something is wrong. Is she having second thoughts? Did she find something else out about my brother? I hurry behind her, and follow her into the bedroom. "Is everything okay? You had a good time tonight, didn't you?"

She peels off her dress, and I fight to keep blood in my brain. "I sort of told the girls that we were trying to have a baby. I ordered a water with lime, and that made them curious and the conversation snowballed from there. I probably shouldn't have done that." She crinkles her nose and I relax a bit.

"It's okay. When it happens they were all going to know anyway."

Her lashes slowly fall and lift again as her eyes move over my face, assessing me. "You're not upset?"

"No, babe. Did you think I would be?"

"It's just, I mean, we were going to say it was an accident, right? Now they know we're actively trying, and you and me, we're just so new."

"We're not that new, Dani. We've been pretty much attached at the hip for a couple years now."

"Even before that, really. In high school and even when I was married." She glances down, and after a moment of silence, asks, "Conner, do you think Alec was jealous, or thought something was happening…" She waves her hands back and forth between us. "Between us? I'd never cheat. Things might not have always been great between us, but people who cheat are...are..."

"Assholes," I offer, and she nods. "No, I don't think he thought that at all. He knew who we were." We just didn't know who he was.

Her shoulders settle in place. "Are you going to say anything to the guys about us trying for a baby?"

"I don't have to. I'm sure there are no secrets between husbands and wives and this is kind of juicy information."

"Juicy?" she asks with a grin. "Now there's a word I don't hear often."

I take off my shirt and kick off my pants. She stifles another yawn, and as much as I want to put my cock inside her, I think she needs a good night's sleep. "Let's go wash up."

She follows me into the bathroom. We brush our teeth, wash up, and she stays behind to put on face cream. I head to the bed and pull the covers down for her, and a moment later she joins me. She slides in and once again goes quiet.

I go up on my elbow, and face her. Lightly touching her chin, to turn her face toward me. "Is there something else on your mind?" From the wrinkling of her brow to the worry in her eyes, I can tell there's something bothering her.

"Was that Summer at the bar tonight?"

Oh, I didn't even realize she'd seen her. "Yeah. She came to see Knox for a second."

"She didn't join us for dinner." She shifts to face me. "I guess I just thought it odd to see her at the bar."

"She said something to us about not being able to be out late. I don't really know. I barely spoke to her."

"Oh." She averts her eyes.

I put my hand on her bare arm, and lightly run my fingers up and down her soft flesh. "Hey, what's going on?"

"Nothing."

Okay, she said that fast, too fast for me to believe she means it. "It's you I love, Dani. You know that, right?"

Her body softens beneath my touch and she smiles and puts her palm on my cheek. "When I got to the bar and didn't see you but saw Summer leaving, then I spotted you coming my way from the same direction she had..."

"First, I'm glad you're telling me this, and second, I think Alec did a number on us both, and his betrayal has left us both very leery." Jesus, she can never see the letter, never know what he really did behind her back. I took it out of my pants that night, and stuffed it between the mattress and box spring until I can dispose of it properly. I make a mental note to do that tomorrow.

She snorts out a laugh full of sadness. "You're not wrong."

"I rarely am."

She whacks my chest and laughs. "Ego much?"

"Come here." I lay on my back and pull her to me. Her cheek rests against my heart, and a soft moan escapes her lips. I close my eyes and the next thing I know, morning is upon us, and I'm the little spoon to her big one. While I love having sex before bed, there's something very nice and profound about falling asleep with my arms around her and waking up with hers around me.

I shift, and try to slip out without waking her so I can have her coffee waiting for when she gets up. Moving slowly, I inch forward, only for her arm to tighten around me. Is she awake? I move again, and she holds me to her, and a soft chuckle reaches my ears. I spin and grin when I catch the playfulness in her eyes.

"Been awake long?" I smooth her hair back and kiss her forehead.

"No, is it the weekend yet?" she asks and groans.

"Afraid not, and you, my sweetness, have to get up and get to work."

"You can't make me."

She rolls over and I throw my arm around her, working to get a grip on my morning wood. I guess my nickname is accurate in more ways than one. I curse under my breath.

"I can't, but I know you're looking forward to taking Lucy to the nursing home today."

She pushes the covers off. "Ugh. You don't play fair."

"Go shower and I'll get coffee and breakfast ready."

"Oh, I thought you'd be joining me." She glances at me over her shoulder. "I think I know a way of helping you with your morning wood."

I burst out laughing. "You felt that, did you?"

"Nearly bored a hole in my back, Wood. But if you want to get lucky, it will have to be a quickie. I can't keep my dogs waiting." She crooks her finger and I jump from the bed, panting like one of her dogs as I follow her into the bathroom. She bends to turn on the shower, and the second I get a glimpse of her sweet, naked backside, I grip her hips, shift her until she's bent over the sink, and slide all the way inside her.

"Oh my god, Conner."

I fuck her fast, sliding my cock deeply into her body. In no time at all, she shudders around me and I throw my head back and groan as I fill her with my seed. I lean over her body as we both pant, and put my mouth near her ear. "Maybe we'll get lucky with this one."

"I'm feeling lucky," she murmurs and I lift her from the sink, put my arms around her body and walk her into the shower. Closing her eyes, she lifts her face. "Feels so good. Best thing I felt this morning." She opens one eye to peek at me, a grin tugging at her face.

"You'd better be talking about my cock and not the rain shower."

She throws her arms around me. "Maybe...maybe not."

I just shake my head at her antics. I fucking love it when she's happy like this. I soap up my hands and wash her and once done, she does the same to me. Ten minutes later, we step from the shower, dry off and go back to the bedroom to dress. I tug on sweats as she grabs her clothes from her side of the closet.

I love that she's occupying the side that never got used before. She should just move all her stuff over. It's ridiculous that we have two big homes but one step at a time. I don't want to rush anything and scare her off. Heck, last night she was questioning me about Summer. This is all so new and scary, so baby steps it is.

She stares at me and moans in appreciation, and I love the way she admires my body. "I'll run down and start breakfast."

"Thanks. I need a minute to dress and dry my hair."

She heads back into the bathroom and I stare at her sweet backside until she's out of sight. Everything is so damn good between us and while I love it, it scares the shit out of me too. You know what they say, when things are too good to be true.

I shake my head to push that thought to the recesses of my brain. It took us far too long to get here, and nothing is going to come between us now. Nothing. In the kitchen I go to work on making coffee and drop some bagels into the toaster. I fix Dani's coffee just the way she likes it and coat her bagel in that awful cream cheese.

The scent of her warm skin, and whatever it is she spritz on her hair reaches my senses and I know she's at the door watching me. I grin as she stays silent, and bend forward jokingly. A small sound fills the air.

"Like what you see?" I tease and turn to face her.

"Yes, coffee and bagel all ready for me. I love what I see."

"I never knew you were a comedian." I cross the room and pull a chair out for her. "Sit. Eat."

"Oh, bossy." She drops into her chair and as she moans over her first bite, I roll my eyes and drop next to her diving into my own bagel, with plain cream cheese, thank you very much.

"I hope the residents at the nursing home take to Lucy the same way they'd taken to Buster. They really adore him and he's such a big teddy bear."

"He certainly has you wrapped around his paw." She sticks her tongue out at me. "Aren't most little dogs yappy and aggressive, though?" I remember when Bear, her chihuahua, didn't like someone, he was a super aggressive ankle biter.

"They can be. Lucy went through certification, though. She's got this. I sometimes just think big dogs make better companions, though."

"Do you want a male or female dog?" I ask.

"I don't know. Bear was male, so maybe it would be nice to have a female. Either sex will be protective."

"What do you think of a name for a female *chienne*?"

"Look at you, knowing the difference between masculine and feminine word for dog."

"I've been practicing." I lift my chin an inch then lean into her. "Our teacher is kind of scary. I don't want to get on her bad side."

"You're actually doing great, Conner."

"Did you know that Korbin's wife Harper used to be an elementary school teacher?"

"I think I remember something about that. They don't get out much, so I don't know her well."

"Right. Well, at the pool tables last night, I chatted with him." She arches a curious brow as she takes a sip of coffee. "I mentioned my dyslexia and how I could talk about the struggle and the support available in the schools."

Her eyes go wide and I love how this makes her so happy. Heck, it makes me happy too. "He's going to look into it for me."

She stands, and throws her arms around me. "I am so proud of you, Conner."

Warmth and love well up inside of me as I hug her back. She presses her lips to mine for a sweet kiss and I tap her ass. "Okay, we'd better get moving. Don't want to keep the dogs waiting or we'll end up in the doghouse." She groans at my corny joke. "Maybe I should leave being the comedian to you," I tease.

We tidy up and head outside. Dark clouds have moved in and I suspect a good downpour. We hurry to her bus, and I take my usual seat. Of course, I'll have to move when Trixie boards. She's pretty possessive of her front row spot on the bus and I don't enjoy the stare down until I move.

We travel and pick up all the dogs and by the time we're done, I'm at the back of the bus. Dani parks and unloads them and I follow her inside. I spend an hour or so playing with the dogs until it's time to take little Lucy to the nursing home. Back on the bus, Lucy sits on my lap, and for a little dog, she's quite snuggly and quiet.

"She likes you," Dani tells me, as she glances over her shoulder.

"What's not to like?"

She rolls her eyes and I pet Lucy as she drives us to the nursing home. I carry Lucy off the bus, and Dani puts on her special vest. Inside, Marta greets us in her usually flirty way, and we make our way to the lounge. As I walk in, I find myself glancing around and listening, remembering the first time I was here. Not that I expect to hear that familiar laughter again. That would be a crazy coincidence, right? Although it is the same day of the week, and close to the same time of day.

The guests laugh and clap when they see little Lucy, and Dani casts me a happy smile as she picks Lucy up and carries her over to one of the ladies. She oohs and awws over the little dachshund, and I follow along behind. I glance over and see a freshly made pot of coffee.

"Is that for anyone?" I ask and Dani nods.

"Want one?"

"I'm good, thanks."

I make my way over to the table at the other side of the room. I pick up the carafe, and fill a paper cup. Just when I'm about to add a splash of milk, that familiar laugh filters down the hall. I go still for a second, waiting. When it doesn't come again, I glance over my shoulder and find Dani busy. Heart beating a bit faster, I step into the hall and look left and right. The laughter comes again and I start toward it, stopping outside one of the resident's rooms.

I take in the woman standing over an elderly lady in her bed, her back to me. I can't see her face, but I'd know that body and long blonde hair anywhere. My heart thuds so hard, I can barely hear. I grip the door to hold on, and just when I think things can't get any worse, a little boy, who can't be much older than one, runs around the bed, coming to halt when he sees me. His big blue eyes—eyes so similar to mine, it's eerie —lock onto mine. Air leaves my lungs in a whoosh as every possible scenario races through my mind. Legs weak, I falter backward, move away from the open door, and brace my back against the hallway wall.

What the fuck is happening?

23

DANI

I study the stick, and my heart sinks into my stomach as the negative pregnancy sign stares me in the face. Dammit, I really hoped this would be it. I'm beginning to believe it's never going to happen for me. I don't want to believe I can't get pregnant again, yet a small part of me is terribly worried. Tonight is the night we're having a party to celebrate Conner's turn hosting the cup. While I wouldn't have widely announced that I was pregnant, as I know how wrong things can go in the first trimester, I would have at least whispered it to a few of the women.

Conner wraps his arms around me. "I'm sorry, babe."

"Oh well, it's fun trying." I put on a brave face as he holds me, and I lift my face to his, trying to shake off my sadness. We do, after all, have a party tonight. All our friends, and relatives are coming, and I'm honestly looking forward to hosting everyone in Conner's house. It will be nice to make this big place feel like a home. "We should get ready. Everyone will be here soon."

I start to back up but he pulls me tighter. "Are you sure you still want to have this party?"

"Absolutely. Even if I didn't, it's too late to cancel now."

"No, it's not."

I put my hands on his chest, and there's just something so comforting about his strong heartbeat. "I really want to have this party."

His face is serious. "Dani, were there any complications after last time?" His eyes narrow even more. "Did the doctors say…anything."

"No, it happens, Conner. It just wasn't meant to be."

"This time, though." He drops a kiss onto my forehead. "It's definitely meant to be." I nod, and inch back. I take in his blue eyes, which hold a lot of concern. While they've always held concern for me, I think something happened at the nursing home a couple weeks ago. He disappeared from the lounge for a few minutes and when he came back he was distracted. I'm not sure what happened. When I asked, he said it was nothing. He's not a guy to lie, so I took his word for it.

I give him a whack on the ass to set him into motion. "Go, get ready. I'm okay. I promise."

"I'm going to give Mom and Dad a call. They weren't sure if they could make it or not." He pulls his phone from his pocket as he leaves the bathroom and I turn on the shower. Being out and in big crowds is still hard for his parents. I do hope they can come for a short time to celebrate and honestly, they seemed so happy about Conner and me together. Everyone has been, and that's such a surprise to me. Back in the day, Conner only wanted to be friends. His nonresponse to the letter proved that. God, I don't want to think about the letter, or the fact that he might never have received it.

I strip off and climb into a hot shower, and when I'm done, I dry off and spend a little extra time on my hair and makeup. Still dressed only in a towel, I stand back and examine myself in the mirror, happy with the woman staring back. I've never felt so content in my entire life.

A curse sound comes from the bedroom, and I hurry into the room to see Conner, dressed only in his boxers, bend over, looking under the bed.

"Are you trying to turn me on?"

He snorts out a laugh. "I dropped my damn phone and it slid under the bed." He lays flat out and struggles a bit to reach it. "How far could it have gone?"

"Let me see." I walk around to the other side of the bed, lift up the bedding, and bend. "It's closer to me than you." I reach out and snatch his phone. "Got it." A little tag is sticking out from the mattress, and I'm about to tuck it back in, when his phone rings and I jump.

"Good God, that scared me."

He laughs as I glance at the screen. "It's your mom. Sorry, didn't mean to check." I hand the phone over and fix the bedding.

"You look amazing, by the way," he compliments me as he slides his finger across the phone. Deciding to play with him a bit, I give a little shake to my backside as I cross the room, open his closet and let the towel fall to the floor.

He groans, and I hear. "Yeah, yeah, I'm okay." I glance at him over my shoulder and chuckle slightly. He gives me a warning glare. I go back to dressing and pull out the dress I bought last week. It's a cute black number that hugs my curves. I knew this was the dress when Conner began to drool. Honestly, I can't believe he wanted to go shopping with me. I probably wouldn't be able to wear this and drive Conner crazy if I was pregnant, so I guess there's something positive about that.

He ends the call with his mother. "They're going to come for a bit."

I pull the dress on and turn to him. "I'm so glad." Lifting my hair, I point over my shoulder. "Zip me up."

"If I get anywhere near you in that dress, the only zipping I'll be doing is down."

I laugh. "Come on, Conner. I can't reach."

"Fine." He reluctantly stomps my way, his knuckles warm on my back as he works the zipper.

"I'm really glad they're coming out. I can't even imagine losing..." I let my words fall off. We all had a loss, and are all suffering in our own way.

His hands slide around my body, and he holds me in a tender way. "I don't ever want to lose you, Dani."

I turn in his arms, and there's worry and hurt in his eyes. "Hey, you're not going to lose me. We made that promise going into this, and it's a promise I stand by."

"Okay," he murmurs, like he's still not sure. Why wouldn't he be? Does he know something I don't? God, I'm just being paranoid, worried that this can be taken away from me quickly.

I go up on my toes and kiss him. "Now get ready. I want you in more than boxers when people start arriving." Inching back, I admire his body as he goes to his closet and pulls on a nice pair of dress pants and a button-down shirt. I continue to smile at him as he dresses, and he just grins at me.

Once we're both ready, we head downstairs, and start putting the hors d'oeuvres on trays and setting out glasses for wine and drinks. Soon enough the bell chimes, and we both hurry to the door, to let in Brighton and Noah.

"You look gorgeous," Brighton says and gives me a hug.

Conner frowns and holds his arms out. "Hey, what about me?"

Brighton rolls her eyes and hugs him. "Always so needy, Wood." I give Noah a hug and usher them both into the living room, where the cup is proudly displayed near the big fireplace.

Noah pats Conner on the back. "Looking good, Conner." He steps up to the cup. "No liquor in that."

"Nah, but I do have beer chilling in the kitchen." Conner throws his arm around Noah's shoulder and they head off. Brighton looks around. "I haven't been here since Conner bought the place. You're making it very homey, Dani."

I smile at my friend. "I've been adding some touches. I've actually been redecorating my own place."

She frowns, and runs her hands over one of the cushions I'd plumped earlier. "If you and Conner are trying to have a baby, are you going to keep both places?"

"I'm not sure what our plans are, but it does seem crazy to have two big places."

"Well, I'd choose this one with the pool," she jokes.

"Me too." Honestly, I do want to talk to Conner about that, but I'm not pregnant yet, so I haven't really pushed the idea and he's not talking about it, even though we're basically living together as it is. "Let's go get wine."

"Wine, yes."

We head toward the kitchen and the bell chimes again. For the next half hour, Conner and I greet his friends at the door, as well as our parents, and my sister and brother-in-law. Rylee grins like the cat that ate the canary every time she sees Conner and me together, especially when he's touching me. I don't hate it, but I don't know why she has that 'I told you so' look on her face. She never told me anything. Or maybe she has.

I don't know or care. All I know is that I'm having a wonderful time celebrating the team's championship with great friends. This, right here, in this house with Conner, is where I belong. I've never really felt a sense of belonging in the house I shared with Alec. This is real and in my heart I know we have a future together.

I catch Gina chatting with Josie, and I don't miss the way Ash is watching her, his face hard as she basically ignores him. Ooh, there's definitely a story there and I want to hear it.

Excusing myself from Conner, I head toward Gina when the door chimes. I pause for a second. Isn't everyone here already? Who the heck did I forget? I walk toward the door and smile as I swing it open. My smile falters slightly when I come face to face with Summer.

"I'm so glad you guys could make it," I greet them. I turn to Knox, as he holds a bottle of wine out to me. "Thank you. Come in."

I guide them in and close the door. "Sorry we're late. Summer had a hard time getting away."

Summer looks almost mortified at that explanation, like Knox said something he shouldn't have. "We're here now. How about we get into that wine?" Summer says quickly, like she wants to change the subject.

"Knox," someone calls out from the living room and he glances at Summer. she gives a little nod, and it makes me think they had a little talk about her not being left alone with me. Knox obviously knows she and Conner have a history. "Get in here."

"You good?" he asks, making this a bit more awkward.

Summer smiles, but it's shaky as she gives Knox a tight nod. "Dani and I are going to get a drink."

He disappears into the room, joining the guys. Since she looks like she's desperate for alcohol to take her nervous edge off, I gesture with a nod for her to follow me to the kitchen.

"Not much has changed," she comments as she glances around, and her words are like a punch to the gut for some reason. Does she want me to remember her time with Conner, or is she nervous, like me, and searching for something to say?

Summer casts me a fast glance. "I...wasn't going to come. Knox really wanted me to."

My heart softens a bit. She's out of place, as out of place as I was when I first started hanging out with this crowd. No one deserves to feel that way, and if memory serves me right, it was Conner who stopped calling her, which led to the breakup.

"You and Knox...things are serious?"

She shrugs. "I'm not sure. I mean he's a nice guy. I really like him. I'm just..."

She lets her words fall off. Clearly something is holding her back, and I'm not going to push. Wait, she's not still in love with Conner, is she? I glance into the living room as we head down the hall, and my heart jumps when my gaze lands on Conner, who's watching Summer very carefully. Every muscle in his body is tight, everything about her presence is clearly distracting him. He'd been around her at the pool party and was fine. Maybe it's because she's back in his house. Maybe it's bringing up old memories. Good or bad memories, I'm not sure.

"You had a hard time getting away," I state, desperate for something to talk about.

"It's fine," she answers, her words fast and dismissive.

Alrighty then.

I find Melanie, Rylee and Emilia in the kitchen. Emilia, a former Olympic figure skater, is the team's assistant skating coach and she doesn't come out much. I'm grateful for their presence. I quickly introduce my sister and Emilia to Summer, and Rylee narrows her eyes as she pours herself a generous glass of wine, like she's trying to place Conner's ex-girlfriend. Rylee had informed me earlier she was going to pump and dump, because tonight she needed wine. I need wine too.

I grab an open bottle and fill two glasses. I hold mine up in salute and we all tap. "To the cup," I say and we all take a drink. "Shall we?"

We make our way back to the living room, just in time to hear Brady tell one of his ridiculous jokes, and as everyone laughs, I note the way Conner is staring again. Summer makes her way to the other side of the room and starts talking with Harper who has been chatting with Gabe—Gabe the Babe, as the bunnies call him—a rookie who came alone tonight. The guys call him Gabby, ironic for sure, considering he doesn't talk all that much. He also doesn't come out much, and he's super quiet. His gaze strays to Emilia, and if looks could kill, Gabe would be six feet under. From what I understand they go way back, childhood friends, I think. Conner told me she seems extra hard on Gabe, the team's right winger, during training.

"Wait, is that..."

I turn to look at my sister. Her eyes are wide as recognition hits. "Yeah, that's her."

"What is she doing here?"

"She's with Knox," I tell her. "The past is the past, and that's where it's going to stay."

She doesn't look as convinced as I am. I'm not sure I blame her, considering the way Conner is watching her. Before Rylee can say more, I hook my arm in hers.

"Help me bring the hors d'oeuvres in."

"Sure." We walk into the kitchen. "She has some nerve coming here."

I shrug. "In this world, the bunnies get around. The guys don't seem to have a problem sharing."

"I didn't think she was a bunny, though?"

"I don't know what she is or was." I open the fridge and pull out a tray of small sandwiches. I set them on the counter, and pull out a couple more trays filled with finger food. We gather them up, and make our way back to the party, but the second I walk into the room and spot Conner in the corner, in deep conversation with Summer, the trays in my hands wobble.

I have no idea what they're talking about, but judging from their body language it's something very serious. Was I wrong thinking those two were done, and that Conner and I had a future together?

● **24**

CONNER

I head to the locker room after a fun practice with the kids. I usually enjoy the camps more than I did today. I tried to put on a happy face, though it was hard with so much shit on my mind. Mainly, Summer's laugh. Had I blocked it out all these years, after hearing it the day my brother called to take Dani to the hospital? Was there a part of me that just wouldn't allow myself to think that Alec wasn't only betraying Dani but was also betraying me—with Summer? Not to mention that Summer was betraying both of us as well.

Jesus Christ, what is going on with my life?

But that laugh. Now that I've heard it again, it untangled something in the back of my mind and took me right back to the day Alec called me, the day I called him back, demanding he get home...the day he died.

Why...why the fuck did he have to want what I had?

Did he not realize he had it all, including the most amazing woman in the world, one who I never thought I'd be good enough for? Neither one of us deserved what he did to us, and no matter what, Dani can never know. I can't hurt her like that.

But seeing Summer with that young boy at the nursing home has left me unsettled, and trying not to be distracted this past week has been nothing short of impossible. Dani must know something is off. She's astute and I'm not that great of an actor. It's true, the party at my house was not the time to corner and question Summer. I hadn't meant to, but the second I saw her standing alone, I pounced. Not my greatest move, I know.

She was the last person I expected to show up at my house. Although I don't know why I didn't expect it. She's dating Knox and naturally he was invited to the party. It's not like she saw me at the nursing home. She had her back to me and after I saw the boy, I bailed. There was no saying the child was even hers, which is why I let it go, until I couldn't hold the question back anymore, because yeah, his eyes are the same shade of blue as mine.

Do I have a child?

She never answered me when I asked the question at my place. My voice no doubt held a shit ton of accusation, and took her by surprise. She became flustered and tongue tied, and when she glanced over my shoulder, I knew Dani had returned to the room. I ended the conversation, but it's not over. No, it's far from over. I don't know when I'll see her next, only that we have to talk. It's not like I can do it around the guys, or Dani. Does she still have the same contact information?

I snatch my phone up, and scroll through it, finding Summer's number. I should send a text off, see if she answers.

I go to my texts, and punch out a message to Summer, telling her we need to talk. I'm not sure if it's still her number or not, but what else can I do?

I hit send and smile when I see the last person I was messaging was Dani. She naturally questioned me the night of the party, and I simply told her I was surprised that Summer showed up at my place. While that is true, it's not the entire truth. Fuck, how was I supposed to tell her I might be a father, when we've been trying so hard to have a baby? She hasn't said anything, but it's clear she's worried she'll never get pregnant again.

"Something on your mind?" Noah asks, coming in and dropping down onto the bench beside me.

"What?" I turn to him, my attention scattered.

He nudges me as he takes off his skates. "Whoa, dude, what's going on with you?"

"Nothing...just...it was weird that Summer was at my place." I'm not sure if I'm making a statement or asking a question.

"I'm afraid you're going to have to get used to seeing her around. She's with Knox." He eyes me. "You don't still have a thing for her, do you?"

"Fuck no," I answer quickly and adamantly. "That was over, before it was officially over."

He nods. "You and Dani, that's where it's at, Conner."

I meet his eyes, and take in the seriousness. "I know that."

He pats my shoulder. "Don't fuck it up."

I snort out a laugh, afraid that I might do just that. "I have to run. The kids want to head to the park and get ice cream. Join us if you want."

I smile, as I imagine that life. It's the life I want, with Dani. But now there might be another child in the picture and dammit, if the child is mine, I want to be a part of his life. How could Summer have kept this from me? Does she not want me in his life?

Okay, slow down, Conner. You're getting ahead of yourself.

"Rain check. I have some things to do," I finally answer when I realize Noah is standing at his locker waiting for a response.

"Sounds good." He closes his locker and gives me a nod before leaving.

One of the boys I coach walks into the change room and holds his hand up. "Great practice, Coach," he says to me with a big smile.

"You did good, Liam. Keep that up and we'll be playing in the NHL together." He gives me a big toothy grin, and I open my locker and grab my bag. The weather is warm when I walk outside, and my phone pings. I pull it from my pocket and read the message from Dani.

Dani: How was camp?

Me: Great. Just finishing up.

Dani: Want to pop by and say hello to the dogs?

I'm about to tell her I'll be right there when a message from Summer lights up my phone. Holy shit. My heart races a bit quicker.

Me: Sorry, I have some things to do.

Dani: No worries. See you for dinner tonight. It's a nice night for a barbecue.

Me: Sounds good.

I stare at my phone for another minute. Three dots appear and disappear. Fuck, I hate not telling her the truth, but how can I? If this turns out to be nothing, then nothing ever needs to be said, right? I don't know if that's logical or not. I only know my main goal is to protect Dani until I have all the facts. I open the message from Summer.

Summer: Come by my place. I'm still in the apartment on Granville Road.

I shove my phone into my pocket and with my heart climbing into my throat, I hurry to my vehicle, a new purpose in my step. I have no idea what faces me when I reach her place. I only know if I have a child, I should have been told. Honest to fuck, anyone who would keep that information a secret, depriving a father the right to know his child, is lower than low in my book.

I pull into traffic and head towards Summer's place. As I drive through the busy downtown core, something niggles in the back of my mind. I pinch the bridge of my nose when I come to a red light, my mind going back to that chaotic day when we lost Alec.

I was a hot mess in the hospital. After calling my brother, demanding he get home from New York, or he'd be dead to me, I called my parents, and Dani's. The light turns green and I start driving. Alec never reached the hospital. In fact, he wasn't that far away when he was sideswiped, hitting a street-light head on.

How was it possible that he'd driven from New York to Boston in less than two hours? Unless he wasn't in New York. Jesus Christ. If he was in the city, does that mean he waited, letting a couple hours tick by before driving to the hospital after I called. I had assumed Summer had gone to New York with him. As my mind goes over a million different scenarios, none of them good, I step on the gas, needing answers, and needing them now.

Twenty minutes later, I reach Granville Road and stare at the apartment building. Summer lived here while she was in college. I figured she'd have moved on from it at this point. I park my car, slam the door and hurry across the busy street.

I buzz her apartment, and she lets me in. Anxious, I take the stairs instead of the elevator and when I approach her apartment, she's opening the door.

"Hey," she murmurs quietly, and I'm pretty sure I've never seen her so worried in my entire life, which gives me an even bigger knot in my stomach.

"Hey."

She shifts from one foot to the other and I glance over her shoulder to see the young boy from the nursing home pick up a toy airplane and run through the living room. He comes down the hall to the front door as Summer remains perfectly still. He stops and stares at me.

"Hi again," I say, and Summer's eyes go wide.

"You...what. How do you know Tyler?" She picks him up and holds him tight to her chest.

"At the nursing home."

"What were you doing at the nursing home?"

I grip the doorframe. "Can I come in?"

She hesitates for a moment, and holds Tyler tighter, like she's worried I'm going to take him from her or something. Does that mean he is mine?

She nods, and moves to the side. I push past her and she shuts and locks her door. I step into the small living room. Not much has changed in her place in two years, except, of course she has a child and the place is filled with toys.

I turn back to her and find her watching me with suspicious eyes. "Dani takes the therapy dogs there on Wednesday. What were you doing there?"

"My grandmother. She was recently admitted."

I nod, standing on shaky legs as I take in Tyler's big blue eyes. "I heard your laugh. It reminded me of a time, long ago." I look back at her, and narrow my eyes. Does she know what I'm talking about?

Her eyes go wide, and okay, yeah, she totally knows I'm talking about the day Dani lost the baby and Alec lied about where he was. "You knew Alec was with me?"

"I knew he was with someone. I didn't know who, until I heard your laugh at the nursing home. It was the same laugh I heard over the phone when Alec called me. So, I went and investigated and saw you."

"You saw me? I didn't see you."

"You had your back to me. That's when I saw Tyler. He came out from around the other side of the bed."

She blinks rapidly, the color draining from her face. "You didn't say anything?"

"I wasn't sure what to say. But I have questions. Lots of them."

She gulps and sets Tyler down. "Tyler, why don't you play in your bedroom." She guides him down the hall, and I drop into her wingback chair, bracing my elbows on my knees as I try to quiet my racing heart and brain.

She comes back into the room, her body tight as she sits on the sofa across from me. She lifts her gaze and it's shaky when it reaches mine.

She gestures toward the kitchen. "Can I—"

"Is he mine?"

"Conner."

I lean forward. "Is he mine, Summer?" My voice comes out hard, and she winces, but fuck, I'm angry. Angry at her, at my brother...just fucking angry.

"He's not yours." Her voice is so low and weak, it's a surprise I could hear her.

"How old is he?"

She gulps. "He's just a little over one."

Okay, we all know math isn't my strong point, which could be why I miscalculated how long it would take my brother to get home from New York—or maybe my brain was protecting me from things it wasn't ready to know—but I'm able to do this math.

"We were together at the time then. If he's a little over one, and you add nine months pregnancy to that, how is he not mine?"

"Because he's...Alec's."

I jump up and nearly send the chair backward. "What the fuck?" Holy Jesus, how did I not even consider that possibility?

"How do you know?"

"I did a paternity test."

I grip my hair and tug as I begin pacing. "Why didn't you tell me this?"

"I didn't want…to lose him. You have a loving family. I was a student with a mom who cared only about herself and a grandmother who wasn't well. I didn't want your parents to take him away from me."

"You denied my parents from knowing Alec's child." I point to my chest. "You denied his uncle from knowing him. If I really am his uncle. I'll be taking a paternity test, Summer." I stomp toward the door. With my hand on the handle, and unable to look at her any longer, I stare at the door and ask, "Was he here, in this apartment with you that day?"

A long beat and then, "Yes."

Just like that, the world as I knew it comes crashing down around me. If Dani finds out, it will destroy her. But how can I not tell her?

DANI

"Are you going to sell your house?" Rylee asks me as she fits Ava with water wings, and adjusts them on her tiny arms.

I take a sip of my iced tea. "We haven't really talked about that yet. It's too soon, don't you think?"

"Too soon. Didn't you just finish telling me you're trying to have a baby together, and yet you haven't talked about sharing a house. I don't think that's the way things are done, sister."

It's true. I did just finish telling her that. I figured if my friends knew, my sister should too, which is why I'm playing hooky this Friday afternoon, and she's here at Conner's place, in the pool. I'd picked her and the kids up earlier since it's hard to wrestle three kids alone. I wanted to have some quiet time with her while Jared was at work.

"Mommy, hurry up. I want to swim."

Rylee rolls her eyes. "Impatient, like her father."

I laugh at that, knowing the impatient one in that relationship is Rylee. She finishes adjusting the water wings, and Ava runs to the stairs, and slowly starts down them.

"Mommy, my turn." Little Jack holds his arms out, waiting for his water wings, and when Brynn starts fussing in her stroller, I pick her up and put her over my shoulder. I breathe in her sweet smell, and my heart thuds a little harder.

Rylee's eyes go soft, full of love and warmth as she watches me. "That's a good look on you," she quietly informs me with a grin as she fixes Jack's water wings. Once done, she stands and puts her hands on my shoulders. "You deserve all this, Dani. You deserve a baby, a guy like Conner and a beautiful house—with a pool—to live in."

Tears prick my eyes and my gaze slides to Jack as he runs to the stairs and jumps in, no fear at all. Will my child be fearless and athletic like Conner, or will they be a little quieter like me? Will I ever even have a child at all? "Thank you."

She cocks her head. "Hey, why the tears? All of this is good, Dani."

Do I tell her? Do I open up and say that Conner has been acting a bit strange lately? Well, ever since the house party we threw last weekend—and maybe even a little before that. He's been making calls and ending them when I walk into the room, and he's even been disappearing at odd times.

He came to visit me at work once this last week, and when I invited him to accompany Buster and me to the nursing home on Wednesday, which I thought he enjoyed, he declined. He's becoming more and more distant, just when I was beginning to believe after everything we'd overcome, it would be smooth sailing from here on out. Is he getting tired of me?

Could it have something to do with Summer?

"I think it's just all the hormones." Not a lie. My hormones have been all over the place lately. Honestly, Rylee has three kids to worry about. I don't need her worrying about me, and maybe I'm in my head too much, and Conner is just busy. We've always spent a lot of time together, but we've never lived together, so this could be the norm for him, and maybe I'm just being paranoid, because I know how fast things can be taken away.

"Mommy, look at me," Ava screams in her loud outdoor voice that I'm sure they can hear down the street.

We both watch her swim, and her happiness helps push down some of my anxiety. "Let's get in. It's hot out."

Rylee grabs the floaty toy for Brynn, and we both ease into the pool. The water is cold, but glorious. Rylee drips a bit of water on Brynn's leg and she squeals. "How's that feel, huh?" she asks with so much love in her voice, I watch on with longing.

"Aunt Dani, over here, over here," Ava yells and I swim to her, circle my arms around her and spin.

Jack, not to be left out yells, "Me, me."

"Anyway, not to harp, but you should think about living here full time," Rylee says as she comes over with Brynn.

I laugh at her. "You're just saying that because you want full access to this pool."

"Okay, so that might be true, but I really am looking out for your best interests." She glances around. "Speaking of your best interests, where is Conner?"

My gaze goes to the patio, to where he loves to lounge. "He had some errands to run. He should be back soon." He left early, and said he'd be home after lunch. It's three in the afternoon. I guess I didn't realize it would be so long after lunch.

She watches me for a second, and I avert my gaze and spin Ava around again. She giggles and it pulls the attention away from me. I'm grateful. I don't want to explain that I have no idea where Conner is, and that he should have been back by now.

"Maybe we'll buy your house so we can live closer," Rylee says with a smile.

I throw my hands up, exasperated. "It's not even up for sale yet."

"Yet?" she exclaims, with a cocky, know it all grin, and I just shake my head at her. She's right though. Maybe it is time Conner and I had a conversation…I think.

"What time is Jared coming to pick you guys up?"

"Ohmigod, are you trying to get rid of us already?"

"No, I was just curious." That and I needed a change of subject. "Stay as long as you like. I was just thinking later I might run to the Airbnb and check on Scottie. He's a new Scottish terrier that is overnight for the weekend."

"Wow, clever name."

I eye her playfully. "Be nice. Besides, are you forgetting you named our chihuahua, Bear?"

She grins. "I miss that dog."

"Me too."

"When are you getting another?"

"What are you talking about? I have hundreds of dogs." She rolls her eyes at me and before she can press, Jack, the daredevil that he is, climbs from the pool and holds his arms out. "Catch me, Aunt Dani. Catch me."

I swim to him and hold my arms out. He jumps into them and we all laugh. We spend the next hour or so swimming, and after we get out and have drinks and watermelon, Jared shows up to collect his family. I give them all hugs and kisses at the door and promise to stop by this weekend with Uncle Conner, who, apparently, they miss greatly. They're not the only ones.

It's nearing dinner and I check my phone for messages. Disappointment wells in my stomach when I find none. Before I begin dinner, I decide to rinse the chlorine from my body, and head up to the main bedroom. I peel off my bathing suit cover up and walk to my side of the bed, and open the nightstand, needing the lip balm I use before bed. As I apply it, I fix the bedding, noting the tag I'd spotted the other day is no longer there.

I snap the cap back on the lip balm, and head to the shower. The warm water is glorious against my chilled skin, and as I wash myself, I miss Conner's body next to mine. God, all the shower sex we've been having has made a mess of me. I never want to shower alone anymore.

Grinning at that thought, and working to convince myself Conner is simply busy and nothing else is going on, I head back to the bedroom, and open my side of the closet. I scan it, searching for something comfy. My gaze goes to Conner's side and I close my door and open his to find his big comfy sweatpants and sweatshirts. It's cold in the house with the air on, so I tug on a pair of his sweats and pull a hoodie off the hook. When I do, it jars the hangers and rustles his clothes.

That's why my gaze slides to the pocket of his suit jacket. I notice the pink paper, the same kind of pink paper I wrote a note on many years ago—and left on Conner's bed. What the heck? I glance over my shoulder, not wanting to invade his privacy, but with curiosity getting the better of me, I tug on it, exposing the paper a tiny little bit.

My words of love practically jump from the aged paper, and I stumble backward. Conner has my letter. Holy God, after all this time, Conner still has my letter! But what the heck is it doing in a suit jacket? I don't know, but what I do know is that it's in his possession, which means he read it all those years ago, and Alec had never taken it from his brother's room.

It also means Conner never wanted me back then.

I stare at the paper like it's diseased, my legs a little shaky beneath me. I can't decide if I'm happy I'd found it or not. Maybe I was better off never knowing. Minutes tick by and I eventually find the strength to shove the letter deeper into the pocket, and shut the door on old painful memories.

I gulp air for a minute and then, needing a distraction, I head downstairs and search for my phone, wanting to check on the animals. Seeing them always makes me happy and now, I'm not sure I want to leave the house. I think I just want to wait for Conner to return. For some reason, I desperately need to see him.

I spot his laptop on the coffee table, and not wanting to climb back up those stairs with rubbery legs, I drop down onto the sofa. In the past, Conner never minded when I used his laptop, so I grab it and boot it up. But the second I do, messages between him and Summer pop up, one after the other, after the other.

With my heart jumping into my throat, and lodging there until breathing is difficult, I'm about to close the device. This is not my business, right? *You're trying to have a baby with him, Dani.* I pinch my eyes shut and when I open them again, I scan the messages. I take deep gulping breaths when I read that Conner has been by her place, more than once, and judging from the last message, he's there today.

What the hell?

I slowly close the laptop, the room nearly fading to black before my eyes. I blink several times, yet nothing can keep the tears from falling as my mind races. Alec never took the letter I wrote Conner. Conner had it all this time. He never wanted me back then. Why then does he now? What changed? He, for some reason, felt responsible for me after Alec's death. Is that the only reason he's with me now? Like his brother, did he never really want me? Is he only interested now because he wants revenge on his brother? Has he been seeing Summer in secret?

Wait, what was that Summer said when I first saw her at the pool? *Always wanting what the other has.* Does that mean she knew what Alec had been up to over the years, and thinks Conner is up to the same antics? But how could that be possible? She didn't know Alec very well. Right?

I snatch my purse and keys off the counter, and even though I probably shouldn't be driving, I stumble outdoors, jump into my car and back out of his driveway. I'm not sure what I think I might see, but everything inside me has compelled me to drive to her address. I'd been to her place when she was dating Conner, and even if she hadn't given him her address, I'd still know how to get there.

Twenty minutes later, I pull up on the street...behind Conner's car. My heart is thudding so hard, I'm sure I'll be hitting up the emergency department after this to mend a broken rib...and maybe even a broken heart. My phone pings and I quickly snatch it up, to see a message from Rylee, thanking me for a wonderful day. I debate on messaging her back, to let her know that mine went completely downhill afterward, but I'm getting ahead of myself. Maybe this is all nothing.

Were you born yesterday, Dani?

No, but I really don't want to think the worst of Conner. He's always been there for me, and I love him. Maybe I should go. Maybe I should let him explain whatever this is when he's ready, because in my heart I know he's not a man to cheat.

I'm about to start my car, only to stop when the front door to the building opens and out walks Conner, his arm around Summer, as he clutches the hand of a small boy who is the spitting image of the man I love.

26

CONNER

As I stand in Summer's kitchen, the DNA results in an envelope in my hand, she holds out a sheet of paper. "These are the results I received after Tyler was born."

I glance at the sheet and scan it. "How did you get Alec's DNA?"

"Hair follicles..." She looks away. "On the bed, and from my brush."

Fuck.

"You knew Tyler was his all along. You didn't question that he could be mine?"

"No, the dates. But I wanted this just for confirmation." She takes a sip of water. "You and I...we hadn't been hooking up much."

"Yeah, that's because you were hooking up with Alec," I blurt out much harsher than intended. Jesus, it's just a lot to wrap my brain around.

She pushes off the island and walks into the living room. "I'm sorry," she murmurs quietly as she takes a seat on her sofa.

I follow her in, my DNA results still in the envelope. I had the results sent to her place, not wanting them to go to mine and risking Dani asking questions. It's awful to keep this from her, it's giving me a damn ulcer, but I don't want to hurt her.

"I'm not looking for apologies," I tell her. "I'm looking for answers." I drop into her wingback chair, Tyler's playful sounds from his bedroom filling the apartment. It's easy to tell she loves her child, and he's well taken care of. Why she thought we'd try to take him away is beyond me. She must not think much of our family. Jesus, my parents would love to know Tyler. They'd be amazing grandparents, despite the circumstances. Having a piece of Alec would do wonders for them.

I peel open the envelope with shaky hands, even though I'm sure the results are going to be the same as Summer's. I open the paper and read it carefully, before I hand it over, and sink back into my chair. How the hell do I tell Dani? I honestly don't know if I can. If Tyler is going to be a part of our lives, and I definitely want that, she has to know something.

"What are you going to do?" Summer asks quietly.

"I want to know him. I want my parents to know him."

"And Dani, what will you tell her?"

"Jesus, Summer. This is so fucked up." I sink deeper into the and cover my face with my hands. My stomach is so tight, I'm sure I'm going to vomit.

"If you told her he was yours…"

I drop my arm and sit up. "I can't let her think Tyler is mine."

"If you're going to be a big part of his life, like you say, what does it matter?"

"It matters." Jesus, there have been enough lies to last a lifetime.

She grips the hem of her shirt and twists it in her fingers. "If you tell her it's Alec's, it's going to be bad, Conner. She's going to hate you for keeping Alec's secret all these years, and she's naturally going to hate me."

Fuck, she's right. She's definitely going to hate me, and what we have will be gone in a heartbeat. "Fuck me." An almost hysterical laugh bubbles out of my throat. This is it. Right here, this is it. The third ball dropping. I thought that had already happened when I found out what my brother had done to Dani and me, but nope. That's nothing compared to what's going to happen when she realizes I've been holding my brother's dark secrets.

I push to my feet. "I need to go."

"Where are you going?" She stands and Tyler comes running into the room.

"I don't know. I need to go figure things out. Figure out how I'm going to handle all this." I sink to my knees in front of Tyler and put my hands on his shoulders. I take in his big blue, vulnerable eyes, and nearly fucking sob. Alec has a son. I have a nephew. This is wonderful news, and so very hurtful to so very many at the same time.

"Tyler, I'm your Uncle Conner." Tyler just stares at me. "I'm going to come back and see you." I realize he can't understand what I'm saying. Heck, he's only fifteen months. "I'm going to take you to see your grandmother and grandfather soon too." I look over at Summer and she nods.

"Do you want me to be with you when you tell them?" she asks quietly.

"I appreciate the offer, Summer. I think it's something I have to do on my own. Let them get used to the idea."

She starts crying and puts her hands over her eyes and Tyler runs to her and wraps his arms around her legs. "They're going to hate me. I was just so scared, Conner." She drops to her knees and hugs her son. "I love him so much. I don't have a lot of support and I would die if he was taken away from me."

I drop in front of them and take them both into my arms, the fight draining out of me. "You're never going to lose him, and think of it this way, your small family will be expanding and you're going to have all the support you'd ever need."

She sniffs. "Dani...she's going to hate me and I don't blame her." She drops her hands and blinks at me. "I'm not that same person, Conner. I was young, and foolish, and you always seemed distracted around me, and whenever I saw you around Dani, it was so obvious that you were in love with her and not me. I was jealous and foolish and wanted to get back at you both. Having a child changed who I was. I've grown up. I'm a different person now. I'm a good person."

"I know."

"I don't want to hurt any more people."

I stand and pull her up with me as she holds Tyler on her hip. "Come on. I think you both could use some ice cream and I need to figure out what I'm going to tell Dani." She sets Tyler down, and we head down the hall to take the elevator to the main floor. When we reach it, I push open the door, and as Summer continues to quietly cry, I put my arm around her and take Tyler's hand in mine, not wanting him to dart onto the street. I don't know him well enough to know if he'd do that, but from the stories Mom told me, boys can be handfuls.

As the sun shines down on us, a car starts from across the street and my gaze goes to the noise. My heart stalls in my chest when my gaze lands on Dani's, who's watching us from her driver's seat. "What the hell?" How did she know where I was? But that's not the question I should be asking right now. Not when she's driving off after seeing me with my arm around Summer and Tyler's hand in mine.

Oh, Jesus no.

I take a step forward. "Dani, wait."

She doesn't wait. Instead, she pulls onto the road and steps on the gas, zinging past us and barely stopping at the stop sign on the corner.

"Oh no," Summer whimpers, as she scoops Tyler up. "She's going to think..."

Panicked, I take the stairs to the walkway two at a time. "I know what she's going to think." For a brief second, I consider letting her think that. At least that way she'd never have to know the depths of Alec's betrayal—my betrayal. Hell, not only have I kept his secrets, the man is dead because of me.

"You better go find her."

I turn back to Tyler. "We'll get ice cream another day, okay?"

He just stares at me with those big, sweet eyes, and smiles, his big cheeks puffing out. "See you, kiddo." I ruffle his hair and take in Summer's worried eyes. "It's going to be okay," I tell her even though I'm not so sure of that myself. "We'll work this out, and no one is going to hate you." They might not hate her, but Dani and maybe even my parents will hate me when they find out what I'd done.

I hurry across the street to my car and jump in. The first place I go to is my house, only to find the driveway empty. I drive to her place, and see the bus, but not her car. I tug my phone from my pocket and call her. It goes straight to voicemail. "Fuck." I shoot off a text, telling her we need to talk. Maybe I should have told her what was going on long before this. I just didn't want to hurt her.

I wait for her to text back. "Come on, Dani." I run my hands through my hair and sit a bit longer. I give up and decide she must have gone to the Airbnb. Seeing the dogs always puts her in a good mood. I back out of her driveway and head across town. I pull into the Airbnb parking lot, and even though her vehicle is nowhere to be found, I hurry from my car and run inside. I find Marley at the receptionist counter talking with Tanya, and they both lift their heads when they see me storming inside.

"Hey," Marley says, and comes around the counter. "Are you okay?"

Breathless, with my throat so dry it's hard to talk, I begin. "Is Dani here?"

"No, she took the day off," Marley explains, her eyes narrowed in concern. "She was spending it with her sister and the kids." I nod. "Is everything okay?"

"No." She opens her mouth, but I cut her off. "If you see her, can you tell her I'm looking for her."

She nods, and I glance at Tanya who's reaching for her phone, no doubt about to call Dani to see what's going on. I meet her gaze. "Please ask her to meet me at home."

She gives a small, tight nod, and I turn and head back out the door. I consider texting Brighton, or Gina or one of the girls. Although, I'm not sure she'd run to any of them. How could she possibly tell anyone that I had a family behind her back, when we were trying to make a baby together? Yeah, she's not going to open up to anyone other than family about that. Family. Shit. She must be at Rylee's.

I get back in my car and check my phone one more time before I start back across town to her sister's house. I try not to drive fast or erratic, but it's damn hard. Relief washes over me when I see Dani's car, and I park quickly and run to the front door. I try the knob but it's locked. I knock, and when it goes unanswered, I circle the house to see if they're out back, only to find it empty.

Back at the front door, I knock again. "Dani, come to the door." I pound harder, and note the neighbors glancing my way. "Dani, please." The door creeps open and I come face to face with Jared. "Where is she?" I try to see past his shoulders but he's tall like me.

"She's upstairs with Rylee. She doesn't want to see you."

"Come on, Jared. Ask her to come down."

He folds his arms, and squares off against me. "Not going to do it, man."

"Fuck, Jared, can you please tell her it's not what she thinks."

"No, what is it then? What should she think?" he asks, his eyes hard as he protects his sister-in-law, and I respect him for that. It's good Dani has people like him in her life. I don't readily answer and he presses, "What is it, Conner?"

Christ, if I admit that Alec was having an affair, and had a child after Dani lost hers, and is having trouble conceiving, it will absolutely destroy her. I can't do that. I won't.

He lifts himself up a little taller. "Well..."

"I...can't."

"You better figure your shit out, Conner." He slams the door so hard, it nearly hits me in the face. I back up and lift my head to see the upstairs window. A shadow moves past, and I'm about to shout. But what the hell am I going to say to her? I don't know, but I do know there are two people I also need to talk to. Maybe they can help me make sense of this and figure out my next move. I just pray that what I'm about to tell them, doesn't destroy them...or us.

It's dinner time by the time I reach Mom and Dad's place and I pull in behind Dad's car. Since their life is very routine, I know I'll be catching them eating, but if I wait, I fear I won't have the courage to do what needs to be done, what should probably have been done a long time ago.

I knock instead of entering, just to give myself a second to pull it together. Mom opens the door and her smile dissolves when she sets eyes on me.

"Conner, what is it?" At the sound of my name, Dad comes to the door and stands behind Mom.

"We need to talk."

They both go pale, no doubt because I'm not only struggling to stand, I'm struggling to speak. "Come sit, Conner," Mom says and guides me into the living room. I drop into a chair and Mom and Dad take the sofa across from me. I lean forward, brace my elbows on my knees as their warmth and comfort curls around me.

"What is it, son?" Dad asks.

I swallow, and pinch my eyes shut. When I open them again, I blurt out. "Alec had an affair a couple of years ago. I knew about it and said nothing. I just found out he has a son, and I'm the reason he died the day Dani lost her baby."

27

DANI

I'm not normally so mopey, and I never sleep this much. I guess sleep helps me forget what's really going on in my life. Honestly, I know I'm being selfish, acting like the entire world revolves around me, when I know it doesn't. I just thought...I thought Conner was a man I could trust, a man I could have a future with. We'd waited so long for our happily ever after, and now, not only is that not going to happen, we've lost our friendship and that was the one thing we vowed never to mess up. Well, we certainly did that, especially after his last text message asking me to please talk to him, and me telling him to leave me alone, that I never wanted to see him again.

I roll over in bed and glance at the pretty pink pictures on the wall. It's pathetic that I'm sleeping in one of Ava's bunk beds, hiding out because I can't face the world right now. I kick off the covers and listen to the sounds coming up from the kitchen. My sister is down there taking care of three kids, and well, now it's more like four kids with the way I'm acting. This is ridiculous.

I push up and climb from the bed. A few steps take me to the window and I pull the curtains open and glance down at the street, half expecting to see Conner. He'd come by four days ago, after I spotted him at Summer's, and I didn't have it in me to talk to him. He called a couple of times, and then after my final text…silence. I guess he's at least respecting my wishes.

How did I not know he had a child, and was seeing Summer behind my back? The man told me he loved me, for God's sake. Then again, so did Alec, and I'm smart enough to know that was nothing but a lie, a hateful stunt to hurt his brother. What is wrong with the Birch men, and how did I get so entangled with both of them?

Out of nowhere, a sob catches in my throat, and my heart cracks just a little bit more. I glance down at my stomach. I can't even get pregnant, yet everyone else around me has no trouble with it. I guess it just wasn't meant to be, and in the end, I'm glad Conner and I didn't procreate. What a mess that would have been when he already has a family and no way can you convince me that the boy isn't his. They look exactly alike, and I'm keeping my distance. I am not a home-wrecker.

Dressed in my sleep shorts and T-shirt, I step up to Ava's small mirror and take in the dark circles under my eyes. I need to get myself together and get back to work. The last few days, Marley has been picking up the slack and driving the bus while I hid and felt sorry for myself. But no more. I need to get back into the real world and give Ava her room back.

I make a quick trip to the bathroom and clean myself up. Laughter rises up from downstairs and the sound of my sister's kids always brings a smile to my face and a pang to my heart. She has everything I've ever wanted. Just like Conner had everything Alec ever wanted, which is the only reason he went after me.

But nope, onward and upward.

"Good morning," I call out my voice chirpy as I enter the kitchen. My sister turns to me, her brows arched.

"Someone's in a good mood this morning." She eyes me, and I know she can see through the act I'm presenting. I don't want my nieces and nephews picking up on my sadness, so I try to be happy around them.

Ava picks up a different crayon and continues with her drawing. "Aunt Dani, when can we go to Uncle Conner's? I want to go swimming."

Just hearing his name sends my brain into a spin. Rylee steps up and hands me a much-needed cup of coffee.

"Ava, we can go to the lake, or maybe we can go to Noah and Brighton's resort and swim in the rooftop pool. I know you love that and you can play with Camryn and Tate."

She claps her hands. "That will be fun."

"I like playing with Tate," Jack mumbles as he jams a spoonful of cereal into his already full mouth.

I take a couple drinks of coffee, and my sister gives me a sympathetic smile. "Are you okay?"

I nod. "I'm good. I'm going to pack up and head home. I need to get on with my life and I miss my dogs." I snort out a laugh. "Maybe I should get a dog. That would be good company."

"Yeah, better than becoming an old cat lady."

"Who's a cat lady?" Ava asks as she holds out the picture to me. "Look, Aunt Dani, I drew my family." She points. "That's you and Uncle Conner."

Jack finishes his cereal and his spoon lands in his bowl with a clang. I jump, my nerves on edge. Rylee frowns at me. "Ava, why don't you and Jack go play on the swings. Later we can all head out and get ice cream. It's going to be a hot day, and maybe we can also go see the pups at Aunt Dani's Airbnb."

"Yay!" They both scream and dash outside. With a heavy heart I glance at sweet Brynn as she sleeps in her bassinette.

"How do you do it with three kids?" I half joke, wishing I had the same.

"It's a juggle, but I love it."

"I know you do. You're a good mom." I drop into the seat Ava just vacated and stare at the family picture—that contains Conner and me. A sob catches in my throat. Rylee drops down next to me and takes my hand.

"You'll be a good mom too." I'm about to counter, and she squeezes my hand to stop me. "Dani, things are a mess right now, I know that. But that doesn't mean you won't have a family of your own one day. You will, I know it." She puts her hand on her chest. "I feel it in my soul."

I try to smile, but tears fill my eyes instead. I don't think she's right, but I don't have the energy to fight her on it, so I say, "Thanks."

She swallows and takes a sip of her own coffee. "I can't understand it to be honest." She snorts out a humorless laugh. "There's a lot of things I can't understand, like why you even started dating Alec when you loved Conner since you first met him in high school." She glares at me, daring me to counter that truth.

"Alec paid me attention," I admit. God I was such a fool. "But now we both know why he did that." She gives me a sympathetic look and I continue, "Conner never liked me that way. He never brought up the letter, which only proves that. For a while I thought maybe he never saw it, but I was wrong about that, obviously."

"I see the way he looks at you, Dani."

"Rylee, it's over."

She shakes her head and briefly closes her eyes, like she's searching for answers. "I still can't understand it."

"What's not to understand." I shrug. "Conner and Summer are back together, and they have a child."

"Do you think he always knew about the child? I've been trying to make sense of this for days. He doesn't seem like the kind of guy who'd abandon his child and then suddenly decide to be there for him. I keep thinking there is more to the story."

"Maybe, maybe not." I guess there could be. I didn't give him the chance to explain anything. I was too shocked and hurt after finding him at Summer's place. He hid that from me. He hid a lot of things from me. I thought we didn't keep secrets, but I was wrong.

"I mean, think about what he said to Jared." I toy with my coffee cup and she continues. "He said it's not what you think and when Jared asked what it was, he wouldn't say. Why wouldn't he say? What is he hiding, and why is he hiding it?"

I pinch the bridge of my nose and work to hold back the tears. I've cried so much these last few days, I'm surprised I'm not completely dehydrated. With my brain a chaotic mess, I say, "I don't know, Rylee. All I know is what I saw. He had his arm around Summer, and was holding a boy's hand. A boy who looked exactly like him."

She gasps and sits up a little straighter. Her movements surprise me, and a strange cold wave moves over my body. I hug myself as she picks up her coffee cup and hurries to the counter, her back to me.

"What?" I ask, suddenly not sure I want to hear the answer. As my entire body chills, I rub my arms, a sick, uneasy feeling growing in the pit of my stomach.

"The letter," she begins, as she puts another pod into the machine. "Conner had it after all these years."

"Yeah." I take a sip of coffee and it suddenly tastes bitter on my tongue.

"I don't understand that. Why keep it? He's moved from his childhood home, why bring it with him? If he wasn't into you back then, wouldn't he have just tossed the letter, not taking it with him when he bought a house?"

"I don't know why Conner does what he does," I answer, wishing my brain would slow long enough so I can have more rational thoughts.

Rylee turns to face me. She leans against the counter, like she needs it to support her as she grips her coffee cup with both hands, cradling it so hard, I'm worried she's going to break it. My gaze leaves the cup and my heart stalls as I take in her pale face.

"What?" I ask again, a measure of panic racing through my blood. I push back in my chair, an odd sense of fight or flight instinct gripping me, because I'm not entirely sure I want to hear what she has to say. What does she know that I don't? Has my brain been blocking something to protect me? I'm sure that's what Melanie, who is a fabulous therapist, would tell me.

"Dani," she begins quietly, her voice low, like she's trying to soften the blow of what she's about to say. I stare at her, my words lodged in my throat. Suddenly, as Summer's words once again come back to haunt me— *Always wanting what the other has*—my brain begins to clear of the chaos, and a new kind of understanding—an entirely different scenario—plays out in my mind. Oh God. Maybe I was wrong. Maybe Summer knew Alec better than I thought she did, and there's only one way that could have happened.

"Rylee..." I try to speak but my words are lodged in my throat.

"What if Conner found the letter in the box, and took it to protect you from being hurt more? What if he loved you all those years ago too? Maybe he didn't want you to know the extent of Alec's betrayal, that he was only with you to hurt Conner."

A cry lodges in my throat. "When I asked Conner if he thought that was true, that Alec never loved me, he said that wasn't true."

"Of course, he did. He wouldn't want you to think you meant nothing to Alec. That you were a pawn in a game of hate."

"But that's exactly what I was. It's the only thing that makes sense in my life. Alec barely touched me. It's the only logical explanation."

She takes a step toward me. "You know way more than Conner thinks you do, don't you?"

I glance at my feet, my hair falling into my face. "I do." I draw in a shuddery breath, knowing exactly where she's going with this. "Conner found the letter in the box...," I state quietly.

"Yeah. I'm pretty sure he did and I'm pretty sure he took it home and hid it so you wouldn't see it."

"It was right after I left that letter on Conner's bed that Alec started pursuing me." Sadness grips me. Sadness for the hurt Alec caused, the years Conner and I lost.

"The boy..." Rylee begins.

My entire body goes weak, and I clutch the table. "He's... he's...Alec's." A sob spills from my lips and I bend forward, putting my hands over my face, as tears fall hard, and I'm not sure if I'm crying from Alec's deceit, or the fact that the baby isn't Conner's and he was simply trying to protect me from the true extent of Alec's betrayal.

"He loves you, Dani. He loves you so much, he couldn't let you think you meant nothing to Alec." I lift my head. "I'm not sure what was going on when you saw him with his arm around Summer, and holding her son's hand, but I don't think it's what you think." I nod in agreement. "Maybe he knew Alec had been with Summer, maybe he didn't. But my guess is that he just found out about the boy and I think you need to go find him."

I hiccup a sob. "I told him I never wanted to see him again." Oh God, how could I have messed this up so badly? Is there any chance of fixing it now? "I...I didn't listen to him, Rylee."

"He wasn't going to tell you anyway, Dani."

She's right. He was protecting me, but I'm no longer that high school girl, the quiet new kid on the block who needed his protection. No, I'm a grown woman who knows what she wants, and what I want is him, dammit. I grab my phone and call him, but it instantly goes to voicemail. In a panic, I leave my sister's and drive to Conner's place, but he's nowhere to be found. Where the heck would he be?

I head to the rink, but his car isn't there. I shoot him off another text and when he doesn't answer, I start driving aimlessly. Okay, maybe not so aimlessly because I find myself sitting in my car across the street from Summer's place—Conner's car parked in the driveway. My heart pounds so fast, the world closes in on me.

My God, was I completely wrong?

28

CONNER

I glance at Knox as he sits next to Summer. She asked me to come by today because she wanted to be open and honest with Knox about our past and what happened with my brother. The whole situation is messed up, and she wanted me here just to help her get the truth out. She's in love with Knox and is terrified the truth will send him running.

After she tells him everything and has given him time to absorb and digest, Knox glances at me, his face tight, but his eyes are full of understanding.

"We okay?" I ask.

"Yeah, man, of course. We're okay."

From the bedroom I hear my sweet nephew playing and it makes me happy and sad. I'm looking forward to getting to know him better, and so are my parents. But the little boy also reminds me of Dani and our failed attempts at getting pregnant. When she told me she never wanted to see me again, it broke my heart into a million pieces, and I stepped back, wanting to give her the space she desired. I needed time to figure out what it was I had to do, too.

I know I haven't been honest with her, and I still don't know what to do about the whole situation. After I opened up to my parents and told them everything, they assured me that my brother's death was not my fault, and that no one, including Dani, would hold me responsible. I'm really hoping that is true, because while I respected her wishes to stay away, I have no intention of staying away forever. No, I have a plan in place, and today, right after I get the call I've been waiting for, I plan to put it into motion.

"Are we okay?" Summer asks Knox tentatively as she twists a long, stuffed snake—one of Tyler's toys—in her hands.

He nods. "The past is the past, Summer. You made mistakes. Hell, we all have. But you're trying to right them now, and that's all that matters."

She throws her arms around him and tears fill her eyes as he hugs her back. I push to my feet. "Okay, I have to run, and I'm sure you two have more talking to do."

Summer jumps up. "You need to go find Dani."

I pull my phone from my pocket. "I plan to. There's a call I've been waiting for before I do, though." The second I see that I have a text and a call from Dani, my throat tightens, and there's not a damn thing I can do to pinch back the tears in my eyes. "She called," I say quietly, my voice shaky as hope fills my heart. The love I feel for this woman washes over me and makes standing a chore.

"That's a good sign, Conner." Summer puts her arms around me. "You two belong together. You always have." She glances back at Knox. "I want us all to be friends."

Tyler comes running into the room and I bend and smile at him. "Not friends," I clarify. "Family." I ruffle Tyler's hair. She nods in agreement and chokes back tears.

"Go do what you need to do, Wood," Knox pipes in, giving me a slap on the back. "The past is the past and it's time to go get the future you deserve."

I nod, even though I still don't know how to tell Dani about Tyler. But it's the lies that got us into this mess, and I'm sick of deceit, sick of my brother's hate, and goddammit, he's taken enough from us as it is, and I refuse to let him continue taking, especially when he's no longer with us. Summer was right. Dani and I belong together. We always have.

Just then the call I've been waiting on comes in and my heart jumps into my throat. "Okay, I have to go."

I see myself out, and hurry to my car. I drive out to the country and hours later, with a very special package on the seat beside me, I head straight to Dani's house. I hope she'll talk to me. I guess the fact that she called means she's open to having a conversation. She's no doubt wondering why I haven't called or texted back, but what I'm about to do needs to be done in person.

Relief rushes through me when I see her car and bus in her driveway. I pick up the bundle beside me, and get everything in place before I exit the car. Hurrying up her driveway, being careful with the precious package in my hands, I reach her door, and set the little bundle on the stoop beside me.

I ring the bell and glance down, shifting restlessly as the door unlocks and swings open. My entire being fills with love as I take in the woman who holds my heart in her palm. Though I also note the dark circles under her eyes. Dani doesn't look like she's been sleeping too well either.

"Conner," she whispers, sounding breathless. Her gaze drops to the ground, to the fluffy Newfoundland pup with a specially made barrel tied around his neck. In the past, Newfoundland dogs were used for rescue missions, and even though this *is* a rescue mission—of our relationship—the barrel is not filled with whiskey. "Conner, what...what have you done?" She shakes her head, tears in her eyes. "Ohmigod, he's beautiful." She bends to pet him. "What is going on?"

"Open the barrel." She glances up at me, uncertainty dancing in her dark eyes. "Just open it."

She opens the little buckle latch, and the barrel opens to expose a bunch of pregnancy tests. She takes them out, and stares up at me. "What are these for?"

"I want to make a baby with you," I explain quickly. "I want us to be a family. I want a future with you, and our new dog, who has yet to be named." She continues to blink up at me and I hurry on. "I know you said you wanted to get a pup when you got pregnant, but don't worry, I'm determined to make that happen very soon, too. If...if it's still what you want."

She stares at me for a second, like she's trying to wrap her brain around that, when the pup gives her a big lick on the lips. She chuckles, picks him up and wipes her face. He snuggles right in with her, and the warmth in her eyes tells me it's love at first sight, for both of them. I get it, little doggy. Trust me, I get it.

Hugging the puppy, she steps into the house, and I say, "I'll be right back." I run to the car and grab the supplies and big, comfy doggy bed. I come back and stand on the steps.

"Can I come in?" She nods. "Good because we really need to talk."

"I know." She blinks rapidly. "I called and texted you. But then I saw your car..." Her words fall off, and my blood drains.

"You saw me at Summer's today?" She nods and inches back to let me in. "It's not what you think."

"That's not the first time you've said that, Conner." The door clicks shut and she follows me into the living room. I set the dog bed down and when the pup yawns, she places him in the middle of the bed. I don't sit—I'm too antsy—and neither does she.

I shift from one foot to the other, fear of hurting her making what I have to say so hard. "Summer wanted me there when she explained things to Knox." Confusion moves over her face and of course she's in the dark. She has no idea that Summer had an affair with Alec and the boy she saw me with is his. "I'll get to that, but you need to know that I'm not with Summer. I haven't been with her for a very long time."

"Okay."

Good, at least she believes that much. "It's you I love. It's you I've always loved." She remains quiet, her eyes sad as she continues to focus on me, clearly needing to hear more. "I thought I was responsible for Alec's death," I begin and her eyes go wide. "I held that pain close to my heart. I didn't want to hurt you because I always thought Alec was the love of your life, and you asked me for my DNA so it could help you keep a piece of Alec with you."

"That's not why I asked, Conner." I blink at her, and she continues. "I asked because I loved you. I've always loved you."

"I know...the letter."

"You found it in Alec's box." It's a statement not a question, and while I want to lie and protect her, there can be no more lies. My loyalties are with her, and if she loves me, and I know she does, my brother's indiscretion will hurt her, but I'm here now, here to help her put her life back together again.

"Yes."

"The boy...he's Alec's," she says again, and my head rears back. Holy shit, she knows...everything.

"Yes."

She nods, and her reaction isn't at all what I expected. Then again, I suspect she's been sitting with this knowledge for a while now.

"I didn't know about him until a little over a week ago," I explain.

"You knew about the affair?"

I exhale, my shoulders drooping and I hope she doesn't hate me for this but here I go. "I kept his secret to protect you. I was torn between loyalties, but now I know where my loyalties stand. With you. Always with you. I'd never do anything to hurt you, Dani. Not purposely. You have my word on that."

"I know that," she murmurs quietly, her voice low and shaky.

"There's something else you need to know. Something that I've kept close to my heart for a long time."

She swallows, her eyes moving over my face cautiously. "We need honesty, Conner."

"You're right." I run my hand through my hair, hoping she doesn't hate me.

She comes closer, and puts her hands on my shoulders. "Now tell me why you thought you were responsible for Alec's death?" she asks, knowing exactly what I wanted to talk about. My God, this woman might know me better than I know myself.

"The day…" I stop when I'm about to choke on my words. "The day you lost your baby…That was the day Alec was with Summer." I pause to let her absorb that. When I finally get a nod, I continue. "As you know, he called me and asked me to take you to the clinic. I knew he was with someone. I didn't know it was Summer. After…you lost…the baby. I called him and told him to get home. I was so fucking angry, Dani." I hold her gaze, as her eyes water. "I told him if he didn't come home right now, he was dead to me."

She slides her arms around me, and I pull her close. We hold onto one another like our lives depend on it. Her touch comforts me, gives me the strength to continue. "I'm superstitious and I believe in karma. I figured I was responsible for his death. I was terrified to say anything. I didn't want you to hate me."

She inches back to see me. "I could never hate you, Conner. I can be mad, or upset, but never hate. I don't have hate in me."

"I know you don't, and it's one of the many things I love about you." Her smile is soft and shaky. "Yeah, so karma. That day…the baby, and then Alec. I spent years waiting for the next ball to drop. I was so terrified it would have something to do with us."

"Losing each other," she whispers quietly.

"Yeah, and we did just that." My aching heart pounds a little harder. "Because of lies and secrets."

"You didn't want to hurt me." She lightly rubs my arms. "I understand that."

"The worst thing that could have ever happened to me was losing you, and then that happened. I was at rock bottom, karma hitting me in the face. Then my parents assured me Alec's death was not my fault, and that I was a good person."

"You're the best person I know."

"When you told me never to call again..." She cringes, and I brush her hair back. "Hey, I get it." I snort out a laugh. "It was then that I'd lost everything, and that's when I knew I had to fight...I had to try. What else could I lose?" She weaves her fingers through mine. "I knew I had the fight of my life on my hands, because I was not letting anyone take anything else away from me...from us."

"No one is ever going to do that again. My whole heart belongs to you." A whimpering sound comes from the doggy bed, and I turn to see the pup having puppy dreams. Dani grins at our new family member. "Well, maybe a small piece of my heart belongs to him now, too."

"And when we have a baby, we'll be sharing our heart even more." I bend and press my lips to hers. "You're going to be a great mom, Dani."

Her eyes fill with tears. "Do you think—"

"Yes, I think," I say, cutting her off, and her worries that she can't get pregnant. "Actually, I know." I brush my thumb over her damp cheek.

Hope fills her eyes. "Yeah?"

"Yeah, I also think—know—that we should go to your bedroom, and start trying again."

She bites her bottom lip, worry in her eyes. "I lost track of my ovulation schedule."

I inch back. "Oh, well then," I tease playfully, my heart so full of love that we haven't lost each other, I'm sure it's going to burst. "If you're not sure if you're ovulating, there's no sense in—"

She whacks me, a huge laugh bubbling up in her throat. "Practice makes perfect, Conner."

I let my head fall forward. "Ah, so it's just my wood you want," I tease.

"Well, I'm not going to lie about that."

"No more secrets," I promise, and she nods in agreement. "But before I give you *wood*, first this." I drop to one knee, and her hands go to her mouth.

"Conner..."

"Je t'aime. Veux-tu m'épouser?" I speak to her in French because I want her to know I've never given up on us, or our secret shared language and what it represents to her, and our future. "And a honeymoon in Paris, if you'd like."

She sniffs, and nods. "I love you too. Yes, I'll marry you, and I'd love to honeymoon in Paris. Now put that ring on my finger, take me into the bedroom and start making good on your promise."

I put the ring on her finger and scoop her up, ready to turn our brand new, small family of three into...four, and hopefully more.

S even months later:

It's the all-star weekend in Toronto, and a bunch of us decided that staying in Boston in February is not our idea of fun, which is why I'm currently stretched out on a lounge chair, beachside in the Caribbean, and the guys are all playing beach volleyball. I've never been to the Caribbean, and I have to say, I'm pretty sure I never want to leave. Although I'm missing my sweet pup, Kai, who's not so much a pup anymore. Brady Fisher, aka Coddy, who's from Newfoundland, helped us come up with the name Kai, which means from the sea and we thought it was perfect for our big, gentle giant.

And while Coddy has been giving us a list of other names, I'm sure Conner and I will be coming up with our own two...for our twins. Yes, I finally got pregnant in November, and we were both over the moon when we found out we were having twins. Although we think that might be fun now, but in reality, I'm sure I'll be run off my feet, especially when Conner is on the road.

But I'll have a lot of help from my family and his. They were all so excited for us, and Rylee was thrilled that her kids were going to have cousins. We haven't announced it widely just yet, as we were waiting for this trip and I wanted to finish my first trimester. But we did sell my house and I moved into his, which he baby proofed from top to bottom.

I lift my eyes from my book as one of the guys yells near the end line, and laughter follows when he faceplants, having missed the ball, giving the other team the point. My gaze strays to Conner and when I find him laughing with his friends, I smile, loving their camaraderie. I always felt like I stuck out amongst the players and the WAGs, but that was silly. We're all a big family and my children are going to have so many people love them. I can't even imagine what I was thinking when I thought I could raise a baby alone. I mean, I probably could, but it's so much better not having to.

Speaking of family, we brought Summer and Tyler into ours. He's a sweet little boy, and I'm so happy he's getting the male influence he needs from Conner, Conner's dad, and Knox. We've put past hurts and mistakes behind us, focusing on what Tyler needs from us, and while Summer and I will never be best friends, we've come to a place of mutual respect and understanding.

Conner wipes sand from his chest, and my gaze rakes over his hard body. I begin to warm. It's not from the sun. It's crazy that I love him more and more every day, and my heart beats a little harder as I think about the little miracles growing inside me.

From the lounge chair beside me, Emilia checks something on her phone, and I lean over to see that she's scrolling through social media. I catch an image of Gabe as it goes by, and then she drops her phone. "I need alcohol."

She looks completely annoyed by something and I gather the courage to ask, "What's going on with you and Gabe? You guys really don't seem to like each other."

She snorts. "That's putting it mildly." Her gaze narrows in on Gabe as he serves the ball. Her face turns a different shade of red and I can't tell if it's anger or something else. "The man drives me crazy." I go quiet as she continues to glare and as if sensing her gaze on him, he angles his head and gives her a big smile that seems to enrage her.

"Wow, what was that?"

"Sometimes I think he enjoys getting under my skin." A fine shiver goes through her and it makes me wonder if she'd like to 'get under' him. "He always has. Ever since we were kids. I almost didn't take the assistant skating coach job with the Bucks. Being so close to him every day, working with him, *ugh*. He never wants to listen to me. It's too much sometimes."

"You guys go way back, huh?"

"Yeah, he played hockey with my brother." She goes quiet for a second, like she's thinking about the past. "We shared ice time sometimes during practices, and he would always fly by me and throw me off. He's such a jerk."

"Yeah, what a jerk."

Her gaze flies to mine, and for the briefest second, I think she's going to defend him. Something on the beach catches her attention and her face softens. "Drink?"

I pick up my water bottle. "I'm just having water for now. Maybe later," I say, not wanting her to guess that I'm pregnant. Conner and I want to make the announcement together. She pushes to her feet and saunters off and I turn my attention back to my book. I read for a few minutes, and when my phone pings, I pick it up.

A smile spreads across my face when I see it's one of the schools wanting to book Conner. I am so proud of my fiancé, turning his learning disorder into something positive to help other kids who feel lost, just like he used to. It wasn't easy for him to put himself out there after hiding his dyslexia for years, after all the bullying he received in school. I love how much he gives back to the community and I know he's going to be an amazing dad. I happily took on the job of booking agent. Now that I'm pregnant, I hired more staff at the Airbnb so I can take it easy. If Conner had it his way, I'd be on bed rest for nine months.

Brighton comes over and sits on my other side. "I just booked us all on the catamaran for tomorrow. It's a full day adventure and we even get to go swimming and paddle boarding." She throws herself back on her chair, and I'm smiling, loving how happy she is, and that she's getting a break from her kids back home. Everyone needs adult time once in a while. Gina was unable to come on this trip, so she's watching the kids.

Ash bowed out of coming with us, and I'm not sure what is happening between Gina and him. If there is anything going on, and I believe there is, they're keeping it under wraps. One thing I do know is there's enough tension between the two to light up Boston in a blackout...for a week.

"That sounds like so much fun."

She eyes Emilia as she comes back with a fruity drink. "She probably won't want to come," she whispers. "I don't think she wants to be in close quarters with Gabe the Babe."

I laugh at the nickname the bunnies gave him. Although he is pretty darn good looking. Not as good looking as Conner, though, but I'm pretty sure I'm biased.

"Sorry, Brighton." Emilia comes back and sits on the other side of me. "I would have gotten you a drink if I'd known you'd be joining us."

"Hey Millie, did you get me a drink?" Gabe yells.

She growls. "I hate when he calls me that."

I chuckle. "I actually think it's kind of cute." Maybe a cute name for our baby if one is a girl.

"He gave me that nickname when I was a freckle-faced girl in pigtails. I've asked him to stop, but he won't because he knows it annoys me." She glances at him. "Get your own drink, Gigi."

Gigi? Okay, that's a new one and it clearly comes from the past, and judging from Gabe's scowl he hates it as much as she hates Millie.

"So, your birthday tomorrow," Brighton says, changing the subject, like she doesn't want to touch on that. "Are you going to come on the catamaran?"

"Not if he's going to be there."

"Oh, come on. I'll run interference," Brighton assures her.

"I think I'm just going to veg on the beach. Is that okay? Quiet time on my birthday?"

I put my hand on her arm and give it a squeeze. "If that's what you want for your birthday, that's what you get for your birthday. Just promise me you'll eat cake."

"I'm eating all the cake," she assures me.

The game ends and Josie joins us. A few of the gals couldn't make it as they're home with children and newborns. Melanie and Brady are home with their toddler Kayce. Conner's mom and Dad, Darcy and Bill have been very involved in Tyler's life and I love that. Kayce, who doesn't really have grandparents to call his own, has been taken in by Darcy and Bill as well. They love all the boys to pieces, and Kayce can use some grandparent love in his life.

As my thoughts return to the present, I watch the way some hot young thing in a thong walks up to Gabe. He casually throws his arm around her. I don't miss the way Emilia is grumbling something rude about him under her breath.

"Glad you're going to eat cake. Can you save me a piece, or three..."

Emilia eyes me when I ask for three, and I can almost hear her brain racing, putting it all together as I jump to my feet and throw my arms around Conner's sweaty body as he steps up to me.

"Time?" he asks, a big grin on his face. He's been dying to tell his friends since we first found out.

"Time," I assure him and squeal as I turn to face our friends. "Emilia, I asked for three pieces of cake because..." A few of our friends' gasp as I turn to face Conner, giving him the floor...or rather the beach.

"Because..." He puts his big strong hand on my stomach, and I close mine over his. "She's eating for three."

"Three!" Brighton yells. "Ohmigod, you guys. We're so happy for you." Everyone comes at us, and tears fill my eyes as we receive hugs and congratulations.

When Emilia reaches me, she says, "I thought something was up when you didn't want a cold drink."

"I wish I could have that, it looks amazing, and I'm parched."

"Oh, is that the drink you got for me?" Gabe asks, and bends down and takes a big drink from the straw. Emilia's eyes go wide, and she shoves the drink against his chest. "It's all yours now."

"I can share."

"Like you used to share the rink?" she challenges.

He frowns. "Are you still mad about that one time you fell?"

She grumbles. "I'm not putting that straw in my mouth after it's been in yours," she shoots back, her gaze sliding to the pretty blonde who'd thrown herself at Gabe earlier and now seems to have her attention on Gunther.

"Rude," he murmurs as she storms off, and wow, the energy between them might just set off a round of lightning overhead.

"What was that all about?" Conner asks, his breath warm on the shell of my ear. My body instantly warms, and the needy spot between my legs lets me know it's time for us to get off the beach and explore our hotel room—our bed, to be specific.

"I don't know," I tell him. "But I can't wait to find out."

ALSO BY CATHRYN FOX

Boston Bucks

Stick Move

Sticking Around

Sticking Out

Hook 'em Hard (Written in the Boston Bucks World)

Scotia Storms

Away Game (Rebels)

Warm Up (Rebels)

Crash Course (Rebels)

Home Advantage (Rebels)

Shut Out (Rebels)

Moving Target (Rivals)

Face Off (Rivals)

Scoring Fast (Rivals)

Opposing Teams (Rivals)

Fake Out (Rivals)

Deal Breaker (Rebels)

Hard Burn (Rivals)

End Zone

Fair Play

Enemy Down

Keeping Score

Trading Up

All In

Blue Bay Crew
Demolished
Leveled
Hammered

Single Dad
Single Dad Next Door
Single Dad on Tap
Single Dad Burning Up

Players on Ice
The Playmaker
The Stick Handler
The Body Checker
The Hard Hitter
The Risk Taker
The Wing Man
The Puck Charmer
The Troublemaker
The Rule Breaker
The Rookie
The Sweet Talker
The Heart Breaker

In the Line of Duty
His Obsession Next Door
His Strings to Pull
His Trouble in Talulah

His Taste of Temptation

His Moment to Steal

His Best Friend's Girl

His Reason to Stay

Confessions

Confessions of a Bad Boy Professor

Confessions of a Bad Boy Officer

Confessions of a Bad Boy Fighter

Confessions of a Bad Boy Doctor

Confessions of a Bad Boy Gamer

Confessions of a Bad Boy Millionaire

Confessions of a Bad Boy Santa

Confessions of a Bad Boy CEO

Hands On

Hands On

Body Contact

Full Exposure

Dossier

Private Reserve

House Rules

Under Pressure

Big Catch

Brazilian Fantasy

Improper Proposal

Boys of Beachville

Good at Being Bad

Igniting the Bad Boy

Bad Girl Therapy

Stone Cliff Series:

Crashing Down

Wasted Summer

Love Lessons

Wrapped Up

Eternal Pleasure Series

Instinctive

Impulsive

Indulgent

Sun Stroked Series

Seaside Seduction

Deep Desire

Private Pleasure

Captured and Claimed Series:

Yours to Take

Yours to Teach

Yours to Keep

Firefighter Heat Series

Fever

Siren

Flash Fire

Playing For Keeps Series

Slow Ride

Wild Ride

Sweet Ride

Breaking the Rules:

Hold Me Down Hard

Pin Me Up Proper

Tie Me Down Tight

Stand Alone Title:

Hands on with the CEO

Torn Between Two Brothers

Holiday Spirit

Unleashed

Knocking on Demon's Door

Web of Desire

ABOUT CATHRYN

New York Times and *USA today* Bestselling author, Cathryn is a wife, mom, sister, daughter, and friend. She loves dogs, sunny weather, anything chocolate (she never says no to a brownie) pizza and red wine. She has two teenagers who keep her busy with their never ending activities, and a husband who is convinced he can turn her into a mixed martial arts fan. Cathryn can never find balance in her life, is always trying to find time to go to the gym, can never keep up with emails, Facebook or Twitter and tries to write page-turning books that her readers will love.

Connect with Cathryn:
Newsletter https://app.mailerlite.com/webforms/landing/c1f8n1
Twitter: https://twitter.com/writercatfox
Facebook: https://www.facebook.com/AuthorCathrynFox?ref=hl
Blog: http://cathrynfox.com/blog/
Goodreads: https://www.goodreads.com/author/show/91799.Cathryn_Fox

Pinterest http://www.pinterest.com/catkalen/